Dark Sight

by

CHRISTOPHER ALLAN POE

PUBLISHED BY BLACK OPAL BOOKS

GENRE: Paranormal Thriller

DARK SIGHT
Copyright © 2014 by Christopher Allan Poe
All Rights Reserved

PRINT ISBN: 9781626941137

Kudos For Christopher Allan Poe

"God, I love Christopher Allan Poe's work. I read Dark Sight in a single obsessive night. That's kind of the way you have to read his stuff. At the heart of the story is the relationship of Victoria and Monique, who could have been my sisters or my friends. He makes you like them the way that Stephen King or John Irving makes you like their characters, and then he has you. Get ready for a late night of reading and a rough day at work or school tomorrow. It's completely worth whatever future pain is coming your way."

—*John Brantingham, Director, SGV Literary Festival*

"This is a real page-turner." —*Wendy Burch, KTLA Mornings*

"Christopher Allan Poe, the author of The Portal, scores big with another killer supernatural thriller. He captures the frustrations and absurdity of high school as a backdrop to this fast-moving, and unpredictable thrill ride with a seemingly average young lady who turns out to be anything *but*." —*Rik Bolman, WEBL/WUMY Memphis*

"Larger-than life characters, vivid imagery and moderate gore makes The Portal a morbid read that will delight many a horror fan. Definitely a recommended read!"

—*Not Now Mommy's Reading*

"Prepare for a page-turner that will keep you reading long after you decided to go to bed. Poe is an author to watch."

—*Genreview.com*

"It doesn't matter when you read this book, it will get to you. If it's cold and snowy, you'll be sweating. If the temperature is a-hundred-and-ugh, you'll get chills. If it's raining, your throat will be parched and dry."

—*Terrance V. McArthur, King's River Life Magazine*

For
Bonnie Hearn Hill

1

WHEN VICTORIA COVERED UP the picket sign that she'd made for her protest rally that afternoon, I worried the day would end badly. When she refused to tell me what we were protesting, I was convinced.

In my rearview mirror, I could see the thing sitting there on the backseat of the king cab next to my makeup bag. She'd hammered a wooden stake onto the frame of one of her stretched canvases and then hid the sign portion from me with a taut, plastic trash bag. The scent of acrylic paint filled the car. Not good. Ditching class today and driving with only a learner's permit were bad enough, but this plan of hers must have been in the works for a while, and yet she had never mentioned it.

As usual, I sucked it up. Unpredictability was the price of being best friends with a savant. Her condition wasn't debilitating. Far from it, but there was no denying that the artistic part of her brain had devoured the region that controlled her people skills. And then it snacked on her common sense for good measure. The beautiful chaos that resulted was Victoria.

Maybe that's why I loved her so much. She could deflect insults with grace and win fistfights against boys, right before stepping absent-mindedly into oncoming traffic. That's why she needed me. To pull her back to the curb sometimes. At the moment, I seriously considered yanking her elbow.

"Monique," she said from the passenger seat. "Snap out of it."

"How much farther is it?" I asked. "My dad will kill me if he finds out we took his truck."

"It's going to be fine."

"I'd like to see my sixteenth birthday," I told her.

"Relax. It's right up there."

Ahead, a procession of cars had parked along the shoulder of the highway, against a rock face of sheared, black granite. I pulled to a stop behind them and got out. Victoria grabbed her sign from the backseat and tucked it under one arm.

"We're here now," I said. "In the middle of BFE, so tell me. What are we doing?"

"Not yet. It's a surprise."

"A surprise protest. Be still my heart."

"Ooh, it's dark Monique," she said, as if I were starring in an old-time Vincent Price movie. "Dreary Monique."

"I'm not going to laugh, so you can quit it."

"Will Monique the Sarcastic make an appearance too?"

"Screw you, Victoria Vinegar-head." I accidentally smiled. Great. That would only encourage her.

"That's better." She pulled out her lipstick from her black fitted cropped jacket and reapplied her red color. Only Victoria. Trying to look gloom-pretty at a protest.

"Any time today," I said.

"Hold up." She pulled open my gray pea coat, glanced at my lint-balled, black turtleneck, and huffed.

"What?" I asked.

"If my girls were that big, I'd put a sign on a tent and charge admission."

"I haven't done laundry this week. Not all of us have maids."

"Hey, you can be a knee-locked virgin forever if you want." She closed my jacket. "Let's go."

"This better be good," I told her.

To the west, the last of the day's sunlight peered over the rolling hills, melting the ice on the roadway to a trickle of gritty slush water. Down the embankment on the opposite side of the highway, a snow-covered trail led to a clearing in the dense forest, where dozens of people gathered.

At the bottom, we entered the clearing through the open chain link gate, which was lined with a slinky of razor wire. Inside, we scooted between several protester groups. Splotches of red snow crunched underfoot, which gave way to green, then purple and blue. The hiss of spray paint came from every direction.

"Looks like Rainbow Brite exploded out here," I said.

"The Jesus lovers are fighting against evil." She motioned to the sign that she'd brought. "We are too."

"We're protesting with a church?"

"Not just any church." She pulled out wrinkled blue flier from her pocket and handed it to me. "The Awakeners Church of Life."

"Where did you even hear about this?" My Spidey-sense wasn't just tingling. It was having cramps. "We don't belong here."

"Quit being such a clit," she said. "These people are harmless."

Next to the gnarled roots of a dead olive tree, a gang of brightly clothed white folks hovered together, laughing and talking, swinging their signs. One guy lifted his proudly. *God Hates Faggots*, it read. He checked its heft, swung it around like a sword, and then set it to the side. Across from him, a woman held her own sign. The fetus depicted sat with a gun pointed at its head. The caption read, *Mommy don't kill me*.

"And they claim that I'm disturbed," I told her.

"These people are freaking rad," Victoria said. "What I want to know, is whose idea it was to bring the butcher's blood."

I searched around. Behind us, a mother grabbed her daughter's hand, dipped it in a bucket from Jackson's Deli, and smeared a small red handprint across her sign. Jeez-us. The crimson mess that we had just stomped through wasn't paint.

"Ick." I wiped my riding boots in patches of untouched snow.

"I know, right?"

"Victoria, we need to get out of here."

"We have every right to protest too," she said. "It's our first amendment duty."

"No, actually it's not." I pointed to a NO TRESPASSING sign that was riddled with buckshot. "This is private property. We can get in a lot of trouble. Or worse."

"Promise?" She grinned. Then she snatched the flier out of my hands and read it aloud, "Do you feel lost? Overwhelmed? Come out and worship at the altar of truth." She glanced up at me. "See, they specifically invited us here."

"Of course, they did. What good are cult killers without their victims?"

The forest of ancient fir trees seemed to agree. It bristled in the frigid wind. God, it had gotten dark too quickly. Around the perimeter of the clearing, parishioners began lighting a circle of torches. What kind of church held a protest in the middle of a forest? Stupid question. Time to go.

"Victoria, listen to me. I don't know where you got that flier, but if you value our friendship at all, we need to go. I'm scared."

"Okay, calm down." She nodded. "We can leave. That's all you had to say."

"Welcome to our camp." A man with hawkish features and a scraggly beard walked up to us, wearing a puffy snow camo jacket. His dark eyes and deep sockets seemed to hold me in place. "I don't remember seeing you out here before. Is this your first time?"

"Sorry," I told him. "I think we've stumbled into the wrong place."

"If you've got a sign, this is the right spot. Mind if I take a look?"

Victoria beamed. "Not at all." She pulled off the black plastic bag before I could stop her, and she held her sign up high.

We were so dead. It might've been her best painting yet. Surrounded by erupting volcanoes, Jesus lovingly cradled a baby dinosaur in his arms. The raptor-type reptile suckled on his breast.

"Victoria." I grabbed her arm firmly and then said to the man, "Sorry to intrude. We're leaving."

I turned and yanked her back toward the gate.

"Hold on," he yelled from behind.

All at once, everyone in the clearing quit what they were doing and stared at us. In my peripheral view, I could have sworn that they all had the exact same smile. I didn't dare look. I just kept pulling her along. We made it through the gate alive, but we weren't safe yet.

"Hey," the man yelled again. From the sound of his voice, he was maybe fifty feet back. Then I heard crunching snow steps behind us. Lots of them. I began to run, pulling Victoria behind me.

We reached the roadway just as a vehicle sprayed by, and then we crossed the street. I glanced back. The cult people didn't follow us. They just stopped by the edge of the road, as if an invisible barrier existed that they couldn't penetrate. We got into the car.

"What the hell was that?" I tried to start the engine to my Dad's truck, but it flooded.

"I was going to ask you the same thing," she said. "What were you thinking with that little scene?"

"Little scene?" I couldn't believe what I heard. *Please start.* The engine finally revved. "We could've been killed."

"They're my friends, Monique."

"Of course, the cult people are your friends. What was I thinking?" I backed up. Headlights approached, so I had to wait. At least the car could be used as a weapon if needed. "Quality people too. Fear mongering gay-bashers."

"If you're talking about that sign," she said. "Justin is gay, dipshit."

"Justin." I nodded. Now she was on a first name basis with them. Hold on. I couldn't have heard her right. "What did you say?"

"He's one of the people who gave me the flier. Did you even read it?"

"How could I? You just threw me out there."

"They're protesting negative messages and all the hateful garbage that everyone spews online these days. Later tonight, they're going to toss all of their signs into a giant bonfire to burn away the negativity. You just made me look like a complete ass."

"Well, maybe if you would've warned me."

"I wanted to surprise you with something cool for once, instead of the tired BS you deal with every day. Do you really think I'd put you in danger?"

What could I say? I knew she wouldn't intentionally try to hurt me, but that didn't mean she always thought things through.

Across the street, the man in the snow camouflage jacket looked unsure of whether or not to approach us. He carried Victoria's painting. In the confusion, I hadn't even noticed that she had dropped it. Now, I really felt stupid.

"I see how it is." Her voice shook as she opened her car door.

"No, wait," I called out as she walked around the front of the vehicle. I rolled down my window and leaned out. "Please get in the car, Victoria. I'm sorry."

"Whatever." She glanced back at me. "You don't need to worry about me anymore. I'll be fine."

The road began to brighten. Then I heard the roaring splash of tires.

"Get out of the street," I shouted and wrestled with the car door.

She spun around and held up her hands. I stared helplessly as a blur of screeching tires and blinding headlights hit her. The sickening thump punched the air from my chest. My best friend crumpled beneath the car, which swerved and smashed through the guardrail and disappeared over the embankment beyond.

2

*D*OWN IN THE DRAINAGE ditch, I held Victoria's head in my lap for what seemed like hours. Despite the cold darkness, I could see the confusion in her eyes, the blood on her broken teeth. I would have given anything right then, my life or my soul, for the power to freeze time. To snap my fingers and pause the flurry of snowflakes that scoured our cheeks.

I would have spent my days alone, leaving tunnels of emptiness in the snowstorm where I passed. I'd study the warm mannequins that used to be people. Even if the air molecules stopped moving too, then I would have gladly suffocated, if I just could have stopped time back in my truck, just before I said the wrong thing. When Victoria wasn't dying in my lap.

I didn't have that power though. Instead, she closed her eyes and stopped breathing. A hand shoved me aside, and several people grabbed her.

Somehow, I ended up in an El Camino with some guy I had never met. And then I was at Eden Springs ER, sitting next to him, drowning in white noise. My temples throbbed.

The guy mumbled something and stared at me with ice-blue eyes that seemed unnatural against his olive skin.

"What?" I asked.

"My name is Ethan."

He might have been our age, but he looked a few years older. A senior, maybe? If so, I'd never seen him at school. None of that mattered. Judging from his survival clothing, I knew he was one of those cult people. I hated him for that.

"I don't know what to say to you," I told him.

"I talked to the nurse. Victoria's surgeon is one of the best in the country, and your friend is strong—"

"Don't." I wanted to believe fairy tales too, but her dried blood still stained my cuticles. No one could live through that accident, and even if she did... "Just don't."

"Really. I overheard the EMTs. They started her heart again in the ambulance."

"To what end?" I said too loudly. A hippie in John Lennon glasses with thinning brown hair gawked at us from the vending machine. Several other people did too. I quieted my voice. "You wouldn't understand."

"I understand more than you think," he said. "You can't blame yourself for this. Accidents happen every day. It's not for us to decide."

"Here we go," I said. "Next, you're going preach about mysterious ways."

"No, I wasn't going to do that." He sat up and leaned forward. "You, above all people, might want to think before dishing out stereotypes."

"Why? Because I'm black, I have some bigger responsibility?"

"Not because of that," he said. "You judged and executed the Awakeners the minute you stepped into the camp. I saw the whole thing go down. You were wrong about us."

"Was I?"

He pointed to the waiting room. "Look around you."

The mother with the butcher's blood from earlier smiled at me, as if to say that it would be okay. Her daughter had passed out, sucking her thumb in the seat next to her. In fact, I think everyone in the waiting room had been at the rally. Through the front sliding glass doors, the cult leader who had approached Victoria and me spoke to Sheriff Acosta. That's when I noticed who wasn't there. Victoria's parents hadn't arrived yet.

"You may not understand why this happened," Ethan said. "But it happened for a reason."

"What reason?" I asked him. "She was going to change the world. It should've been me."

"Yeah," he said. "Maybe it should've."

"Excuse me? Who the hell are you again?"

"Good." He nodded. "It's about time we broke up your pity party."

"My friend is dying in there because of me."

"Your friend just got hit by a truck, and she's still fighting. If she hasn't given up, what's your excuse?"

His words stopped me. He was right. If anyone could survive this, Victoria could. I wanted to believe it, but he hadn't seen the tree branch stabbed through the side of her abdomen. Or the glass nuggets embedded in her cheeks.

"I don't know what I'd do without her," I said. He grabbed my hand, and I pulled away. "I'm fine."

"It may seem like no one understands," he said. "But some of us do."

He reached inside the front of his green flannel shirt, pulled out a twine necklace, and took it off. The pendant was some kind of canine tooth, too big to be a wolf's.

"Some Native American tribes practice bear medicine." I could see the sadness in his smile. "My mother wore this when she got sick a few years ago."

He took off the necklace and handed it to me. Feathers had been woven into the twine. An ivory circle surrounded the tooth. Latin words were etched around the perimeter.

"Did this necklace help?" I asked.

"That depends on how you look at it. She lived years beyond any of her oncologist's predictions. So yes, to a scared eight-year-old boy, it was magic." I started to hand it back to him. He reached out and closed my palm around it. "I want you to have it."

"I can't take your mother's necklace. You don't even know me."

"Give it back when your friend gets better. I want you to bring it to Victoria for me." He glanced around the ER. "From us."

I realized that everyone had stopped what they were doing. They all watched Ethan and me. Many of them were crying, but it was really the sincerity on their faces that moved me. They were just a group of people who wanted my best friend to live. Yeah, they were weird, but seriously, who was I to judge normal? At this point, we needed all the help we could get.

"Do you think it will work?" I asked.

"I'd put more faith in the doctors here and her will to live. I don't know. Maybe my mother fought the breast cancer into remission on her own. Either way, it can't hurt."

He was right, and it did make me feel better to hold something. I glanced down at it again. The tooth itself was still sharp. The inscription around the edge had worn down with time. Why would a Native American talisman have Latin on it?

Don't do that, Monique.

Sure, these people were Cuckoo for Cocoa Puffs, but they weren't dangerous. Besides, even if they were demon-worshipping orgy freaks, I didn't believe in that nonsense. I slipped the cold ivory around my neck, grateful for the gesture. Still, why would a Native American medallion have Latin written on it?

"Here's my phone number." Ethan wrote it down. "If you ever need to talk, call me."

A doctor in surgery scrubs rushed down the hallway to the head nurse's station. The woman behind the front desk pointed at me, and he walked over to us with a grim look on his face.

"I need to speak with somebody from Victoria's family," he said.

"That's me." I stood. Technically a lie, but so what? "Her parents are on their way."

"You may want to sit down," he said, and my heart caught in my throat.

3

T HE DOCTOR'S WORDS RAINED like meteors on my small world, each impact crater more devastating than the last. Victoria had died for six minutes on the road before they restarted her heart. No one knew if she would ever wake again or how extensive her brain damage would be when she did.

"I have to see her." I pushed my way past the doctor.

He yelled something from behind, but I didn't care. After Dad's surgery last spring, I could navigate the hospital's rat maze blind. I reached the critical care section and hit the red button. Mechanized glass doors hissed open, and a burst of pressurized air seemed to freeze me in place.

I stared down the dark, lemon-scented corridor. At 2:00 am, all foot traffic had stopped on the high-gloss floors. The dimmed lights barely fought back the shadows.

I shivered. At the end of this hallway, lay a special place that I knew too well. Hidden away from the regular patients, with their broken fingers and tonsillitis, was a different realm, where the damned endured endless torment, wondering if their loved ones would survive the night.

I hurried down the hall and reached the head nurse's station, which sat like an oasis of light in the center of the ICU's octagon. Jeannette apparently still worked the night shift. Her red hair looked like flames under the warm lamps above. Her skin seemed to glow.

"Monique." She pulled out a single iPod ear bud. "Honey, I am so sorry."

"Where is she?" I demanded.

"Just out of surgery, but it's after hours. You know that only family can be back here now."

"Victoria and I have been sisters since kindergarten." I glanced around. Two hospital rooms per side on the octagon. Sixteen total. I'd search every one of them if I had to, with or without her permission. "I won't let her be alone. Not in this place."

"Monique, please don't make me call security."

"You don't have to do that," I told her. "You've broken the rules before."

"Your father was a different story. He's your blood."

"The accident was my fault—" I choked up, so I paused to compose myself. She glanced nervously down the hallway from which I'd come, so I added, "It's just us."

"Fine, you can check on her from outside her room, but then you need to leave," Jeannette said, and I nodded. "We have to keep her contained until she heals."

She stood, and I followed her over to room eight. Ethan's talisman felt warm against my skin, so I pulled it above my shirt.

"Where did you get that necklace?" Jeanette asked me.

"From a friend," I said.

"There's a lot of power there," she told me. "Be careful."

What the heck did that mean?

A girl shrieked as if she were being stabbed. It sounded like Victoria! Jeannette raced forward and wrestled with the door handle. It didn't budge. Another scream. This time, I knew it was her. I ran to the room's front window.

Through the reinforced glass, I saw Victoria lying on a gurney with her head turned away. Cybernetic attachments surrounded her bed, which sat in the center of the room. Underneath the blanket that covered her body, she twitched. I grabbed a chair and smashed it against the glass, but it bounced off without leaving even a crack.

"We have to get in there," I yelled at Jeannette.

"It's not time. Not yet."

I glanced back inside the room. Victoria's bed sat empty. Next to my faint reflection in the window's glass, something twitched. I spun around. She now stood inches away from me with her eyes closed, wearing only a hospital gown.

"Help me." She mouthed the words, but only a metallic whisper came out.

Her eyes snapped open. They'd been carved hollow. Hundreds of spiders began crawling out of them. Several thick tarantula legs poked through her left eye and rested around her socket.

"Victoria," I said. "I'm so sorry."

Someone grabbed my arms. I struggled to break free. A flash of light stole my sight, and I screamed.

"Honey," my dad said. "Are you hurt?"

Suddenly, I was sitting at Spic 'n Micks. Everyone in the restaurant stared at me, and I realized that I had just screamed out loud. A mud-caked construction worker grabbed his son's chin and forced him to look away. My god. What had happened? One moment, I was in the hospital. Now, I was here in this restaurant twenty miles away. Was I losing my mind? Psycho people in movies lost hours of time like this while they were busy chopping up coeds.

"Are you okay?" Dad asked. He put his hand on my wrist, although he looked unsure of whether or not he should touch me. Then he motioned to a waitress in a halter-top and butt-muncher shorts. "Can I get some water for my daughter over here?"

She nodded and rushed through swinging doors into the back kitchen area. Everyone still stared.

"No big deal," Dad said loudly. "She just saw a cockroach."

"What do you think this food's made out of?" a graveled

voice called out to an assortment of snickers. "I got a good idea. Why don't I send the pretty lady a drink to calm her nerves?"

"She's fifteen, Don," Dad said. "If I ever catch any of you meatheads near her, I'll snip off your cock and staple it over my doorstep."

The bar erupted in stomping and fits of laughter. I covered my face, positive that I had never been more embarrassed. Some metal band began playing on the jukebox. The conies and hardhats settled down, clinking their metal forks against ceramic plates as they began shoveling food in their mouths again.

The waitress arrived with my water. "Here you go, honey."

"We need a moment before we order," Dad told her. She nodded and walked away. He turned to me with a furrowed brow.

"I'm fine," I said. "Really."

"You just fell asleep while I was talking to you." He kept his voice hushed. "With your eyes open. You're telling me that's fine?"

"I'm just a little tired. That's all."

Right then, reality flooded back. I'd been spending too much time down at the hospital watching over Victoria in her coma, so Dad had picked me up for lunch. We had just sat down to eat when...what happened? That daydream hit me. No, *hit* was the wrong word. Daydream wasn't right, either. A steamroller smashed me into another universe. I had been wide-awake here, yet in that nightmarish hospital, I had no clue that what I felt wasn't real. The rasp in Victoria's voice sent prickles of ice up my back. *Help me,* she had said.

"Dad, I'm sorry." I stood and grabbed my pea coat on the back of my chair. "We have to go back to the hospital."

"Not until you get something in your stomach."

"I already ate."

"I mean real food," he said, as if either the Irish or the Mexican menu here provided any nutrition except lard and carbs, fortified with E-Coli.

"Victoria needs me," I told him.

"Lita and Carl are there for her right now." He took off his cement-dusted beanie and placed it on the wooden bench table. "You haven't left that hospital in three days."

How could I possibly explain to him what happened? It felt like Victoria had somehow mentally reached out to me for help. If I said anything that crazy, he'd ban me from the hospital forever.

"What if I order something to go?" I asked.

"We're going to have dinner here together as a family, and that's final."

"Don't give me your old man tone," I said. "I'm not six anymore. I contribute plenty to our household."

"I don't care if you're a hundred-year-old, toothless banker," he huffed. "You're my daughter, and you always will be."

I couldn't risk working him into a fit. Though he tried to hide it, he was out of breath. He still hadn't fully recovered from his heart surgery. His cheekbones showed on his gaunt face, and I couldn't shake the thought of those zipper tracks of keloid scars up his sternum.

"I don't want to argue," I told him.

"Just sit down," he said softly. "We need to talk."

Something was wrong. Robinsons didn't discuss ideas or share feelings. Especially my dad, the king of grunts.

The bar's track lighting dimmed. On the stage across the room, Friday's Open Mic Night started with no announcement. A female knife juggler spent the first thirty seconds picking up the blades she dropped. Even morbid curiosity couldn't bring me to watch her nearly slice herself open with every toss.

I sat back down. "What do you want to talk about?"

"You remind me of your mother sometimes." He grabbed some peanuts from the center tray, cracked one open, and contributed to the sawdust of shells on the concrete floor. "You know what I always said about her?"

"Never trust a white woman?"

"Yeah." He chuckled. "Never jump the broom with one either."

"I'll keep that in mind if I decide to lez out," I said.

He smiled with such sadness in his eyes that I almost had to turn away.

"She was tough sometimes because she had to be," he said. "You got all the best parts of her. None of the bad."

I didn't know what to say. This was the first time we had spoken about her in years. Watching him chew on his lip was strange too. I'd never seen him so nervous. This was far worse than when he used a carton of eggs to explain the birds and the bees to me. For months, I thought that human babies hatched as well.

"Why are you bringing this up now?" I asked.

"You got the best parts of me, too, I think," he continued as if he hadn't heard me. "When somebody's given a lot of gifts, God sees fit to test them sometimes."

What the hell was this? He never talked about God, and he wasn't a philosopher. That's when I noticed that his eyes had welled up.

"What's going on?" I demanded.

"Listen to me—"

"We haven't been to this restaurant in years. Why did you bring me out here?" He didn't seem to know how to respond. "Answer me."

"Victoria's tests came back this morning."

"And?"

"Her parents didn't want you to be there."

"Why wouldn't they want me with her?" I asked. *Help me*, she had said in that dream. "I don't understand."

"They need to be alone so they can grieve."

"Grieve for what? She's not dead."

Oh no. There was only one reason why they would want me gone. They were going to pull the plug.

"Dad, you have to listen to me. Take me back to the hospital. She's not dead."

"This is their business now. Lita specifically asked me—"

"Of course, she did," I yelled. Everyone stared again. "She's always hated Victoria. Take me back there now."

"Dammit," he said. "Their daughter is dead, Monique. Leave them be."

"You lied to me." I couldn't hold back my tears anymore. "To keep me here while they kill my friend."

I turned and barreled through the front door.

"Monique," he shouted from behind. "Come back."

Screw him. Only five miles to town. I'd sprint the entire distance if necessary. Next to the neon sign along the highway, several big rigs started to pull out of the parking lot, so I headed toward the closest one, which had no trailer attached. Maybe I wouldn't have to run after all.

I waved my hands at the driver, and his brakes squealed. I climbed up on the passenger side window and motioned for the guy to roll it down. He did.

"I need a ride into town," I told him. "I don't have money."

"Hop in."

"Hold on. Are you going to chop me up or sew girl suits out of sections of my skin?"

"Sounds pretty messy." He laughed, but it wasn't funny.

"Well?" I said.

"Why don't I just take you someplace safer than this dump?"

"I've got pepper spray," I told him, opened the door, and climbed in. "So don't get any ideas."

"My mind is blank." Judging by the monster truck magazine on the seat, I believed him.

He shoved the vehicle out of park. Something under the hood hissed, and we pulled away.

Help me, my best friend had begged. That was just what I planned to do.

4

YES, HITCHHIKING WAS RECKLESS and stupid. So was my father for putting me in this position. Had the trucker chopped off my head and used it as a hood decoration, it would have been Dad's fault. Instead, the creep chattered endlessly about his wife and their swinger lifestyle, which involved a little dark meat every now and then. I told him I was fifteen, which shut him up, but the silence was almost worse as we traveled down that dark slush highway.

I called the hospital on my cell. Just like in that waking nightmare, Jeanette was working the late shift. She reluctantly told me that Victoria's parents hadn't gone through with it yet. They were across the street at the church, collecting their thoughts.

Fifteen minutes later, Chester the Truck Driving Molester lived up to his word and dropped me off in front of Eden Springs Cathedral. As I entered the church's cold darkness, my boot steps echoed off the epic granite archways.

Directly in front of me, Victoria's father sat alone in the third row pew, lit only by the hundreds of candles that dripped days-old wax over the memorial of flowers, stuffed animals, and framed family pictures.

Help me. Victoria's SOS had been real. Somehow, she had found a way to reach out to me, but how could I explain that to him without sounding insane.

I approached him. "Mr. Malakoff?"

Carl barely turned his head. I couldn't shake my nerves. I'd rarely spoken to Victoria's father because his emotionless face always seemed to be calculating the best way to strangle me. Now, with his puffy eyes glistening in this low light, he looked infinitely more dangerous.

"I heard about the test results." I sat a few feet from him. "I don't know what to say."

"Sure you do. This is the part where you try to stop me." Without taking his eyes from the flickering candlelight of the shrine, he reached inside his trench coat and pulled out a flask-sized liquor bottle that was wrapped in a sweaty paper bag. "Nothing you say is going to help, so get to it. Let's hear your pitch and then leave me the hell alone."

"I'm here to ask for more time."

"Time." He nodded with a sarcastic smile.

"If you could just wait for a few days to get a second opinion—"

"I've already paid for the best opinions. Even the cowards on my hospital payroll couldn't bring themselves to lie to me."

"What if they're wrong?" I asked.

He answered with a long swig of booze. What could I even say to somebody like him, especially in this condition?

One of the parish cats strolled down our pew, paying mild attention to the cooing sounds of a pigeon somewhere in the rafter above. It jumped into Carl's lap. For a second, he glared at the puff of gray and white fur. Then he began to pet it. Blood streaked its hair. Had it been in a fight? No, the mangled knuckles on Carl's right hand looked like he'd wrapped his fist in barbed wire and fought in a cage match.

"Please," I said. "I'm only asking for a few days."

"It won't make any difference," he slurred. This was more than just drunk. Pills, too, or something worse. "It's better for her this way."

"She's not better off dead."

"You're not a Malakoff. You wouldn't understand."

"I understand your daughter needs her father to stand up for her. Not your drunken BS."

"Watch yourself." His face twisted. The candlelight splayed across the hard angles of his cheekbones, making him appear deadly sober. "Don't think for one second that I've forgotten who drove my daughter into those hills to her death."

"It was an accident," I said, but his words cut me like daggers. "She's not dead yet, unless you pull the plug."

"Okay." He shooed the cat off his lap. "You got my attention, little girl. What information do you have for me?"

"Victoria is alive."

"Medical science disagrees with your expert analysis," he said.

"They're wrong. I know it."

"Ah. You know it." He enunciated every single word.

I searched for an argument that wouldn't land me in a straitjacket. Screw it. I couldn't possibly sound crazier than he did right now.

"She reached out and talked to me today," I said.

"Don't lie to me." He pointed in my face. "Don't you dare."

"I wouldn't lie about this. Do you think I'd want her to live on those machines if she really was dead?"

"Lita's been filling your head with garbage. Victoria is my daughter. Not hers. You hear me? I make these decisions."

Was Queen Lita trying to save Victoria's life too? I'd assumed that she'd be hovering next to the respirator with one finger on the switch. Still, she wasn't Victoria's biological mother. The decision really was his. Somehow, I had to make him understand.

"If I'm wrong, a couple of days won't matter," I told him. "But what if your daughter is alive?"

"That crippled thing across the street is not my Victoria," he said. "No Malakoff wants to live like that, and the sooner that you and Lita get that through your heads, the better off we'll all be."

"Oh my god. You don't want her to come back." All my life, he had showered her with love and praise. Given her everything. I had never even considered that he wanted nothing to do with imperfect offspring, staining his precious legacy.

"Just get out of here," he said. "There's no point in arguing. Doctor Weston is taking her off life support."

"What? Now?"

"As we speak." He turned away from me. "I already told you that nothing you said would change this."

That bastard. I stood and raced back down the aisle. My vision that I'd had at the restaurant was coming true. Victoria had tried to warn me, but I didn't know how to read the images. In the dream, I tried to smash a window because someone had locked me away from her, but the glass wouldn't break.

Not this time. Carl. The doctors. Hospital security. It didn't matter who it was. I barreled out of the chapel toward Eden Springs ICU, ready to smash anyone who got in my way.

5

I'D NEVER FELT MORE HELPLESS than I did racing down the hallway that led to the ICU. What exactly did I intend to do when I got to Victoria? Stop the doctor from doing his job? I needed Lita. If anyone could convince Carl to give his daughter more time, his wife might be able to.

As I turned the corner to the nurse's station, my boot steps chirped on the hospital's high-gloss floors. I glanced over. Déjà vu stole my breath. Jeannette sat at her desk, tapping her keyboard. Her red hair glowed under the oasis of track lights above in an otherwise darkened room, exactly like in my dream.

"Monique." She pulled out an ear bud. "Honey, I am so sorry."

Chills raced up my neck. Word for word, my hallucination had officially become a psychic vision. That meant I was almost out of time. Those spiders would be here soon— whatever they meant.

"Where's Lita?" I demanded.

"You can't be here."

"Please, I have to talk to her."

That's when I saw her through the window to Victoria's room. I raced over and shoved the door, half-expecting it to be locked like in the dream. Instead, the force of my shoulder slammed it open against the wall. Lita and Dr. Weston stood on either side of Victoria in her bed, clearly stunned by the outburst.

None of the attachments wired to her body appeared to

beep or flash. Had they already done it? If so, it must have happened just seconds before because Lita still held Victoria's hand.

"Turn the machines back on," I said.

"Honey, you shouldn't be here." Lita stepped into my path. Her raven hair was drenched, and her white blouse clung to her thin frame, as if she had stood outside in the rainstorm with no coat for hours.

"She's alive," I said.

"I'm going to have to ask you to leave." The doctor gently grabbed my shoulder and then looked past me to the nurse, Jeannette, who now stood in the doorway.

Get security, he mouthed the words. She nodded and rushed away.

"You have to turn the respirator back on," I told Lita as he nudged me. "Just give me a day. I'll find a way to pay for it."

"Monique, it's not my decision to make." She looked down to the floor.

"Victoria," I shouted. "Help me. I don't know what to do."

"It's time for you to leave." Dr. Weston shoved me backward, looked at someone behind me, and said, "Get her out of here."

"They're going to kill you," I shouted. "If you don't wake up, you're going to die."

A security guard rushed in and grabbed me. I shoved back, and we struggled. The doctor leaned in too, and something stabbed my sternum. What sort of idiot doctor would try to inject tranquilizers through my breastplate? I glanced down. Actually, there was no needle. Ethan's bear tooth necklace had partially ripped through my blouse and dug into my chest.

In everything that had happened since the restaurant, I'd forgotten about the medallion. It had been in my hallucination too. In the vision, Jeanette said that it had power. Was this what Victoria tried to show me? So what if those church freaks were crazed? The cult leader's son said his mother beat cancer for years because of that tooth.

I yanked on the necklace and snapped the twine. With all my strength, I pushed free from the guard and ran up to her. Both Lita and the doctor hopped back, as if the necklace I wielded were actually a butcher knife. I grabbed Victoria's hand, which shocked me with static electricity. The lights overhead flickered.

"Wake up." I touched her cheek gently, careful to avoid the gauze patches that covered both her eyes. I put the medallion in her hand. "Please don't leave me."

Then what seemed like a frenzy of people grabbed me, yanked me backward, and snapped my cheek against the room's glass window.

"Be gentle with her," Lita said. "She's grieving."

"Victoria," I shouted.

Something wicked and inhuman shrieked. The short, piercing burst sounded like a wild animal caught in a rototiller.

"Christ Almighty." The guard let me go.

I spun around to find Victoria sitting up in her gurney. With wires and feeding tubes stretched taut around her arms and neck, she looked like a human marionette, dangling from the life support machines.

Then she screamed again, but this one was so much worse, as if the barriers between this reality and a hellish ice realm had ripped, giving birth to something with scissor claws and brutal teeth.

Victoria's head twitched. Despite the gauze patches taped over her eyes, she turned her head and seemed to stare directly at me. Violent spasms erupted through her body, finishing with a chomp of her jaw, which looked painful with her missing front teeth.

For the briefest moment, I saw it. I wish I hadn't, but we were best friends, and I couldn't pretend. Her lips twitched upward, ever so slightly. She smiled at me and then collapsed back on the bed, still clutching the medallion in her white-knuckled grip.

6

SECONDS AFTER VICTORIA WOKE from her coma, the guard regained his composure, and he shoved me out of the hospital. Carl and Lita then proceeded to shut me out of her life altogether. I understood why they needed space, but it had been two days. Why wouldn't they let me see her? Had she talked yet? How long until she could come back to school? Then came the worst thought of all.

She's never going to forgive you. You know that, right?

Early Monday, I called her house again and waited for Lita's prepared remarks. For the first time, the line went straight to voice mail. That's when I knew if I ever wanted to see my friend again, I'd have to make it happen. Instead of walking to school that morning, I turned left toward her house.

Down Castel Lane, shrouds of fog concealed the behemoth oaks that evenly lined the street. Frosted in ice, their clutched branches created a tunnel above the road, daring outsiders to stroll down Death's gauntlet.

I approached the Malakoffs' gate of ornamental wrought iron and antiqued brick. It never ceased to amaze me how creepy rich folks and their houses could be, especially in winter. Still, I knew my fear was irrational. I mean, come on. I stood outside my best friend's house. Not the black gates of Mordor.

With a gloved finger, I pushed the intercom.

"Hello," I said into the microphone. "Is anyone home?"

Up on the hill, Lita's second-story bedroom curtain

moved. Seriously? A grown woman hiding in her own house like a ghost. From me, no less.

"I can see you up there," I said into the intercom. Maybe I shouldn't have been so forward, but this game was getting old.

"Monique." Lita's voice crackled back at me through the speaker with disturbing pep. "Shouldn't you be at school?"

"Can you open the gate? It's freezing out here."

"Victoria's not ready for visitors," she repeated that same monotone script.

"Actually, I'm here to see you. I'd hop the fence, but I wore a skirt today, and I don't want my name and address out there for everyone to see." No laugh. Just silence, as if she believed I might actually scale the wall like Victoria and I did when we were eight. "Just give me five minutes. After that, I'll leave you alone if you want."

Finally, the gate popped and groaned open. I walked inside to find the hedge sculptures frosted in the same windswept tundra that crunched underfoot. I turned the corner. Lita already stood outside next to the pond, where the absent Koi had been hibernating for months.

Normally, she wore lipstick to bed and eyeliner to breakfast. Now, her straight black hair had been tied in a knot. Puffs of her breath fogged on contact with the air, yet she wore only a white bathrobe, slippers, and a tacky red scarf.

"I need you to stop," she said as I approached. "I told you I would let you know when Victoria was ready."

"It's been days now, and I've heard nothing."

"You don't know how serious it is." The circles below her eyes seemed to accentuate her point.

"Yes, I do," I said. "Victoria wouldn't be alive today if it weren't for me."

She also wouldn't have been in the accident in the first place. My inner bitch voice wouldn't shut up.

"I know you don't understand," Lita said. "But you have to trust me. It's not safe for you here."

What could possibly be so dangerous? I could only think of Ethan's talisman and the crazy cult people. In every horror movie, from Wes Craven to Stanley Kubrick, idiots always took too long to notice the obvious, and idiots always ended up as meat for the grinder.

"That necklace," I said. "Where is it?"

"What are you talking about?"

"The pendant. The one that brought Victoria back from the dead."

Lita gave me a strange look. I didn't care if she thought I was nuts. She was only ten years older than I was, and she slept in the same bed with Carl.

"This is not one of your movies," she told me. "It's serious. I asked your father to take you away from the hospital that night for your own protection. Do you understand what I'm saying?"

"My protection?"

Somewhere outside the front gates, brakes squealed. She pushed me behind her and glanced around the shrubs. The car must have driven away because her shoulders relaxed.

"Listen to me." She put cold fingers on my cheek, and her ridiculous scarf dipped low, revealing dark splotches on her neck. Were those finger marks?

"Go home," she said. "This will blow over, but you can't keep taunting Carl like you did at the church."

"That bastard." I pulled down her scarf to reveal a full handprint bruise. "He did that to you?"

Lita jerked away, covered back up, and said, "Don't worry about it."

"Are you kidding me right now?"

"Our family has been dragged through hell. That's all you need to know."

"I'd like drag him behind our pickup," I told her.

"Stick around for a while," she said. "If he ever does it again, you just might see that happen."

I could tell she wasn't kidding. Lita was no punching bag. Darkness hid inside of her, a fingernail's scratch below her flawless skin, but it was there. It was the good kind too. The kind that helped a girl in a pinch if necessary.

"Why would you stay with him?" I asked.

"I can't leave." She glanced back at the house with concern. "Not yet. Maybe when things calm down. I don't know. If I'm not around..."

Suddenly, I understood. Lita could leave if she wanted.

"You can't take Victoria with you," I said.

"I'm not her mother. Not legally."

"But she's alive," I said. "Why is he still acting crazy?"

She stared across the pond, clutching her robe. On the far side of the lake, the twelve-foot rock waterfall appeared to have frozen in time, leaving behind blobs of flowing glass.

"Victoria never came back to us." Her lips started trembling. "From the ambulance ride on the night of the accident. She never came back."

"That's not true. I saw her in the hospital."

"You saw something," she said. "Believe me, we all did, but that girl up there is not her."

I thought of Victoria's scream as she woke. Her malicious smile.

"She needs me." I tried to push past Lita. She grabbed my arm, so I said, "Let go."

"It's not your fault. God knows that it's not, but if Carl sees you here, I don't know what he'll do."

"I'm not scared of him."

"I've already lost my daughter. I won't lose you too."

A lump swelled in my throat. It wasn't just the way that she talked about Victoria as her daughter. Did Lita actually care about me? Now, I felt ashamed for all the names we'd called her over the years. Dollar Barbie. The Trophiest. Through all of this, she seemed to be the only person who cared.

I knew only one way to fix this situation. I had to bring the real Victoria back to her family.

"Carl's not here now," I said. "Let me see her."

"He's coming back this afternoon."

"So what? I've sneaked in and out of this house a million times without you knowing."

She laughed and wiped the corner of her eye. "Not as many times as you think."

"Trust me," I said. "I can help."

She seemed to consider it. Finally, she said, "If you're going in, you need to brace yourself."

"I'm ready."

"No, you're not." She put her arm around me and began walking me through the front door. "God help us, sweetie. You're not."

7

THE COLD WINTER LIGHT that trickled through the arched windows didn't ease my fear as I followed Lita up that staircase to see Victoria. Would anything be left of the girl I'd known and loved since kindergarten? The girl who literally kicked a hornet's nest behind Fallbrook Elementary to prove she was tougher than Lisbeth Salander and her stupid dragon tattoo. I had to hope. After all, she had sent out that mental beacon. To me, no less. Monique the weary, dark, and dreary, who'd never been psychic or gifted in any sense of the word.

So she wasn't gone forever. Lost maybe, in some subterranean part of her mind. I had to bring her back. Lita continued to the end of the hall and stopped outside their personal museum room. Inside, a muffled rendition of Moonlight Sonata played.

"When we go in," she said. "Talk softly. And no sudden movements."

I nodded. She opened the thick oak door, and I realized the music wasn't prerecorded. An older man—way heavier than Dad at his largest—sat at their baby grand. Wearing a full tuxedo, he caressed the keys with the grace of a ballerina's pirouette.

"It has to be live." Lita seemed to read my mind. "Or she doesn't respond."

Dead ahead, faced away from us toward the crackling fire, an antique wheelchair squeaked. My heart raced. It had to be Victoria, but why would they sit her in that decrepit thing? With its wooden back and tarnished brass handgrip, it looked more like a medieval torture device than a wheelchair. Victoria's cooing noises were interrupted by gasps for air. I started to move to her, but Lita grabbed my shoulder.

"You need to prepare yourself."

"I'm ready, but...." I glanced at the fossil skeleton of the sabre-tooth tiger. Its hollow eye sockets and bone spear incisors seemed more threatening than usual. "Can we move her? She hates this room."

"Not anymore, she doesn't." The finality of her words scared me. "This is the only place where she's comfortable. Besides, any movement could set her off."

The pianist finished his piece and started right back in. No wonder she wasn't doing well. How long had he been playing that same song? In my absence, the circus had come to town, complete with a carnival barker freak show.

"I need to be alone with her," I told Lita.

"Honey, that's not a good idea."

"I'm not allowed, but it's okay for a strange piano player?"

"It's not that," she said. "She needs the music."

"He just plays Beethoven over and over. How's that working out for you?"

"You think I don't know how this looks?" she asked, and I immediately regretted my tone. "This room. That disgusting chair."

"Then why are you using it?"

"It's her grandfather's heirloom. I don't know why these things calm her, and I don't care. I can't take the screaming. It's too much."

"Nobody's judging you." I hadn't realized how close to the edge she was. "I can't talk to her openly with people in the room. Especially Pavarotti's sweaty cousin over there."

She smiled, and I was grateful for the break in the tension.

"No matter what," she said. "You can't remove her restraints."

"I just want to talk. That's all."

"Mr. Henson," she said to the pianist. "Take a break."

He shot me a dirty look, apparently perturbed that he didn't get to play his song, yet again. The minute he stopped, Victoria began moaning like a mother who'd just lost her child.

"I'm going to get dressed in something more than my robe," Lita told me, and then she followed the pianist out into the hallway and shut the door behind them. I crept over to Victoria and stood in front of her.

Lita had been right. Nothing could have prepared me for this.

She wore a white nightgown, wet down the front with drool. Both of her wrists had been secured to the armrest with leather cuff straps. Her ankles and chest had also been fastened in place. Gauze bandages covered her road rash of scabs from the car accident, while an IV drip had been taped down to her forearm.

None of those things could compare with the swimmer's goggles though, tinted black with large oval lenses. She looked like a genetic experiment gone wrong.

"I'm so sorry," I told her. "This is all my fault. You never would have gotten out of the car that night if we hadn't fought."

I touched her cheek.

Help me, the words screeched inside my brain. The taste of nine-volt battery zinged my tongue. Had that happened just from my touch? The urge to help her escape overwhelmed me. She had to get out of this place. I leaned down and unstrapped one of her wrists.

Immediately, Victoria shoved me and began clawing at her own right arm. Was she trying to free herself? No. She tore off her bandages and began digging into her scabs, yanking her feeding tube loose in the process. Fresh blood poured from the new wounds. Her mouth twisted in a painful grimace, revealing those same broken front teeth.

"Victoria, stop it." I tried to hold her wrist against the armrest, but I couldn't strap her in at the same time, so I shouted, "Help."

The door burst open, and Lita hurried over to me. An older woman with her hair pulled back in a bun followed behind. She wore blue scrubs.

"What happened?" The nurse shoved me aside and cinched Victoria's wrist back in the cuff.

"Dammit, Monique," Lita said. "I told you not to let her out of the restraints for a reason."

"Who is this person?" the nurse asked Lita with a Russian accent. "Mr. Malakoff said no visitors. No exceptions. The patient is far too worked up."

"The patient has a name," I told her. "I don't know what came over me. It's this chair, the room, everything."

"We don't have a choice," Lita said. "She keeps hurting herself, Monique. Do you understand?"

Suddenly, the goggles took on new meaning. Had she tried to claw at her own eyes? Either way, it didn't matter. *Help me.* That message couldn't have been more clear.

"I'll get the disinfectant." The nurse walked over to a medical storage unit that had been wheeled underneath the stuffed boar's head. "We're going to need to sedate her to get the feeding tube back in properly."

"I need more time with her," I told Lita.

"Absolutely not," the nurse said.

Victoria let out a short, piercing shriek. Then she leaned against her chest strap and tried to gnaw on her own shoulder.

"Get her out of here," the nurse demanded. "She's making this worse."

"Do you even know why she feels safer in this room?" I asked. "That window doesn't lock because we broke it. I always sneak in here. She's been waiting for me."

"Nonsense." The nurse pulled out a syringe and shoved it into a vial. "Victoria doesn't even know what day it is."

"How would you know?"

"Just look at your face," she said, and I realized in the excitement, Victoria had clawed my cheek. "She attacked you and hurt herself again."

"No, I just happened to be in the way. She's deathly afraid of needles, and you have one permanently jacked into her arm."

"Why am I arguing with a child?" She turned expectantly to Lita. "Get her out of here. Now."

"Excuse me?" Lita's back stiffened. "This is my house and my daughter. I tell you what to do."

"Please," I said. "I only need five minutes to try something. If it doesn't work, I'll leave, and I won't come back until you call me."

"You've got three." Lita pulled the nurse back. "And we're staying in the room."

"Victoria." I kneeled in front of her. Open palmed, I gently put both my hands on her cheeks to recreate what happened just before that voice entered my head. "Come back to us."

"I won't be held responsible if something happens to either of them," the nurse said over my shoulder.

"Victoria, you sent me that message," I said. Nothing. She continued struggling against her restraints. "I don't know what you want from me, but if you don't show them something now, they're going to split us up for good."

With a jolt, my heartbeat sped up. My knees weakened, but I held strong. Victoria stopped screaming and sat motionless. Both our bodies felt connected, like a single rigid animal. A pulse of nausea washed through me, but I still held tight.

"That's it," I told her. "You have to show them something, or they're not going to let me see you anymore."

Victoria opened her mouth and released a raspy gurgle.

"We," she said in a breathy voice.

I think she said *we*. It could have been *way*. Lita gasped behind me.

"We." Victoria dragged out the word this time, as if trying to relearn its pronunciation. "We."

"That's right. We," I told her. Another wave of exhaustion hit me. My muscles felt ready to give out, so I clasped her cheeks with all my strength. "We. You and me. Forever and ever."

"We, are, you." Victoria raised her voice. "We are you."

Another jolt drained me. I could barely lift my arms.

"What's going on?" Lita moved to my side. "Monique."

"Stay back." I tried to shout, but my voice cracked.

"We are you," Victoria said more frantically now. "We are you. We are you."

Finally, I couldn't take anymore, so I pulled my hands away and collapsed onto the floor.

"Honey, can you hear me?" Lita rushed to my side and snapped blurry fingers in front of my face.

"It's okay," I said through gasps. "I'm okay."

Above me, I could see Victoria's blurred face past the wheelchair's armrest. She remained still, but not completely silent.

"We are you," she whispered now, barely moving her lips. "We are you. We are you."

8

EVERYTHING CHANGED AFTER Victoria spoke. With haunted eyes, Lita started popping Xanax from her purse like Tic Tacs. The nurse refused to make eye contact with me. I mean, come on people. Yes, Victoria's words had been disturbing. *We are you.* Only a fool wouldn't notice it, but after witnessing the horror of her condition beforehand, I couldn't help my excitement.

Now she remained calm without the aid of the pianist. We removed the restraints, and she didn't try to hurt herself anymore. As a precaution, the goggles stayed on, but during those few minutes when I was with her, she had made real progress.

That's why I sat behind her wheelchair now, brushing her hair. I had no clue what caused her to speak. Physical contact had something to do with it maybe, although it didn't seem to be working now. Or it could have been the sound of my voice. Either way, I needed to be close to her.

When the nurse finally left for the afternoon, I turned to Lita and said, "I don't think she's coming back tomorrow."

"You must be a mind reader. She just gave her notice."

"Really? I was only kidding."

"Carl will be home soon." Lita closed the door to the hallway. "We need to talk."

I pointed at Victoria and shook my head. *Not in front of her.* If she was trapped in there listening to our conversation, I didn't want her to overhear what her father had done to Lita. At least not yet.

Lita motioned to the fireplace on the far side of the room. I squeezed Victoria's hand and put it back in her own lap.

"Deadness," she muttered. "Falls, catacomb press, lead the light, stitched skin."

"Her vocabulary is growing." I tried to lighten the mood.

"Yeah," Lita said with a creased brow. "I can hear that."

I stood from my seat and stumbled, latching onto the wheelchair for support until my vertigo passed.

"Are you okay?" She put her hand on my shoulder. "We need to get you to a doctor."

"No," I told her. That hospital was the last place I wanted to be.

"You could be hurt. I don't even know *what* I just saw."

"I'm fine," I told her, but actually, I felt as if I had gone twelve rounds with a chimp. "I'll go to bed early tonight."

"Fine, but you're not walking home."

I nodded, and then followed her out of earshot to the other side of the room next to the sabre tooth cat fossil. Inside its chest cavity, the black wig still remained where Victoria had given kitty a hairball last Halloween. Outside, the thunderstorm kicked up a notch. Flecks of hail pecked the arch window glass.

"I'm going to need as much time with Victoria as possible," I said quietly.

"That's all you have to say to me?"

"Are you mad at me or something?"

"No," she said. "But you need to explain what's going on with my daughter."

"I don't know. I think her brain is rebooting." That didn't feel right, though. "No, it's more like she's reinstalling her operating system."

"Monique, you're fifteen-years old, and somehow you know more about her condition than her doctors."

"It's not my fault that nurse was clueless. How can someone possibly help Victoria if they've already given up on her?"

"It's not just the nurse," she said. "Phillip Kensington is the head of the neurology department at Cedars-Sinai. Persistent vegetative state has been everyone's diagnosis across the board."

"Then she needs better doctors. I mean, those morons pronounced her dead at the hospital. They could have buried her alive."

"These people don't get it wrong, Monique. Last week, Victoria barely stopped screaming long enough to breathe. Now you arrive, and she's speaking sentences within an hour."

"If we can bring her back, does it matter how?"

"Yes," she said. "To me, it does. Have you listened to the things she's been saying?"

"Who cares about that? Let me see her again tomorrow. She'll probably start chattering about butterflies."

"There won't be a tomorrow if you don't start talking." She reached inside her purse and pulled out a handkerchief. She unfolded it in her hand and held out the medallion that Ethan had given me. "You mentioned this to me earlier today."

I reached for it. "I need that."

"Not until you answer my question." She pulled her hand back. "You gave this to her that night in the hospital."

"It doesn't belong to me."

"Then who gave it to you?" she asked. "Answer me, or you can't come back here."

What could I tell her? Lita wouldn't be able to handle any truth that didn't fit in a convenient box. Me? I didn't pretend to have answers. If you see a ghost, then ghosts exist. If your best friend sends you a vision of the future, well then, there you have it.

These events were stacking up, though. Victoria shouldn't have survived that accident. Then came my vision, and now my physical touch had shocked her brain into functioning. These occurrences floated like bubbles of lawless magic in a universe with gravity. How fragile was a miracle? Certainly this one wouldn't stand for Lita poking at it with her worry stick. She wasn't going to back down. I had to give her something.

"I'm not sure what is going on, but she could still die." I knew that to be true, though I didn't know why. "One of those Awakeners gave the medallion to me. He said it helped his mother who had breast cancer."

"You mean those church people who brought her to the hospital?" she said. "Christ, Monique. All week long, they've refused to leave us alone."

"They might be a little schizo—"

"A little?"

"They're not evil, I think. Now I've told you everything. Please, I need to be here tomorrow. Let me come after school."

"You don't understand," she said. "Carl was angry with you before. Now he's livid."

"Why? His daughter is alive. She's getting stronger."

"That's not how he sees it," she said. "You brought back a shell to him, and a few incoherent words aren't going to change his mind."

"Is that what you think?"

"No." She absently fingered the bruise on her neck, which she'd hidden underneath a charcoal turtleneck. "I mean, I don't know."

"Now you're giving up on her too?"

"Of course not." She glared at me as if the idea were ridiculous. "You don't understand what's been happening. I almost left him for good yesterday. It's that serious."

"Why are you still here then?" I asked.

"I don't know what he'll do if I leave."

"He wouldn't hurt his own daughter," I said. "Would he?"

"Maybe not intentionally, but it's not just her that I'm worried about. The only person I know who's more stubborn than Victoria is you."

"That's not true."

"Of course not," she said. "Except that I used to work as an assistant at Chester Abbey Daycare."

"You had a job?"

"I wasn't always Queen Lita," she said. Again, I felt embarrassed of our little nicknames for her. "I met you before Victoria. I also made the foolish decision to take away your blocks because you kept throwing them at the other children."

I smiled. "Were they mine?"

"You didn't speak to me for weeks after that. No eye contact either. You just sat on a tiny chair, facing the corner. When I came to talk to you, do you know what you said to me? 'I wonder where my babysitter went.'" Lita mocked my voice. "'She must've died.'"

"That's pretty funny."

She smirked. "I can promise you I didn't think so at the time."

"I've been coming over here for years. Why didn't you tell me this?"

"I don't know. I guess it was just easier to avoid. You have to remember, this was nine or ten years ago, right about the time your mom—"

"Got it," I said. No need to dwell on the past. *Left us.* I pushed it away. "So what if I'm a little stubborn? I'm not scared of Carl."

"You should be."

I shivered at the look in her eyes. The running joke at Lucido's—always spoken in hushed voices—was that Carl Malakoff never operated in sunlight because it agitated the flies. I never understood what they meant. I think maybe I did now. Still, that didn't matter.

"We can bring her back," I said. "Isn't that worth some risk, even if cult boy's necklace is responsible?"

"I don't care about that. I'll glue it to her skin if it really helps."

"Good," I told her. "Do that."

"My concern is that Carl comes home early and catches you with Victoria, being weird in some way."

"It's a necklace."

"Is that all?"

"Yes, that's all. What, you think I've got pentagrams and chicken's blood hidden in my purse?"

"Of course not."

"Then what?" I asked, and she paused.

I thought about the child's bloody handprint on that sign at the rally. In her hand, I could see my own blood on the medallion's tooth from where it had cut my chest. A chill swept over me. *Please don't let blood be part of the magic.*

"I'm just worried," she said. "About how he'll react if he sees you—"

"Being weird."

"Monique, you tell the truth when it doesn't suit you. You fight for causes that are beyond lost. You have more heart than anyone in this town, and yes, you are the single oddest child I've ever met."

"I'm not a child." I corrected her to cover up the lump in

my throat. It might have been the nicest compliment anyone had ever given me.

"If we do this," she said. "You have to be careful."

"Don't worry about me. My dad has a shotgun if Carl gets any ideas."

"That won't be necessary," she said.

"An axe?"

"We're not going to chop up my husband."

"Then I'll come over early every day so we don't get caught," I told her.

"What about your school?"

"I can be here at lunchtime. You just handle Carl."

"Fine," she said. "Today, it's getting late, though. I'll call you a cab. Be here tomorrow at noon."

I nodded and started making plans. I would have to rearrange my school schedule. Work might be a problem, too, not to mention Dad. Still, it could be done. I didn't know how, but Lita and I were going to get Victoria back. No matter what the cost.

9

DESPITE THE HARSH WIND mixed with snowflake grit, I arrived at North Hills High the next morning determined. In order to see Victoria, I needed to switch fourth period Algebra II for study hall. Combined with lunch, that space in my classes would give me the perfect opportunity to sneak off campus every day.

I climbed the school's front steps. The massive five-story rectangle building of weathered brick loomed dark overhead, as if the pecking status, lunch-fight, sexting, high school petty drama had veered into a much more sinister script.

When the muffled bell ended first break, I went inside. A sneaker squeaked, and the last classroom door slammed shut, leaving me alone in the hallway with the smell of wet wool and fruit bubblegum. I walked upstairs to Mrs. Hall's office on the third floor and knocked on the frosted glass.

"Come in." She didn't bother to look up as I entered. Instead, she scribbled something in her organizer. Behind her, a motivational poster of a butterfly emerging from its chrysalis read, *Believe and become.* God, spare me.

"What is it?" She finally glanced up and immediately pressed her lips together, giving her jaw an even more beaklike appearance. Her canary yellow skirt suit didn't help matters.

"Monique," she said. "I'm glad you're here. Have a seat."

"I need to adjust my schedule this semester."

"Okay." She dragged out the word. "I'm not sure that's going to be possible."

"Why? Mr. Doyle teaches Trig during fourth and fifth periods. It's an easy switch for study hall."

"I take it you didn't get my phone calls?" she asked. I shook my head. "And your father didn't either?"

"He's still recovering."

"We're not insensitive to your hardships, but..."

"What?" She'd always been a prim, proper pain-in-the-butt, but after everything that had happened, I didn't have the patience to sift through her snarky politeness.

"Monique, there is no easy way to tell you this, and your father really should be here, but given the circumstances of his recovery, I'm just going to come out and say it. The school administrators met yesterday. We've set up an expulsion hearing for you next week."

"You're going to expel me? For what?"

"Right now, it's just a hearing."

"What have I done?" I demanded.

"North Hills High has a long-standing reputation for excellence, and we've come to believe that this school isn't the best fit for your specific needs."

"What are you talking about? I'm not some preggers burnout. I get A's and B's."

"The high school experience isn't just about grades."

"Experience?" I couldn't believe her. "It's high school. You get good grades and graduate. That's how it works."

"No, that's not the way it works," she said calmly. "This is the beginning of the second semester. Your absences were already beyond the acceptable level for the year. Then you missed all of last week."

"The circumstances were a little rough," I told her. "Some of us have responsibilities beyond house parties and cheer squad."

I couldn't resist the dig at her daughter Alexis.

"In addition," she said. "I find it impossible to believe that your father is aware of the amount of absences. We know you've forged his signature at least once."

"That's not true," I told her.

It was more like a thousand times, on everything from rent checks to new credit card offers. In fact, they'd be hard-pressed to find his original signature anywhere.

"Be that as it may," she said. "You're well beyond the legal limit."

What could I do? Really, I didn't care if this place burned down, but the next school was in Linton County. Way too far for me to visit Victoria every day. I'd be permanently separated from her.

"How can I fix this?" I asked.

"I'm sorry, but our hands are tied."

"I get it. I'm not like the other kids here, but that's no reason to expel me."

"Young lady." She looked offended. "This isn't about your African-American heritage."

"Don't throw the race card in my lap," I told her. "I dress differently than the other kids. I think differently. So what?"

"You wouldn't be strange if you put in a little effort." Her face softened, and I could almost see her liberal bleeding heart warring with her insufferable self-righteousness. "A new start might be just what you need, especially with this unfortunate business with your friend."

"You know her name, Mrs. Hall. It's Victoria. Your daughter Alexis knows her name too."

"Yes, well, nobody blames you for the accident." She paused to choose her language carefully. "Or the odd circumstances that you girls found yourselves in that night."

Unbelievable. That's what this was really about. I could only imagine how deep the gossip hounds had gnawed that bone.

"There's nothing strange about it," I told her. "She was hit by a car. It was an accident. That's it."

"Well, she won't be attending this school anymore. Have you thought about what you're going to do without her?"

"I'll be fine," I said.

"Every time Victoria was sick last semester, I saw you in the quad by yourself at lunch."

"That's called reading. And what are you doing spying on me, anyway?"

"I wanted to be sure that you're okay. We are all worried." She gave me a longing stare.

What did she expect me to do? Gush to her about my true feelings? Tell her that I didn't want to be trapped in this crab-bucket town. That reading alone was better than dealing with a barrage of shitty comments, just like the ones she was making now.

Hey, Monique, you're not thinking of doing anything to yourself this weekend, are you, because it's Super Bowl Sunday, and we'd hate to spoil the party?

"I prefer to be by myself," I told her.

"How would you know that? You've never even tried to meet new people."

"I've tried. You stopped Alexis from hanging out with us."

"That wasn't my decision," she said. "I don't control who my daughter chooses to spend time with."

I knew she was right. After eighth grade, Alexis had become a snarling radioactive bitch all on her own.

How could I get through to Mrs. Hall here though? Alexis always said that her mom loved saving people. No, that wasn't the right word. Craved. I glanced at that poster of the Monarch cocoon on the wall. *Believe and become.* Maybe I could be a pretend butterfly for a few weeks, until this blew over.

"Please give me a second chance," I said. "I won't miss any more classes. I'll be the best student at this school, and I'll even try to meet new people."

"I don't know what the board will decide."

"But you can put in a good word, if I make a real effort."

She stared at me suspiciously. In her eyes, this offer was clearly too good to be true.

"Attendance isn't enough," she finally said. "Perhaps you could help Alexis plan the Winter Formal."

"Are you kidding? I already have to work at Lucido's."

"Also, I'd like you to attend the dance. And no more bloody horror movie talk or offensiveness. That's the deal."

"You'd better give me a glowing freaking review," I told her.

"The hearing is this Friday at four. Your father needs to be there too."

"Fine." Crap. The minute he found out about this, he probably start taking measurements for my coffin. One problem at a time. "I need you to change my schedule so I have a better chance of fitting in. Can you switch my study hall for trig?"

"Whatever you need," she said. "Don't make me regret this."

As I walked out the door, a terrible knot settled in my stomach. Though we hadn't really spoken to each other since the night I hitchhiked, I had to tell my dad that I was about to get kicked out of school as well. It wasn't his yelling that scared me so much. Or being grounded. Or that he'd probably torch all of my possessions in the barbecue pit.

There was no easy way to break news like that, especially to a quick-tempered Robinson. I prayed that his heart would be able to take it.

10

I ARRIVED ON MY FRONT DOORSTEP that night with a sinking feeling. The flickering television light through the front curtains didn't help. Dad was still awake. There was no way around this conversation. He needed to be at my expulsion hearing. The fact that we hadn't really talked since last week at Spic 'N Mick's only made things worse.

Yes, I'd hitchhiked back to the hospital, but I wasn't the only one who had screwed up that night. He lied to me about Victoria's parents pulling the plug. We didn't do that to each other. Embellished, sure. What good was a story without a little spice? And we omitted things. I didn't need to know the details of his nights out at the bars with the boys. At least he never dragged the trash back home with him. We did all of those things, but we didn't lie.

I hurried up the front steps, opened the screen door, and walked inside to find him on the couch. He sat up and rubbed his eyes.

"Hi," I said.

He grumbled something. Then I saw the Hardee's bag on the coffee table. Son-of-a—I snatched it, threw it in the trash, and started doing the dishes.

"Do you want to take it down a notch in there?" he said. "Kirk's on."

"He's always on somewhere." I purposely clinked a ceramic plate in the dishwasher. "I don't know why you like him anyway. Picard's better."

"Picard's got no soul," he said, clearly agitated.

Good. That's what he got for eating garbage food in his condition.

"It doesn't matter," I said. "Both of them would get their butts kicked by Janeway. And neither Enterprise would be a match for her Voyager."

"You're out of your mind. Kirk has Spock on his team."

"Janeway has a pet Borg, who never lies to her loved ones. Even when the truth is upsetting."

"Well, if that woman wasn't so pigheaded," he said, "folks wouldn't have to lie to her."

"That's because she can take care of herself."

"Yeah, hitchhiking rides through the galaxy in a stranger's ship. That's real smart, if she's looking to get killed or raped."

"Maybe if the Federation didn't force her to go on that mission, everything would be fine. Wouldn't it?"

"Well—"

"Just quit." I was sick of our little game. I finished the dishes and went back into the living room. "Victoria would be dead right now if it wasn't for me. You do know that, right?"

He started to point at me, but he stopped mid-thought. Then he leaned his recliner forward, looked down with a furrowed brow, and began picking at glue or something on his fingers. "How's she doing?"

"Every last one of her doctors was wrong. She talked today." I paused to calm the shakiness in my voice. "But she's not all there."

"Shit." He shook his head. "I'm sorry about that. She's alive, though. That's good."

I thought of her in that wheelchair and hoped he was right. "Yeah."

"Eventually we're going to forgive each another," he said. "So we might as well get it over with."

"Fine."

"Good," he said. "And don't you ever hitchhike again."

"Don't lie to me."

"Fine," he said.

"Good."

"I know you've had a really rough couple of weeks, but you'd better understand something." He stood, walked over to me, and gave me a hug. "Picard couldn't even touch Captain James T. Kirk in a fist fight."

I laughed into his chest. "Not on any planet."

I didn't have the heart to tell him that I really didn't like *Star Trek*. I only watched it sometimes so we could have something to talk about. Besides, Kirk wasn't all terrible. He did kiss Uhura. I know that meant something back in Dad's olden times. Not as much as cool George Romero casting a black lead in *Night of the Living Dead*, but it meant something to Dad nonetheless.

I felt better. At least we were speaking again, which meant the moment that I had been dreading was here. It was now or never.

"I need to tell you something." I sat on the arm of the couch. "But you have to promise not to get angry."

"Never ask that of a grown man. If I get mad, then I'm mad."

"I'm serious. I can't handle the hospital again if you decide to pop your valves."

"My heart problem wasn't because of our argument that day." He grabbed a water bottle and chased an aspirin down. "That was from three tasty decades of chicken-fried steak and corn on the cob with butter."

"That's not funny," I said. "And what's the deal with the Hardee's bag?"

"Relax, doc. I ate a dry grilled chicken sandwich tonight,

no fries." I gave him a don't-BS-me look, so he said, "Look in the trash if you want."

"I'll pass, but I have to tell you something. Just don't stress out."

"Is this about you getting kicked out of school?" He pulled something from his back pocket. Crap. I'd forgotten to check the mail yesterday. He set a letter down on the kitchen counter. "You're not quite as slick as you think you are."

"Are you angry?" I asked.

"I was about to go down to that hearing with a blowtorch and a hammer to teach those fools a lesson, but I got to thinking. Not one of those bureaucrats has ever picked dirt from under his fingernails. They have no clue where we're coming from."

"Thank you for being on my side."

"Don't thank me," he said. "If you were in the wrong, I would've thrown your body on the pile too."

"Shut up." I slapped his shoulder. "You would not."

"This has nothing to do with your absences."

"Mrs. Hall doesn't like me, Victoria, her dad, or the crazy church folks out in the Black Hills. It's a perfect storm."

"It goes back farther than that," he said.

"What do you mean?"

"We'll just leave it at that." He must have been talking about my mother. "Maybe this is the right time to think about moving."

"What?" I asked. "That's not what I want."

"I talked to Frankie the Jew this morning."

"Don't call him that."

"Doc says I can go back to work in a few weeks, but construction has dried up around here. Frankie's got nothing."

"So what? I have my job at Lucido's."

"No. As soon as I'm healthy, you're going to focus on college again."

Keep dreaming. Not with that surgery bill. Just the Chase card's minimum alone was close to five hundred dollars.

"We'll make it work," I told him. No need to ruin his fantasy.

"You don't get it," he said. "There are no jobs for me here."

"We've done fine so far."

"Take a good look around this house." He pointed at the living room. A sad fifteen-inch computer monitor replaced his flat screen. Stereo, gone. Nana's slave-time knickknacks, gone. "We're running out of Craigslist fodder."

"What about bankruptcy?" I asked. "That's what it's for."

"We've been through this."

"Yeah, yeah," I said. "Robinsons pay their bills, but do Robinsons run away when things get tough?"

"We do when there's nothing left in this town to fight for."

"Victoria—"

"Isn't herself," he said. "She won't be at school with you anymore. Probably not for a while."

"Yeah, but if we move, I'll never see her."

"We don't have to go far. Just over to Jackson County. Soon you'll have your regular driver's license."

"Just give me a couple of months," I told him. "Maybe I can find something for you."

"Whether you want to face it or not, this situation is coming to an end."

"So you're willing to give me two months then?"

"What would be the point?" he asked.

"If I figure some way through this, great. We get to stay. If we do have to move though, it's on our terms. I want to go to that hearing tomorrow and make them eat their snooty words."

That got a laugh out of him. I knew it would. I also knew that if I got kicked out of school on Friday, we'd be packed and moved by the weekend.

"Fine," he said. "You've got thirty days. That's it, but you'd better be ready to go."

"Good."

"Just so we're clear though," he said. "If I ever catch you hitchhiking again, the CIA won't even be able to find your bones."

"You're going to murder me if I hitchhike because you're worried that somebody might murder me?"

"You're my daughter, and I won't have you killed by some stranger."

"Whatever, Dad."

"That's right whatever, Dad. Now we should get some rest. It's been a long day."

For once, we agreed.

11

I RETURNED TO SCHOOL THAT Wednesday on a mission. Head down, mouth closed, Monique. No exceptions. Dad wanted to move to a different city. Mrs. Hall was just itching to expel me. I couldn't give either of them a reason. Problem was, in order to see Victoria every day, I had to leave our closed campus at lunch without raising any alarms. I needed to make sure that the students forgot that I existed. Not an easy thing, considering Victoria's accident, but I had to try.

Luckily, my first classes back had been manageable. Dirty looks were easy enough to ignore, especially with my earbuds sealed tight, volume cranked. Some anonymous twit passed me a note in World History, which I crumpled and threw on the floor without opening. Nothing good would be in there. After four hours of epic self-control, the lunch bell finally rang. Now for the hard part.

I grabbed my backpack and hurried from American Lit. Within seconds, the hallway teemed with students laughing and shoving books in their lockers. The pre-lunch chaos would be my best chance to escape unnoticed.

As I hurried toward my locker, the chatter died down to tense whispers. Everyone stopped and stared. Even Jeremy Whitley, Caucasian Gangsta, stopped giving his poor girlfriend Stacey her daily tongue bath.

"Seriously?" I mumbled.

Mouth shut, Monique.

Victoria's accident had been a big deal, but it happened two weeks ago. Certainly, the Ritalin zombies should have found shinier objects to gawk at by now.

"Hey," a boy shouted from behind.

Not falling for that trap. I picked up my pace.

"That's not yours," he shouted again.

Hold on. That was Pete's voice. I spun around. Two idiots had snatched his baseball hat. They were tossing it over his head, playing a sick game of keep away. Of all people, Terrence Cranston—who might have weighed a hundred pounds soaking wet—was picking on Pete.

"Do you want this, Grendel?" Terrence dangled the hat up high.

"That's not my name." Pete chased after it, but with his extra bulk, he'd never get it back.

Let it go, Monique. Victoria needs you.

With the other students distracted, this was my best chance to get off campus unseen. The teachers were probably already on their way. Principal Rademacher would deal with this. Somebody would step in eventually, except the parents of these trust fund babies made sure their douchebag offspring never got what they deserved. Damn it. I turned and hurried back toward them.

Terrence tossed the hat again. Pete tripped over his feet and fell onto his stomach. The slap echoed down the hallway.

"Oh shit," somebody shouted, and most of the kids around started laughing. A few girls seemed horrified, but those cowards didn't try to help.

I raced to Pete's side and put my arm around him. "Get away from him."

"Monique," he said with shaking lips. "My hat."

"Don't cry," I whispered. "It's what they want. Don't give it to them."

"My dad gave me my hat. I can't go home without it. My dad—"

"I'm going to get it back. I promise. Now wipe your tears,"

I told him, and he did. "We're going to be tough, you and me, right?"

He nodded reluctantly, and I helped him up. I had no clue what doctors called his condition. Mentally challenged fit the bill, I guess, although most days he seemed to have a complex hard drive upstairs with a smaller chip processor to get those ideas out.

"Looks like Grendel has a new girlfriend." Terrence tossed the hat.

I jumped in and caught it mid-air. Then I shoved his chest. "What is wrong with you?"

"Don't get your panties bunched. We're just playing."

"Does this look like fun to him?"

"Why do you care so much?" Terrence said. "Are you two together or something?"

"Screw you." I turned back around. This little scene had already gone too far, and I had to get to Victoria. I grabbed Pete's hand. "Come on. Let's get out of here."

"You *are* together," Terrence said loudly for his audience. A few people snickered. "Does your father approve of your new boyfriend?"

"I don't know, asshole." I turned back to face him. "Is your dad ashamed that you always get picked last for sports teams?"

"Ooh," the rest of the mental giants around us said in unison.

"At least I'm not a devil worshipper."

"Maybe you should consider Satan," I told him. "You might need the backup tonight when you're alone in your room, because that's when I'll be coming for you."

He stepped backward. "Whatever."

"Just leave Pete alone."

"Or else what?"

"You've heard that I know Voodoo, right?" I said. Thanks to Alexis Hall, even some of our teachers believed that stupid lie. "Well, sweet dreams, Terrence. I'll try to leave your teeth intact so your parents can ID you."

"This is lame," he said, but I saw real fear in his eyes. He turned to his friend. "Let's go eat."

"See you tonight, Terrence."

Both members of the clown patrol scurried off. All around, the rest of the students looked at me as though I'd just butchered their mothers. Not good. Overkill. Always the best defense, unless you were trying to be a Wilma Wallflower. With everyone watching, I couldn't leave campus through this exit now.

"Let's get out of here." I gave Pete his hat and hurried him away.

"Where are we going?" he asked.

"Secret mission stuff. I need you to walk with me so I don't look suspicious."

That seemed to please him. We headed toward the school's second best ditching exit, in the opposite direction of the cafeteria. Finally, we arrived.

"Are you going to be okay?" I asked, and he nodded. I fixed his collar. "Whatever you do, stay away from those kids. They're jerks."

"They don't think that I'm smart."

"You're ten times more brilliant than the rest of these sock puppets." I made a talking motion with my hand.

Apparently, this was one of the funniest things he'd ever seen. I don't know why his laughter made me feel so awful. To be trapped away like that. Could there be a worst fate? I was probably just projecting, though, because of Victoria. Would people treat her this way if we couldn't rehabilitate her? No. It would be much worse.

"Don't be upset." Pete seemed to read my thoughts. "Those kids don't hurt my feelings."

"I know," I told him, except that no matter how many times I had made that same statement, it was never entirely true.

"We're tough." He showed me his muscles to prove it.

"It's not that."

"Victoria?" he asked, letting me know once again that he understood more than anyone gave him credit for.

"You're going to be just fine now." I pointed to the main office on the second floor. "Go see Principal Rademacher. Tell him what happened."

"Are you coming?"

"No," I said. "My friend needs me."

He hugged me and then walked upstairs. When he was out of sight, I opened the door and raced toward Victoria. The stakes of her recovery seemed so much larger now. I couldn't let her down.

12

*A*FTER SUCCESSFULLY ESCAPING campus that day, I arrived at Victoria's front door, clanked the brass knocker, and checked my phone. 12:23pm. I'd already wasted a third of my lunch hour just getting here. After the incident at school with Pete, people would notice me absent in fifth period. I couldn't afford to skip today, or Mrs. Hall would expel me for sure. If I wanted to spend even twenty minutes with Victoria, we needed to hurry.

I knocked again, more urgently this time. Beeps from the home security system sounded, followed by the muffled clack of dead bolts. Lita finally opened the door. Wearing a black turtleneck with her straight dark hair pulled behind her ears, she was once again in flawless form.

She glanced nervously around the front yard. "Come inside."

"It's fine," I said. "Your husband isn't out here."

"I have something to show you." She closed the door behind me and re-bolted it. Then she took me upstairs.

Outside the bathroom on the second floor, she stopped and said, "Wait here."

Then she closed the door in my face. Whatever. I understood that people loved surprises. People also loved the ingredients of sausage meat and McDonald's hamburgers. Surprise.

"What's taking so long?" I asked her through the bathroom door.

"Hold on," she called back, and something metallic clattered.

"I have to be back at school soon."

Or they're going to kick me out, I almost added. Probably best not to reveal the whole situation.

"Okay." Lita finally opened the door with flushed cheeks. "We're ready."

She stepped aside. In the center of the massive circular bathroom, Victoria sat in her antique wheelchair, which seemed filthy against the pristine marble tile and countertops. She appeared to be sleeping in a sitting position.

"Do you notice anything different about her?" Lita asked.

"I can't believe it." I tried to sound positive, but the large looping curls and black dress looked kind of perverse. Victoria wasn't a doll. "You did her hair and dressed her up."

"No," Lita said. "Well actually, yes, I did dress her this morning, but that's not the surprise."

She grabbed Victoria's goggles off of the bathroom sink and waved them at me.

"She doesn't have to wear them anymore?" I asked.

"Doctor Kapur doesn't think she'll try to hurt herself again." She stepped on the lever that lifted the waste bin's cover and dropped the glasses in. "I don't ever want to see these disgusting things again."

"That's wonderful," I said, but it didn't seem like enough reason to make me wait in the hallway.

"We're not done yet." She turned to Victoria, gently held her wrist, and helped her stand.

This too was nothing new. Although I'd only managed to see Victoria for a few minutes yesterday, that visit had produced an evolutionary leap in her behavior. She walked around without assistance, and she'd even begun to communicate. So what if her language skills weren't perfect. I understood her.

When she rotated her head and said the words *spine claw,*

she wanted me to brush her hair. A finger clinching motion combined with the words *dark sight* meant she wanted her handheld mirror, which she stared at endlessly. Now, she just stood there like a store mannequin though.

"Victoria?" Lita whispered in her ear. "Are you ready to show her?"

Nothing.

"Lita, don't get me wrong," I said. "I'm excited. I really am, but I have to get back to school soon."

"We are you," Victoria repeated her favorite creepy saying without opening her eyes. "We are you."

Oh Jesus. Her front teeth.

"You fixed them," I said.

"I brought in the dentist yesterday." Lita was clearly pleased with herself. "Carl doesn't even know about it. I want him to see her all at once, as she was. I think then he might start acting like her father again."

Right then, it hit me. The magnitude of fixing her broken smile. Though I tried to hold back, my eyes welled up.

"What is it?" Lita asked.

"I'm sorry." I held my hand over my mouth. "It's just stress."

"That's okay." She hugged me. "I've been crying all morning."

This was the first real crack in the suffocating darkness that had swallowed everyone the night of the accident. With the exception of a few scabs, Victoria was again the same girl—at least physically—who dragged me out to a cult rally revival two weeks ago.

Now we just had to get her mind back too. I didn't know how to do that, but I had some ideas that started with this mansion, which had all the warmth of an eighteenth century mausoleum. Worse yet, Carl's poltergeist toxic anger seemed to ooze from the walls. It wasn't healthy.

"I've been thinking," I told Lita. "We need to get her outside."

"Honey, that's not going to happen."

"She'll open her eyes once she feels the sunshine on her face. It will help. I know it."

"It's a good idea," she said. "But Carl has been acting strangely, more than usual. I think he knows something is going on."

"We don't have to go far. The backyard will be fine."

"Not with our neighbors. I've seen those vultures peeking over our fence, and if he even catches word that you're here, I don't know what he'll do."

"Yes, but she's come so far. Why don't we just tell him?"

"Tell me what?" a deep voice growled behind me.

Chills sprouted all over my body, as if my skin had been doused with Listerine. I spun around to see Carl standing in the doorway.

He wore a dark business suit, but he hadn't shaved in days. Resting against the doorjamb, he peeled an apple with a knife. The last time I saw him, he was drunk and high, wallowing in grief. Not today. His maniacal eyes never strayed from Lita.

"Carl," she said. "You're home early."

"I asked you a question." He spoke so softly that I almost couldn't hear him. "What were you going to tell me?"

"Just that we're working with Victoria." She reached out and rubbed his shoulder with one hand.

"That's interesting." He slowly set the apple down on the bathroom sink, and then he deliberately removed her hand from his arm. "Because I already told you that thing is not my Victoria."

"Don't say that," Lita said. "She's making progress."

"Really?" He shoved his way over to her, still pinching that knife with a slice of apple peel between his fingers. With his other hand, he snapped his fingers in front of her face. "Can you hear me? Anyone in there?"

She just stood with her eyes closed.

"Quit it," I told him. "She's your daughter."

"I was almost willing to forgive you." He turned to me. "For the accident. For butting into my family's affairs. Now you've crossed the line."

"Monique," Lita said. "Go home."

"She can run anywhere she wants." He smiled and looked around the bathroom. "Here. There. It won't matter."

"Go," Lita said, but I could only think of those bruises on her neck.

"I'm not leaving you here alone," I told her.

"I don't think I heard you correctly, little girl," he said. "It sounds like you're doubling-down."

"She doesn't mean anything by it." Lita tried to step between us, but he shoved her aside.

She slipped and latched onto the wood-slat mini blinds, which pulled free. Sunlight flashed my eyes, blinding me in the clatter. Lita fell to her knees. I could see the bastard gearing up for something violent. I raced to her side.

"Get out of my house," he roared at me.

I almost ran for it right there, but I wasn't sure if that would set him off. He just called his own daughter a thing. Besides, I couldn't leave them behind with him.

"It's okay." Lita stood. "I'm fine. Just go, Monique."

"Victoria, come with me." I grabbed her hand. "I'll take you to your room."

"Leave her and get out of my house." He pointed the knife at me. "Or I promise, you'll regret the day you ever heard my name."

Victoria began to squeeze my hand tighter. Searing pain shot up my arm. All my limbs felt starved of blood flow. My heart skipped beats, just like that first day.

"Get out of my fucking face," he shouted at me.

Desperately, I tried to yank her into the hallway. With my last bit of strength, I latched onto the bathroom counter with my free hand for support. Victoria released my other hand, and I could breathe again, but my vision felt coated in a reddish blurry haze.

Carl reached for me. "I warned you."

"No," Lita shouted and grabbed his arm to pull him back.

"Get away from her," a demonic-sounding whisper called out. I turned to see Victoria's bright green eyes wide open. She had spoken a real sentence. Dressed like a doll, her entire appearance was unnerving. Carl turned and stared at his daughter, clearly unable to believe what he saw.

"I said get away from her, Carl," she shouted this time.

The knife dropped from his hands and clattered onto the floor.

"Victoria, can you hear me?" I hurried over to her. "Are you there?"

"We are you, Monique," she enunciated each word carefully. "We are you."

"I don't know what you mean," I told her.

"We are you?" she seemed to ask with fear in her voice this time. Then she reached her hands forward and felt the empty space before her. Suddenly, I knew what she meant this entire time. Somewhere in her healing, she'd confused the word *we* with *where*. Where are you, she was asking me. Where are you, Monique? Now, even *dark sight* made sense when combined with the hand mirror.

She'd been trying to reach me all along, but she couldn't see me.

Where are you, Monique, she been crying out.

My best friend was blind.

13

I SAT BESIDE VICTORIA in her bedroom on her comforter, trying to wrap my head around everything that had just happened. Twenty minutes ago, Lita had rushed a speechless Carl out of the house. With his ghost-pale face, he looked as if someone had just pulled apart the foundation on which he'd built his petty life. Good. Served that SOB right.

Lita had only one request before they left.

"Don't leave Victoria's side," she'd said.

I never would, until the sun popped supernova if necessary. I just hadn't expected the empty small talk between us, followed by bouts of terrible silence. Who could blame Victoria for not wanting to speak to me? What could I possibly say to make any of this better, especially with her easel in the center of her room? That stretched canvas resting on it would now stay blank forever, and it was my fault.

Maybe I didn't push her in front of the speeding vehicle as some at school had whispered, but she never would have gotten out of the car that night if we hadn't argued. I hoped she could forgive me someday. Until then, Lita didn't need to ask. I wouldn't leave her side for anything.

"Are you hungry?" I asked.

In the creeping dusk, I could barely see her shake her head. I grabbed the matches next to her brick fireplace and lit a few scented candles. Outside, a mild wind ruffled her flowing maroon drapes. She pulled her arms close to her chest.

"Are you cold?" I reached up and closed the window. "I can get you a jacket."

"My father," she said with the slightest accent, as if the words were new to her.

"He went out with Lita to calm down." Really, I didn't want the jerk with her either, but I couldn't stop them. "It's just us here."

"This is my...old housing?" she asked, and I realized the pauses in her speech gave her time to fill in the blanks in her vocabulary.

"Yes, this is your bedroom." I tried not to sound like I was correcting her.

She nodded and felt around on the nightstand. Her hand came to rest on one of her wooden brush handles, spattered with paint. She pulled away as if it had burned her fingers. A lump formed in my throat.

"I don't think they moved anything," I told her.

"How long was I...missing?"

"It's been twelve days since the car accident."

"Days?" She gently touched her own lips and nose. Then she pinched one of the large loop curls that framed her face.

"I'm sorry about your hair. Lita doesn't know what to do with it, and I didn't have the heart to stop her."

"Days?" Her lips began to tremble. "It felt like years."

"What do you remember?"

"Everything." She stared directly at me and then slightly to the side, trying to triangulate my voice. I'd never felt so low.

"Victoria, about the night of the accident—"

"I don't want to talk about that." She wiped underneath her eyes, smearing the dollish mascara that Lita had applied. "You should not...be at this place."

"My dad said it's okay that I spend the night."

"You can't be near me."

"I'm not scared of your father," I told her.

"That is not what I mean."

"I don't understand." I grabbed her hand, and she flinched. "Please don't shut me out."

The house's heater kicked on. One of the hardwood floorboards in the hallway popped. Her body tensed.

"What is it?" I asked.

"Shhh." She spun her ear toward the door and pulled her hair back. A few moments passed.

"Victoria," I whispered. "What is going on?"

"I know you are worried about me." She finally turned back with a strained smile. "I am...happy to be back. Aren't you excited that I'm back?"

"Of course I am, but I can't pretend that you're not blind."

"The car crash doesn't matter. I am here, and we are happy," she said firmly, complete with a don't-you-agree look. "Aren't we?"

Why was she acting so strange? Was she trying to warn me that somebody was watching us?

"I'm extremely happy to have you back," I played along.

"Since everything is better now, you should go home, Monique. Where you can be safe."

Jesus. Who had scared her enough to talk in code? Victoria wasn't afraid of her father, and certainly the NSA hadn't decided that Monique Robinson's smart mouth finally warranted a drone strike. Then I noticed candlelight glinting off of Ethan's medallion around her neck.

"Are you worried about the church people?" I whispered. She shook her head. Even in this dim light, her green eyes seemed to burn with frustration. "I won't leave here alone. So if anyone is listening to us now, they can go straight to hell."

"Do you remember the dead...boar we found in the field behind my house a few years ago?"

Actually, it was a possum but close enough.

"What does that have to do with anything?" I asked.

"Do you remember where we hid that day? We have to go there now."

"No way," I said. "It's icy out there, and you can't see."

"Hooker, take me there now or get out of my house."

"You don't have to be like that," I said.

Deep down though, I was grateful for the first flash of her true personality. Of the Victoria Malakoff who'd bloodied Johnny Henshaw's nose because he said that girls couldn't throw. So what if neither of us could toss a stupid baseball? She could throw a punch. I saw that same determination on her face now, and I felt better.

"Fine. Let's go." I walked her downstairs and then outside through the sliding glass doors.

Over the dark forest line, dirty gray clouds smothered the horizon. In murky light, I moved her down the slippery path and then inside her greenhouse. Orchids and overgrown vine flowers spread into the central walkway. The trapped sweet scent, combined with the humid environment, nearly overwhelmed me. I pulled branches aside for Victoria to pass and cleared her path of loose bedrock gravel.

Against the far wall, I stomped around on the damp wooden floor until I heard a hollow thunk. Then I pulled back the rug, found the hatch door, and pulled it up. The steep staircase of wood slats descended ten feet to a clay cellar floor. Carefully, I helped her down into the darkness. I felt around and flipped on the rusted toggle switch.

To my surprise, the dangling light bulb flickered to life. Even the vintage record player started turning without the needle down. A bolus of cobwebs began to form around its spinning center prong. The empty stills, covered in decades of grime, smelled of stale bootleg whiskey.

"Okay," I whispered. "What's going on?"

"It's probably not safe here, but it's all I could think of. The flowers and life and plants might...hold back death."

"Victoria, you're scaring me."

"You have to go home now," she said. "We don't have much time."

"I already told you that I won't leave you."

"While I was underneath everything—"

"You mean in the coma?"

She nodded. "I was alone. It looked just like this world, but it was darker there. And colder. At first I thought I was dead, but then I saw myself...broken on the hospital bed. Tubes came out of my arms and mouth. My eyes were bandaged, my teeth smashed."

"That was the ICU." I'd always chalked up out-of-body experiences to Internet morons and their junk science, but there was no way she could have witnessed those moments.

"I tried to get back inside my body, but it didn't work." Her speech patterns strengthened, as if each breath brought a neuron surge. "I wanted to escape, but nothing existed beyond the hospital's parking lot. No street signs or buildings. Just a black nothing that kept creeping in. It swallowed the cafeteria first and then the children's wing. I screamed, but no one was listening."

"Victoria, you have to believe me. I was by your side every day."

"Then the darkness took me," she continued. "And I was nothing too."

"You only died for a few minutes after they pulled the plug. Then you came back right away."

"You don't understand," she snipped at me. "I'm trying to tell you that I wasn't alone. The voices in the darkness kept me company. Sometimes it was an old woman, and then a little boy or a chorus of whispers, but I knew it was always the same...presence, because it only ever wanted to know one thing. How to get to you, Monique."

The air seemed to leave the room. "Excuse me?"

"Every second down there," she said, "I wanted to die, but the voice wouldn't let me."

"How did you send me the message for help then?"

"Will you listen for once?" she snapped. "At first, I refused to speak to it. For what seemed like years, but then the pain started. It was like barbed wire tearing into me. I could feel the stinging coldness of its touch, feeding off of me, and I broke."

"This is my fault." I grabbed her hand. "I am so sorry for what I said that night in the car before the accident."

"Don't you ever apologize to me." She pulled away. Her voice was frantic. "I never contacted you. Don't you get it? That wasn't me. It sent you the message."

Suddenly, coming down in this dank cellar didn't seem like such a hot idea. "What does it want with me?"

"I don't know," she said. "But we came back together. I can feel it out there. It's probably listening to us now. That's why you need to stay far away from me."

"No. Whatever the danger, we're in this together. It's you and me. Best friends until death ends."

"Don't say that," she told me. "Don't you ever say that. There are worse things than death. I don't know when that voice will come for us, but it will. And it's hungry, Monique. It's always hungry."

14

AFTER I FINALLY CALMED Victoria down, she fell asleep on the couch, but I was restless. Two weeks ago, I would have thought her warning nuts, but I couldn't hide from the truth anymore. She had actually risen from the dead. In every story that I'd read or watched, resurrection always had a price tag.

No, she didn't eat raw steak out of the fridge and lick the blood from the Styrofoam tray. Nor did she sleep all day or grow cranky when exposed to morning sunlight, but payment would be due soon. I could feel it. The voice from *underneath everything* would come for us. Every moment wasted only cinched the noose tighter around our necks, and I wasn't about to let some sketchy demon eat my soul when plenty of tastier brain-dead students littered my high school.

I needed answers. Only one other person knew what was going on here. Ethan. He told me his necklace would help Victoria, and yet, he'd conveniently forgotten to mention the curse attached to it. I pulled out my phone.

We need to talk, I texted him.

WNDRFL!!! MEET @ NORTH PRK 8p, he responded in text gibberish, caps lock. I tried not to hold that against him.

Lita returned that night with Carl, and I hurried out before she could insist on driving me home. I headed directly for the park. Fifteen minutes later, I sat on a wooden bench next to the main fountain. A snowflake flurry danced around the circle of lampposts that lit the bronze statue of one of the city's founders, Chester North.

Yeah, I knew it. Horror movie 101. Never meet cult boys

alone in the park after your best friend predicts that hungry things would pick your bones clean, but I could see Lucido's from here. The rest of the downtown shops were visible, too, complete with shoppers.

To my left, a tall silhouette emerged from the tree line. That wasn't Ethan. It was the Kool-Aid drinking cult leader!

"I'm sorry." I stood to leave. "This was a mistake."

"Don't go." He pulled off his gloves and shoved them in the pockets of his dark coat. "Forgive me. Most people like to start simple with us, so we don't ask too many questions on first contact. We never officially met. My name is Roman Santo."

"I thought I was texting Ethan."

"Ah." In this light, I couldn't tell whether his dark eyes brimmed with disappointment or bone-crunching rage. "Why do you need to speak with my son?"

"He's your son?" I was so blown away that my statement bordered on rudeness. They looked nothing alike.

"My stepson, actually."

"Oh," I said. "I didn't mean to bother you. I thought he gave me his personal number."

"Our members only have the one cell phone between us, which he usually answers."

"You have one phone line for the whole church?"

"Unfortunately, a certain amount of technology is necessary for day-to-day business," he said. "Paying bills. Meeting new converts."

Me a convert? Not likely. What would happen when he figured that out? I glanced behind me. The foot traffic next to the shops had thinned. Even the park lights seemed way too dark now. Like hide-the-body dark.

"I'm sorry to waste your time." I backed away toward civilization. "Can you please let Ethan know that I'm looking for him?"

"You must have questions. I can answer them."

"It's kind of private."

"I see." A knowing smile crossed his face, or at least, his creepy version of a smile. "If it's about our proper customs for dating, it might be easier to talk to me first."

"Customs?" I asked. First of all, gross. Was the whole church going to sit around our bed and chant while we consecrated our wedding night? Ick. Bleach my brain. "I don't want to date Ethan. I just want to talk to him."

"I haven't seen him in a few days." He shrugged, as if his son's whereabouts couldn't be less important.

"Ethan is missing, and you don't care?"

"I know our ways might seem strange to an outsider, but I assure you, I could drop that boy off in the arctic, and he'd be eating polar bear by dinner."

"Okay, but even adults let somebody know if they're going to be gone for a while."

"You know, you never answered my question." He squinted. "Why are you so interested in speaking with him again?"

I held up my hands as if to surrender. "Jeez. Paranoid much?"

"It's my job to watch out for potential threats."

"You got me. I'm actually a government agent looking to storm your compound." That clearly struck a nerve. Not smart. "A car hit my best friend, and Ethan was there for me. I just wanted to talk to him about it, but if that's too much for you, forget it."

"Wait." He scratched his scraggly beard and finished behind his ear. "We're getting off on the wrong foot. You have to understand, our members must always be vigilant. People aren't wild about our message of coexistence."

"Who would have a problem with that?" I asked. Then I

remembered butcher's blood Jane, smearing her daughter's handprint all over that sign at the rally.

"Folks don't want to see the truth," he said. "The Awakeners work every day to stamp out the sickness that's plaguing our world."

Here we go. The big reveal. Which brand of hate had they chosen? Muslims? Fornicators? Illuminati reptile aliens?

"To which plague are you referring?" I asked.

"Science and the abominations it produces," he said. Wow. I had to admit, I wasn't expecting that one. "Our guiding principle to avoid technology whenever possible has a tendency to unnerve people, especially those caught up in the psychotic delusion of scientific advancement. Our members have awakened from the electronic chains of mental slavery. Anyone who thinks freely is a threat to the mainstream system, and we're treated accordingly."

Great. I'd clearly set off his sermon tripwire, which might be useful. Maybe Roman knew something about the medallion that had kept Ethan's mother alive.

"Your wife," I said. "Was she a member of the church?"

"Ethan told you about his mother, did he?" He sounded irritated.

"Just that she had cancer. Did she turn down the treatment?"

"I wish she hadn't gone through with the chemo." His voice turned grim and quiet. "I warned her. All the gadgets and radiation ate away at her body until there was nothing left."

"I'm sorry."

"Don't be," he said. If he felt anything for her, I couldn't see it. "After she died, I knew what needed to be done. She delivered me to this path."

"What path is that? You said everyone is welcome at your church. What if they practice a dark religion?"

"Is that what this is about?" he demanded. "Why you need to speak with Ethan?"

"I'm trying to understand. That's all."

"I know what the hatemongers in town whisper. We did not try to sacrifice Victoria Malakoff."

"I didn't say that."

"In this world, you can preach love and tolerance all you want, but don't touch the iPhone or mention Monsanto's genetically altered Frankenfood. Those sacred cows are beyond reproach." He motioned to the downtown area, where pedestrian foot traffic had nearly disappeared. "Those fools bathe in their own ignorance from cradle to grave."

"I can't argue there," I said.

"Victoria's death was an accident. That's all."

Victoria's death? He must not have known that she'd been released from the hospital. Did that mean he didn't know about the medallion as well?

"You know she isn't dead, right?" I told him to see his reaction.

"Brain death is the same thing."

"I just talked to her an hour ago."

"That's impossible. Dr. Wynn showed me her scans."

"I assure you, it is." Why would her doctor show Roman any part of her file? Was that even legal? "And I thought you didn't trust technology. Why would you look at her charts?"

"You're telling me she's alive and talking? Why would you keep this miracle from us?"

"I don't know you."

"That doesn't matter anymore." He stared off to the side as if realizing some greater truth. "This is bigger than us now."

"What are you talking about?" I demanded.

"It's no mistake that her accident happened right outside

our compound." He started backing away from me. "I have to convene the members."

"What about Ethan?"

"I told you. I haven't seen him since last Friday."

Then he disappeared into the darkness and left me alone in the park with my mind spinning. Ethan had been missing since last Friday, which just happened to coincide with Victoria's resurrection.

Worse yet, Roman had been oblivious to her condition until I just opened my fat mouth. Judging by the way he raced away from here, I couldn't shake the feeling that I'd inadvertently played the part of Pandora, unleashing something inside of that man that would never again be contained.

15

I WALKED DOWN THE school halls Friday morning, still freaked out from my meeting with Roman Santo. I wanted answers. Instead, that man dumped ten kinds of crazy on me, infecting my poor brain with questions. Where had Ethan gone? Who was responsible for Victoria's resurrection? How could we stop the voice in the darkness?

I pushed those thoughts away. I couldn't afford to lose focus, not today with my hearing after school. If I didn't give those pencil pushers a spectacular performance, Dad would move us to a different city. So far, I'd made it through the last week of school without incident. I just had to get through the rest of this day, which wouldn't be easy considering the stink face I'd been getting from the other students.

I walked into fourth period trig and sat at my desk. The rest of the horde filed in. Mr. Doyle stood at the dry erase board with his back to us, removing the remnants of equations from the last class.

Out of the corner of my eye, I saw Alexis Hall walk up to me with two of her underlings in tow. Perfect. The one person I needed to avoid today. Not only was she Mrs. Hall's daughter, but she was also Victoria's arch nemesis for valedictorian next year.

Her grayish-green eyes matched the color of her skintight cotton sweater. Combined with long bangs that swept across her forehead, her dishwater blond hair with maroon highlights framed her porcelain face for perpetual battle. Somewhere in Iceland, Viking village was missing a stone statue bitch. She motioned to my ears.

I pulled out my headphones. "Lexi."

"It's Alexis now." With a flick of her wrist, she waved away her two minions.

"If you insist, Alexis," I said. "What is it?"

"How are you?" she asked with a look of faux concern that would've made a news anchor jealous.

"You don't have to pretend to be my friend," I said. "Just get to the point."

"Have it your way." She sat in the stool next to me on the double desk.

Then she just stared at me, with that left eyebrow raised in its permanent accusing arch, as if she were trying to solve a perplexing problem.

"What do you want?" I asked.

"Yeah," a voice called out from behind. "Why are you talking to the freak show, Alexis?"

I didn't need to look. It had to be Tim Donnelly. He was the only idiot who called me that name to my face. Scratch that, to my back. Alexis gave me an irritated smile.

"That's right," Tim's yippy dog of a friend added. "The freak show has returned."

"Hey, dick breath." Alexis turned to face them. "Why don't you take your boyfriend's balls out of your mouth for once and pop a Prozac."

"Oh snap." Jeremy Whitley, Caucasian Gangsta, almost fell out of his seat across the aisle. Tim's cheeks couldn't have flushed redder if she'd slapped him.

"Now." She turned back to me. "Where were we?"

For a second, I didn't know what to say. With one sentence, she reminded me of why we used to be close in middle school.

"Thanks," I said.

"Don't thank me. You're my real problem."

"Excuse me?"

"Monique, you don't fit in at North Hills High. You know it, and I know it, even if my mother is clueless."

And with that, she reminded me why we'd never be friends again.

"Nobody asked you to come sit here," I told her.

"No actually, that's exactly what I have to do, or else my mother is going to take away my car. Do you know what that means?"

"Famine?"

"You think this is a joke?" she said.

"No, I think both you and your mother are pests."

"Well, she chose this moment to put her foot down. Now she expects me to help you prepare for the dance, whatever that means."

"Not my problem." I started to put my ear buds back in, so she grabbed my hand.

"Admit it," she said. "You don't care about the Winter Formal or any of it."

"Not even if every pretty princess there contracts syphilis," I told her.

"So why are you on the dance committee then?"

"Your mom is making me do it," I said. "Talk to her."

"Why do you even want to stay at this school? Your only friend is gone. Lincoln Heights is perfect." She tapped my wrist. "You'd fit right in there."

"You'd like that, wouldn't you? To remove any trace of Victoria from this school."

"I don't have to remove anything," she said. "You already did that for me."

"You can go to hell and take your mother with you."

"I can make your life miserable here. I don't want to, so don't force me. Just volunteer to go away. Everyone will be happier."

"You know." I leaned in close and spoke quietly. "Some of these people here are actually scared of you, but I still remember the girl who used to stuff her own training bra with her mother's panti-liners at sleepovers."

"Who cares what you remember?"

"I have the video of it saved on my phone," I lied. "YouTube is calling me, and it's hungry for content, Alexis. So hungry. You might want to be a little nicer."

That left eyebrow inched just a bit higher, as if she thought I'd finally made a breakthrough in life. Threats and blackmail. To her, this must be what communication looked like.

"Stay if you want." She pulled out a compact mirror from her purse. Then she gazed into it and wiped the edges of her lipstick. "We're still going to have to deal with my mother. She's a problem, wouldn't you agree?"

She snapped the mirror shut.

"Yes." What could I say? The girl had a point.

"She wants me to tutor you after school until you catch up from your absences."

"Hold on. She never mentioned that to me. I don't need your help."

"That's her deal."

This was nuts. What, if I didn't let Alexis tutor me, would Mrs. Hall revoke her offer to speak on my behalf tonight?

"Why does she care so much about me anyway?" I asked.

"Have you met my mother? She doesn't even need this job. She's just bored and trolling for pet projects." She motioned her hands up and down, as if to showcase me. "Now she's found the Promised Land."

"My grades are fine. I don't need a tutor."

"If that helps you touch yourself to sleep at night." She huffed. "Why is this even an issue? It's in your own interest to have her forget about you."

"All right then." At least she was being honest. I could appreciate that. "What do you propose?"

"Come out next Monday to help build sets for the dance. Let her see you there, and the minute she leaves, you can go too."

"What's the catch?"

"We're going to have to meet once a week," she said. I started to protest, but she held her up her hand. "If you do this a couple times, she'll feel that she's fixed you, and I promise she'll go away. You can bask in your loser-ness. I get my Lexus back, and everyone will be happy."

"Fine."

"What's your cell number?" she asked.

I tore off a piece of notebook paper and wrote it down.

"If you try to dump pig's blood on me or any other stupid pranks." I handed it over. "I will get you."

"Do you have yogurt for brains? Why would I drag it on? I want out of this arrangement worse than you."

Mr. Doyle cleared his throat. I glanced up to find him staring at us. Apparently, class had started.

"Sorry," I told him, and he turned back to the board and began yammering about tangents and cosecants.

My phone buzzed. I glanced down at the text.

Library Monday, Alexis texted me.

"Whatever," I told her.

A loud pop made me jump. I glanced up. Mr. Doyle had slammed his textbook down on the floor. His push-broom mustache twitched. The entire class giggled at his trademark move.

"Nice of you to join us." He pointed at the dry erase board. "We were just discussing how to simplify this problem. Perhaps you could help us, Ms. Hall."

$(sin^2x)(cos^2x)+cos^4x$

Alexis glared at him like he was a cockroach that had crawled across her plate of cookies. Finally, she mumbled, "I don't know."

"What's that?" he asked. "I couldn't hear you."

"I don't know," she said clearly this time.

That was a shocker. I thought for sure she'd have already studied through to the end of the textbook. How the heck was she supposed to tutor me? Maybe if I needed assistance in blowjob etiquette, I'd give her a call.

"I'm confused." Mr. Doyle walked around the front of his desk and sat on it. "I was certain that you had all the answers because you obviously don't need to pay attention in class. Ms. Robinson, perhaps you could be of some assistance to your friend. Why don't you stand up and fill us in."

This was the last thing I needed.

"Get up," he said loudly.

"Okay." I stood next to my desk.

Suddenly, the room grew dark, all except Mr. Doyle, whose gleaming bald head appeared to glow under a single panel light above. The students around me blurred. A low drone noise filled my ears, like a million tiny machines vibrating in sync. My stomach turned.

"I'm sorry," I said, "but I'm not feeling well. Can I go to the nurse?"

"We've just begun class." From the way he looked down his glasses, he wasn't buying any illness unless I coughed up blood. "We're going to need all the time we can get since you've barely paid attention or shown up this year for that matter."

I glanced back at the board, and my legs felt weak. The trig problem had been replaced with the words, *Help me.* My god. It was happening again! Victoria's SOS. No, she'd never sent me that first message. The voice had. What if this wasn't her? Didn't matter. I couldn't take that chance.

"Please," I said. "I have to leave. It's an emergency."

"It always is."

This vision was different somehow. At the restaurant with Dad, I'd been completely hallucinating, but this was the real world with extras added.

"I'll try to make it back as quickly as possible," I told him.

"Tell you what." He folded his arms. "If you help us solve this problem, you can go."

I glanced back up at the board. The words *help me* had been replaced by the original problem. *(sin²x)(cos²x)+cos⁴x.*

"It's cosign squared x." I picked up my backpack, put it on, and leaned against the desk for support. "Factor out the sin squared x plus cosign squared x, which equals one."

For a moment, he stood motionless with a clenched jaw. The darkened room returned to normal. The buzzing in my head died down to the patter of raindrops, which pecked at the classroom's fogged window glass.

"Very good," he said.

No, it wasn't. I'd never seen a grown man look so irritated, and that included my dad on salad night.

"I'll try to make it back before the end of class," I told him.

"Don't worry about it." He nodded slowly. "I'll see you this afternoon, four o'clock sharp."

Hold on. That was the exact time of my hearing. He was going to be there? I glanced at Alexis, who struggled so hard to contain her smile that it seemed her head might pop into a spray of confetti and glitter. What could I do though? Victoria was in trouble. I had to go.

"Thank you." I tried to downplay the moment.

Then I raced out the door to get to my friend before Mr. Doyle could change his mind. I didn't know if Victoria or the voice had contacted me, but it didn't matter. Either way, I knew she needed my help.

16

*S*LUSH PUDDLES SPLASHED UNDERFOOT as I hurried around the corner onto Victoria's street. Yes, I just ditched school in plain view of half of the faculty, which meant I'd probably get expelled tonight at my hearing, but I had no choice. When your best friend sends a psychic signal for help, you respond. I just hoped she'd been the one who actually sent the message this time.

I reached the end of Castel Lane to find some kind of scuffle happening outside her gate. The Malakoff's private security guard nudged a camera crew back. What the heck was Amber Gonzalez from Action News 7 doing here? Somehow, I had to get inside that house without anyone noticing.

I ducked and ran down a row of hedges that bordered their estate. When I reached the gap in the fence, I climbed through and kept to the outside of the yard to avoid leaving a trail of fresh footprints in the virgin snow. Luckily, the window to the trophy room was still unlocked. I climbed inside.

"How am I supposed to know?" Lita's voice came from some distant room.

"Well, somebody told the press about her," Carl said. Something slammed, a drawer maybe.

I grabbed my phone, ready to dial the police in case he decided to go all Jack Nicholson in *The Shining* again.

"The entire ER saw her wake up from that coma," Lita said. "How long did you think we could keep this a secret?"

"I'm calling Flynn," he told her. "We need to get out in front of the story."

As I snuck up the back staircase, their argument faded into an echoed jumble. I slipped into Victoria's bedroom.

"Hey?" I whispered, closed the door behind me, and walked into darkness. "Victoria, are you in here?"

My eyes took a second to adjust. When they did, my heart sank. What had she done? All of her paintings had been ripped from the walls and piled in the center of the room like bonfire kindling. Giant X's had been slashed down the center of some of the canvases. I should have known she'd do something like this, especially considering her temper.

She'd always mistreated her own artwork. Left unvarnished paintings on the floor face down. One time, she even spray-painted a Joker grin over one of her oil portraits, but this was something else. I had no words.

The curtains to her balcony rustled in the breeze. I walked outside. Above, a flock of crows smothered the skyline, writhing and cawing with no apparent sense of direction. I turned to my left to find Victoria huddled on the ground in the freezing drizzle.

"Oh god." I ran to her side. With her soaked white night gown plastered to her skin, she looked as if she'd been out here for hours. "Honey, what are you doing? Why did you destroy your paintings?"

"Help me." She latched onto my shoulder. Her bare feet slipped on the wet deck as I lifted her up. Then I walked her inside the bedroom.

"Here, sit on your bed." I rubbed her arms and then wrapped one of her blankets around her body. "Are you crazy? What were you doing out there?"

"We have to leave...Monique." She shivered violently. "Now."

"What's going on? Why did you send me that message?"

"I didn't send you...you anything. It found us."

"You mean the voice?" I flipped on her nightstand lamp and searched the room. "Is it here now?"

"It wants to take me back down," she said through chattering teeth. "I can feel it inside my skin, digging, pulling me underneath. We have to get out of...here."

"And go where? Your parents are downstairs right now. They'll never let you out of this house."

"I don't care."

"Hold on. Just give me a minute to think."

"There isn't time," she said.

"This doesn't make sense. If some demon wants you back in a coma, why did it tell me to come here and help you?"

"I'm, I'm run—ning out of time." Her facial tick returned. "Help—me."

Crap. She was getting worse. Her word-glitch stutter was back. She really was regressing, Algernon-style. At this rate, she'd be gone in minutes.

"I don't know what you want," I said to anyone or anything that might be listening. Wind shoved in her curtains and rattled the blinds. "She's wearing the stupid necklace. Do you hear me? What am I supposed to do?"

No answer. *Think, Monique.* Yesterday she'd told me that the voice had come back into this world with her. Now, she'd just said that it was somehow inside of her skin, pulling her down again. Why would it change its mind?

It's hungry, Monique, she had told me last night. *It's always hungry.*

Could it be that simple? It needed to be fed. What do you feed a psychotic demon voice? It couldn't be a coincidence that after each of the leaps in her recovery, I'd felt drained from her touch.

"Victoria, listen to me." I grabbed her cheeks and then her neck, which felt deathly cold. She just stared off into space.

"When you woke up a few days ago, I touched your hand, and then I got dizzy. The same thing happened when you came out of your coma. I think you're doing something to me. Feeding off me, I don't know, but you have to do it again."

She shrank back against the wall. "I'm—I'm."

"Do the energy drain," I told her, but still she didn't move. "Dammit, Victoria, do you want to die?"

I slapped her face hard. Instantly, she bared her teeth and snatched my wrists. I could have sworn her feral eyes burned hotter, a bright Photoshop green that locked onto me with ravenous hunger. I stared into the face of the thing that had used Victoria to cross into this realm. It really was inside of her.

My muscles began to shake, and then violent spasms erupted through my body. Sparks exploded everywhere in my vision. I gasped for air, which poured down my throat, slick and freezing, as if I'd been submerged in a bath of ice water.

I tried to pull away, but she squeezed tighter. My vision began to constrict to a shrinking circle. Then I was falling, struggling to glimpse the last moment of light. Struggling.

Please don't pass out. I didn't want to die today.

***

I wake up. I think it is the middle of the night because it is dark in our blanket tent castle in my bedroom. Did Victoria go home? If she did, I'm going to be mad at that chicken bird. She was supposed to spend the whole night with me for my birthday. One, two, three, four, five, six-years old tomorrow. We sneaked pizza upstairs for a late-night snack, but now I am alone, and I'm not hungry for pepperoni.

Wait a minute. Is it tomorrow yet? I get up and turn on the flashlight. Time for birthday presents now that Daddy came home. Sometimes construction people have to leave town for jobs because the rent doesn't pay itself, but he made sure to be here for my big day. Rent can wait. I crawl out of our tent and see Victoria sitting on the window seat, staring outside.

"Why aren't you asleep?" I shine my light at her. The look in her eye scares me. "What's wrong?"

"Shhh." She holds a finger over her lips and whispers, "I saw your mom in the hallway packing up her stuff. I don't think she's coming back home."

I run over to the window. "Yes, she is."

There is a red car in our driveway with the roof down. She is in the passenger seat. A stranger is in the driver's seat. He starts the car, but he doesn't turn on the headlights. I try to pull on the window, but it will only open a little bit.

"Hey," I shout through the crack. "Mommy. Victoria is lying again. Where are you going?"

She looks up at me for a second. Then she says something to the man. He starts to back up in our driveway.

"What about cake for my birthday tomorrow?" I slap the window. Then I run downstairs and outside into our front yard, but I am too slow. The red car is by the stop sign at the end of our street.

"Come home," I shout at her. "I'll be good." The car drives away. "I promise."

"It's okay," Victoria says. "I won't ever leave you."

"Shut up," I tell her. "She's coming back."

"Then I'll wait for her with you." Victoria grabs my hand, and we sit on the curb together.

I don't know why I'm crying. She's coming home tomorrow. I know it. She just needs to go buy presents for me. Victoria will see. Mommy will be home soon.

***

I woke in a darkened room. My cheeks felt wet. I must have been crying in my sleep. That nightmare had been too real. Even now, I smelled pepperoni and cigarettes. Could that have been what happened that night? I had few memories from my childhood, especially of my mother, but why would she leave us in the middle of the night without a goodbye, and why would Victoria have been there? I glanced around. I was in her bedroom now.

I shot up on her bed. Victoria! The energy drain. Had it worked? I turned and found her hunched in a ball, rocking gently against the headboard.

"Monique?" She sat up straight. "Is that you?"

"I think so." No matter how deep I breathed, I couldn't stop my heart from racing. "I feel like an EMP fried my brain though. Did it work?"

She threw her pillows aside and hugged me. "I thought you were dead."

"Hold on." I leaned back. "I can't take another hit like that last one."

She let go of me. "Got it."

That's when I noticed the bluish haze that surrounded her. The room looked normal, but her eyes seemed to glow. Her teeth too. She looked like she loved spending her summers in Madame Curie's Radium Clock Funhouse. Perfect. Now, *I* was hallucinating. Just what I needed. Brain damage.

"How do you feel?" I asked.

"Strong," she said. "I don't feel the pull anymore."

"How long will it last?"

"I don't know."

The glow around her began to fade. Her once rain-soaked nightgown and hair were nearly dry.

"How long were we out?" I rubbed the sleep from my eyes. "What time is it?"

"Let's see." She held her wrist up to her blind eyes, as if trying to read her nonexistent watch. "It's fuck-you o'clock."

I laughed, and she did too. That probably topped the list of epically stupid questions. I pulled out my phone from my jacket pocket. 3:58 pm.

"Crap. I have to go." I stood on wobbly legs, staggered over to her bedroom door, and peeked out into the hallway.

"Don't leave me here with those two," she said. "They haven't stopped arguing yet."

"The school is going to kick me out if I miss my hearing that's happening right now."

"What is it for?" She looked terrified. "Because of me?"

"Not really. Well, maybe a little. I've been missing a lot of classes since your accident. If I get kicked out, my dad said we have to move."

"That can't happen."

"I know. I never would've made it here in time today if I lived just ten minutes away. Now I'll explain everything when I come back to check on you later, but I'm late."

I turned and snuck out the door.

17

TWENTY MINUTES AFTER leaving Victoria's house, I arrived at the North Hills High administration building. I tried to compose myself, but considering what I'd just been through, that task was nearly impossible. The butterflies in my stomach were a tweaked-out hot mess. Outside the hearing room, I pulled my mop of hair back with a scrunchie. Then I went inside and walked down the center aisle.

Although a dozen chairs had been set up around the perimeter of the oval desk that filled the room, only three people sat on the far side. On the right, Alexis's mom, Mrs. Hall, seemed worried as she checked over some papers. To the left, Mr. Doyle still looked angry from trig class this morning. Sandwiched between them, Principal Rademacher glared down at me from his tribunal podium throne.

Dad had already shown up. On the near side of the oval table, he sat with his back to me, wearing his nice suit, the navy blue one with the razor pinstripes. I walked over to him, took off my gloves, and undid the buckles on my black jacket.

"I'll explain everything later," I whispered as I sat down.

"No need," he said quietly. "You made me look like a jackass here today by showing up at your leisure. If you want to stay in this school, you'd better explain it to your teachers damn good, because you're on your own."

Perfect. He was pissed off at me. Again. *Hey, karma, how about a break for stressed Monique? Just this once.*

"Hello?" I said to the teachers and noticed my voice was slightly amplified. What was with the microphones? Two of them had been set up in front of each of us, with additional ones across the table in front of each teacher. Although the room was large, they weren't that far away.

"We're taping this session." Principal Rademacher seemed to read my mind. "We don't want anything to be misconstrued later."

"What, you think I'm going to sue the school or something?" I asked, not really as a threat. Well, kind of as a threat, and a lame one at best. It wasn't like we had money or time for that kind of nonsense.

"An expulsion hearing is a serious event," he said. "A fact that seems to have been lost on you because you're twenty-three minutes late."

"I'm sorry. I got caught up."

"We're sorry too," he said. With those acne scars, he could have given Edward James Olmos a run for the worst skin Oscar. His pasty face and wispy comb-over to cover his balding head didn't help matters. "This hearing was to determine your ability to take your schooling seriously, and I think we have our answer."

"I know I have some absences, but you haven't heard my side of the story."

"You were put on probation last week." He traced a finger down the page on the folder in front of him. "You've already missed four more classes since then. Two just today. Now you're late for this hearing."

"Wait a minute, Phil." Mrs. Hall covered her microphone with one hand, but it didn't really muffle her voice. "She's a good kid in a tough spot."

At least she held up her end of the bargain.

"That may be," he told her in a hushed voice. "But what kind of example are we setting for the other students?"

"Just hear her out."

I don't think they understood the concept of microphones. "Fine." He turned to me, took off his glasses, and pinched the bridge of his nose. "You're lucky to have such a dedicated counselor on your side, young lady. You've got five minutes."

"Thank you," I said. "I want to stay in school. Now my dad is healthier, he's going back to work, and..." I almost brought up Victoria. Knowing this town, mentioning the accident that occurred outside the cult's compound would be a mistake. "I promise I can do better."

"Do you know the maximum number of allowed absences?" he asked. I shook my head. "Nine. You had more than sixteen last semester. Unexcused I might add."

"My dad had a double-bypass. What was I supposed to do?"

"The board is aware of your hardships, but that doesn't exempt you from showing up to school. This year alone, you've already missed the first week."

"I kept a 3.4 GPA last semester," I told him. "And it wasn't a bunch of fluff classes either. I don't see what the problem is."

"One day you're going to have a boss. Or be somebody's boss. What would you say to an employee who didn't show up for work?"

"I don't know. Does that employee make me lots of money?" I asked. That clearly irritated him, so I added, "I have a job now, and I've never called in sick."

"And yet, our time isn't valuable to you."

"My dad and I have bills," I said. Grumps Robinson shifted uncomfortably in his seat next to me. "Lucido's pays me to show up."

"Who do you think pays your teachers' salaries? The electric bills at this school? The rent?"

"Taxpayers like me."

Dad snorted a quiet bit of laughter, which seemed to irritate Rademacher even more.

"Well, you're wrong," he said. "The state doesn't pay when students don't show up. We can go round and round on this, but the policy here is clear. You were put on probation last week, and it didn't work out. Can you please leave the room? I'd like to talk to your father alone."

"She needs to be here for this," Dad said like he was trying to teach me some life lesson. Jerk.

"Have it your way," Rademacher said. "Whichever school she attends next, these absences are going to be a problem."

"I can't go anywhere else," I told them. "Please, Victoria needs me. If we have to move, there's no telling what will happen to her."

"You mean your friend who was in the accident?" he said. "The one the police are still investigating?"

The doors creaked behind me, cutting him off. I spun around. Victoria stood in the center aisle, except she was no longer the feral child of Malakoff Manor. Her hair had been combed straight, and she'd somehow managed to apply precision mascara and blood red lipstick. Large snowflakes flecked her favorite black jacket with the matching skirt.

"I would like to speak on behalf of the defendant," she said to the faculty.

"What are you doing?" I asked, and then realized that Carl and Lita were nowhere to be seen. "How did you get here?"

"I hope you don't mind." She strolled toward me carefully, so I stood up to help her. We reached the desk. She felt around, found the microphone, and pulled it free. "I brought some friends with me today."

A camera crew pushed open both doors behind us and entered, followed by Amber Gonzalez from Action News 7. Victoria must have grabbed her in front of her gate.

"I am alive today because of the actions of Monique Kathleen Robinson," Victoria said. "I think everyone here can agree, that it is a testament to the smallness of this school and its faculty to try to expel this bastion of the community."

"Who let them in here?" Rademacher demanded. "Get those cameras out. This is a closed session."

"The defendant has the right to have witnesses appear on her behalf," Victoria said.

"Young lady, this is not a court room."

"The world needs to see how North Hills High treats its only hero. A woman scorned by society—"

"That's it," Rademacher said. "I'm calling the police."

"Be quiet, Tom," Mrs. Hall told him. She clearly couldn't believe her eyes. "Do you know who that is?"

I glanced at Victoria, whose smirk must have been evident to everyone.

"When my own family gave me up for dead and tried to pull the plug on me, Monique Robinson stopped them. She worked tirelessly to make my life better, never giving in when the odds were against her. Yes, she's, weird." Each word came with a beat of her hand on the desk in front of me. "A condition that began at birth. The daughter of a schizoid psychosocial, but hey, who isn't a little crazy these days? Am I right?"

Each teacher sat in various degrees of dumbfounded horror.

"What the hell is that girl doing?" Dad muttered.

"Helping me," I whispered. "I think."

"I don't think she's helping."

"You told me that I'm on my own here," I said. "You made that clear. So this is me. On my own."

"Fair enough," he said. "I'll start packing tonight."

"Young lady," Rademacher said to Victoria. "I don't know

who you think you are—"

"Victoria Malakoff." She smiled back at the camera crew. "I died one cold bitter night, but then I came back to life to protect the dignity of Monique Kathleen Robinson, our city's proudest treasure."

"You might want to tone it down a notch," I told her.

"It takes a big man to admit when he's wrong." She waved me away. "So how about it, Principal Rademacher. Anything to add here tonight?" He just sat with a nasty sneer. "Didn't think so."

Shit. After that barb, I'd have to help Dad pack.

"Victoria, you shouldn't be here," I told her. "You need to be getting rest."

"Absolutely." She held out her hand. "Our work here is done anyway. Let's go."

"But they haven't ruled yet."

"Do you trust me?" she asked.

"With my life."

"Good." She pulled me up, and I grabbed my jacket. "Then let's go."

"You'd better know what you're doing," I said.

"One more thing." She turned to face the camera crew. "Due to Monique Robinson's tireless efforts to save my life, my father Carl Malakoff has decided to donate a new technology wing to the school's library. The Monique K. Robinson Bridge to a Brighter Tomorrow room, where a fifteen-foot steel statue will immortalize her for all time."

"Are you crazy?" I asked.

"So, Amber Gonzalez from Action News 7." She glanced back at the reporter. "Why don't you ask these socially conscious teachers up there why they feel it's so important to expel a girl for being absent, while she was literally saving another student's life?"

Then Victoria squeezed my hand and pushed past the photographer, who immediately shoved his camera and lights into Rademacher's face. We hurried away from the barrage of questions behind.

"Victoria, you have finally gone and lost it." I cinched my jacket to protect from the biting cold. "Does your father even know about any of that?"

"Of course not, but how can he say no to such great press?"

"I don't want a ridiculous statue. The other students will deface it."

"Big deal," she said. "We'll tag it first. Besides, it doesn't matter. Think about the backlash. There's no earthly way they can expel you now."

My god. She was right.

"How did you get here?" I glanced at the news van that had parked out front.

"Just walk me home. We can talk about it on the way."

A hand grabbed my shoulder. I turned around to see Dad, who stood with a strange grin on his face. Apparently, he knew what Victoria had done as well.

"Do you two need a ride?" he asked.

"Nope," I said. "We're fine *on our own.*"

"Be home by ten." He kissed my forehead and then motioned to Victoria. "And make sure Sister Souljah gets home safe too. I suspect that she has a lot of explaining to do."

She beamed. "Bye, Mr. Robinson."

He chuckled and walked away, and I realized just how much I appreciated my dad sometimes. For the respect he commanded. To Victoria, her father was Carl, but my dad—who owned no property or stock portfolios—had always been Mr. Robinson. And he always would be.

"Now take me home, slut," she said. "I already told you our work here is over."

Screw the blindness and the circumstances by which she came back to me. This was my best friend. Sure, she was amped like a crack head. Had that come from our encounter earlier? What if that voice had something to do with this?

Quit it, Monique. Enjoy the moment.

I'd asked karma for a break, and here it was.

"Let's go," I said. "I'll walk you home."

We turned onto the snow-covered bike path that bordered the road, and I kicked something. A dead crow rolled to a stop next to a lifeless squirrel. Gross. Animal Control needed to step up its game. Both were missing their eyes, as if their irises had exploded.

Then I saw another bird cawing on the ground, flapping one extended wing against the snow bank. My heart began to race. As far as I could see, the bike path was littered with dead crows and other small animals. That's when I noticed where the trail of death led.

Directly from Victoria's house.

18

A GIRL HAS A LOT OF TIME to think when she's picking up dead bodies, especially on a dark bike path at night. It didn't matter that they were animals. I'd like to see Clive Barker spend an evening collecting Tweety and Thumper carcasses without gagging. Worse yet, after what had happened in Victoria's bedroom earlier, I had no doubt that she drained these poor creatures, just as she'd almost done to me.

So here I was. Something like a vampire's familiar. How proud my dad would be if he could see me now, stuffing an armadillo thingy into my Hefty bag. Monique Robinson, undertaker to the Walt Disney extras. I should have guessed that my fairy tale in which my best friend returned without serious consequences would sour into Grimm territory.

I mean, Cinderella's stepsisters chopped off their own toes to fit into the glass slipper. In the original version, Red Riding Hood barely escaped with her life, only after being eaten. Why would I be surprised that Snow White didn't wake with a kiss from her true love, but instead with a scream so horrid that it still gave her best friend nightmares, cursed to feed on her forest friends?

How much of her was really Victoria now? How much was the voice? One thought haunted me more than anything, though.

What would happen when the snacks ran out?

I pushed it away. I needed to clean up this mess and get Victoria home before anyone came along and made this situation worse.

"Am I going to get the silent treatment all night?" she asked from a snow-crusted iron bench across the path from me.

Above, a cone of light from the park lamp barely fought back the night fog, leaving Victoria little more than a shadow in her all black jacket, skirt, and tights.

"Until I'm done picking up dead things," I told her. "Yes."

"It's Friday. Let's go out."

"Are you kidding me? After all this, you want to hit the town?"

"Someone will come along and report the animals," she said.

"Yeah. That someone will probably be Amber Gonzalez with her ten o'clock news crew." With two fingers, I picked up another crow by its extended wing. "I'm going to burn these gloves when I'm finished."

"There's no way she can know what happened," Victoria said.

"Let's see. Girl mysteriously comes back from the dead. Then piles of animals stack up around her house. Oh, and let's not forget about the crazy cult folks involved in her accident. We're lucky that people aren't swarming all over this place right now."

A car whooshed closer on the overpass above, vibrating the tiled tunnel walkway next to us that cut underneath the roadway. I paused to listen.

"Hey," Victoria shouted up at the car. "We're doing delinquent stuff down here. Come get us."

"Are you out of your mind?" I prepared to run.

The car slowed for the speed bump on the bridge, and then it passed.

"See," she said. "Nobody cares what goes on down here."

"Keep it up." I picked up the final crow and stuffed it in

the bag. "When the crazed town folks come for you in the night, I'll be on the side of the road selling pitchforks."

"Don't be like that," she said.

"I'm finished now. I'll take you home."

"Seriously. I didn't mean to worry you."

"This isn't a game, Victoria. You almost died today, and I'm pretty sure that I almost did too."

She stood and walked carefully over to me. "I know."

"I have no clue what the hell happened out here," I told her. "I'm up to my eyeballs in death. I'm stressed beyond...I don't know, but I don't have the patience to play around with you. Between my dad and the school and the animals and the strange voices that want to suck the freaking life out me, I'm about to pop."

"I'm sorry."

"You're just saying that."

"I mean it," she said. "I was being stupid. I'm scared too, which is why I don't want to be here."

"You have a strange way of showing it."

"I don't deal with my emotions very well. At least according to my pedophile therapist. I swear, he spends more time trying to look down my shirt—"

"Victoria, focus. What happened out here?" I rustled the bag so she could hear it. "It looks like you devoured the whole forest in one sitting."

"You have to believe me. I didn't know they would die." She looked down at the ground. "The animals just kept coming closer, like they were drawn to me or something."

"Did that voice call for them?"

"Maybe. I don't know. I only knew that you needed my help, but I couldn't see." Her voice shook. "I just didn't want to be helpless anymore."

"How could the animals possibly help with that?" I asked.

She gave me a look like I was being intentionally dense. "What?"

"I thought it was obvious when I showed up at your hearing by myself."

"You mean you can see again?" I asked, and she nodded. In this carnage, I'd been too distracted to notice. I hugged her. "I just assumed that you came to the hearing with the camera crew."

"I told them to meet me there."

Actually, that made sense. Otherwise, they would have noticed this mess.

"Hold on. If you can see." I shoved the Hefty bag against her chest, and she grabbed it. "I am not your Renfield. You can clean up your own nasty mess, Dracula."

"Nobody asked you to do this." She dropped the bag. "Besides, it doesn't work like that. I can't see the bodies."

"That's convenient."

"No, really." She glanced all around. "Almost everything is pitch dark. The ground, the snow, and the houses, but I can see you in front of me, in millions of vibrating threads of blue light." She pointed to the fir trees that bordered the path. "Their roots and needles spread out like luminescent pink veins all around us, even underneath our feet. That's how I can see the ground. It's about a foot above where the roots' light ends."

"That sounds beautiful."

"And I can see this." She whipped out her hand and turned it over. Her fingers had twisted like a claw. She loosened her grip. A large moth flew away.

"When did this happen?" I asked.

"I could see shapes and glowing blobs after you gave me the boost earlier."

"Why didn't you say anything?"

"And jinx it? No, thank you. I'll tell you another thing. Now that my sight is back, I am not going to waste another minute at my house. You and I need to celebrate in town or something."

"Absolutely not," I told her. "We don't even know what we're dealing with."

Her unflinching bright eyes seemed to cut through the fog. She wasn't going to back down. After this day, I didn't have the energy to fight with her. Truth was, I really couldn't stop her once she put her mind to something anyway. I had to be smart here.

"Fine," I said. "I'll go out with you. Alexis Hall will be glad to hear it."

"You can quit with the reverse psychology, hooker. We're not in second grade. It doesn't work on me anymore."

"I'm serious," I told her. "No games. I talked to Alexis yesterday."

"What exactly did that two-faced talentless worm suck tell you?"

"Just that she was happy to have you gone from North Hills High. After your TV appearance, everyone will be anxious to see you at school. You could really stick it to her by making a big entrance. If you go out tonight, you'll ruin the suspense though. That's up to you."

"Fine." She sounded irritated. "We'll wait until Monday."

"I'll walk you home then," I told her.

"Can we just stay here a little longer? I can't take my father and Lita fighting all the time. I think they're going to get a divorce."

She was probably right about that.

"Give me a second." I walked over to the closest oak tree and hid the bag behind it.

No need to carry around a smoking gun. I could pick it up

on the way home and ditch it in the dumpster near my house. I moved back over to Victoria, grabbed her hand, and we sat on the bench together in silence, but my mind raced. I couldn't wait for Ethan any longer. Whatever it took, I had to find him. Like right now.

Otherwise, Victoria's future victims might have curfews and legal rights.

19

I WATCHED THE CEILING for hours that night, but sleep never came. Ever since Victoria awakened from her coma, my dreams had become violent, even by my standards. Children with filed teeth and wolves with human faces hunted me endlessly. Given the bird apocalypse, I now had proof that a physical threat actually existed. I needed to talk to Ethan. He just happened to give me his mother's necklace, and I was supposed to believe that it had nothing to do with all this? Please. Not to mention that he had conveniently disappeared.

Last time I tried to call, his psychotic father intercepted me, and I wasn't about to search for him back at that compound. Luckily, the Awakeners set up shop at the farmer's market every Saturday to recruit new mind zombies. That would be my best chance to find him before Victoria crossed a line that she couldn't come back from.

Before sunrise the next morning, I dressed and hurried into town. My gray pea coat and riding boots did little to block the breath-freezing chill, but I had to leave early. My double shift at Lucido's started at noon.

By the time I reached the edge of town at dawn, the church people had already set up six booths with striped awnings like a mini travelling circus. None of the people seemed to notice me as they arranged their carrot and zucchini displays.

Near the tree line behind the market, I spotted Ethan's car. The attached thirty-foot Airstream camping trailer looked way too big for his rust-bucket El Camino. I hurried over to the far side of the trailer and glanced back, but no one had followed me. I bumped into someone.

"Watch out," a young voice said.

I spun back around to find a girl with a lopsided ponytail, wearing a purple nylon windbreaker and blue jeans. Her sneakers had charms sewn into them. The shoes made a cool shooshing sound as she set down a milk crate filled with potatoes.

"Hey," I said quietly. The last thing I needed was a bunch of cult crazies figuring out why I was here. "I need to speak with Ethan. Is he around?"

"Well, that's rude." She blew wisps of her dark hair away from her eyes. "I haven't even met you yet, and you're already making demands. I'm not his receptionist," she said as if she were royalty.

"Sorry," I told her. "I'm Monique."

"I know who you are." She shoved out her hand, and I shook it. "My name is Tara Elizabeth Ann Michelle Mossri."

"Quit making things up, Tara." Ethan opened the screen door to his camper.

"I'm not," she told him.

"You don't have any middle names." He put on a gray hoodie and walked down the trailer's front steps.

"I would if my parents had better sense," she said.

"Take that stuff up front," he said. "Give Monique and me a second to talk."

"I turn twelve next month. I'm more than old enough to hear anything you have to say."

"Go," Ethan said. Then he barked something at her in what sounded like Italian.

"Someone should have taught you manners." She jutted out her chin. "It's impolite to speak foreign languages in front of people who don't know them."

"How do you know Monique doesn't speak Portuguese?" he asked.

She turned to me. "Do you?"

"I only know Pig Latin, honey."

"Ooh." Her eyes brightened. "What is that?"

"Seriously?" At her age, Victoria and I had spoken nothing but that stupid language for an entire summer. "Trust me. It's not that big of a deal."

She clapped her hands. "Say something."

"Hat-way ooh-day ooh-yay ant-way eeh-may o-tay eeh-shay," I told her.

She looked up toward the mountains, tapping her thumb and forefinger together in a strange rhythm. Then a huge smile lit her face.

"Ave-hay ooh-yay and than-yay ad-hay ex-shay et-yay," she said back to me.

Have you and Ethan had sex yet?

"Excuse me." I wanted to flick her. Then I realized what had happened. Sure, it was a boneheaded language, but she'd dissected and assimilated it from one sentence. "No, we have not done that."

She giggled. "Why not?"

"I've only met him once. And because I'm not a hoochie coochie."

"Tara, what did you ask her?" Ethan said. Then he turned to me. "What did she say?"

"It's not so much fun when somebody does it to you, huh?" She smirked at him.

"How did you learn that so fast?" I asked her.

"Her parents are linguists." Ethan grabbed the back of her neck and she scrunched up. "She speaks seven languages."

"None of them are so exquisite as Pig Latin." She squirmed away from him, and I realized how much she reminded me of Victoria at that age.

"Let's go in my trailer," Ethan said, and then he glared down at Tara. "Where we can be alone."

"Try to keep your clothes on." She picked up her milk crate and scurried off with her charm shoes jingling all the way.

I followed Ethan up the steps, which squeaked underfoot as we entered the dark trailer. Inside, my eyes struggled to adjust. A potted plant or something brushed my face. Ethan hit the light switch, and I stopped.

WTF didn't begin to describe this place. Plants smothered every square inch inside the trailer. They grew up the sides of the walls. Carrots and tomatoes sat on platform shelves. Onions, I thought, and other kinds of leafy vegetables too. A lattice of clear plastic tubes supplied water to their roots.

"It's a hydroponics bay," Ethan said.

"You think?" I walked forward into his mini-jungle.

"It's too cold outside during the winter to grow anything."

"I thought you guys didn't believe in technology or something."

"That's my stepfather." He flicked on a couple of the UV lamps that dangled from the ceiling, revealing the back end of the trailer.

Along the far wall, a sleeping bag had been rolled out on top of a yoga mat. Did he live in here too? At the far end, massive pot plants grew against the back wall. Ladies and gentlemen, here it was. The real reason for this ridiculous setup.

"Don't worry about those," he said. "I sell weed to Sheriff Acosta twice a month."

"Is that smart?"

"Is this really why you came all the way down here? To talk about my plants?"

"I want to know what you did to Victoria." No, it wasn't

tactful, but accusing people in their own homes of sinister plots was a nasty business, and I wasn't going to wrap it up with a bow.

"What are you talking about?" he asked.

"She was dead. I was in the hospital room that night. Lita had already pulled the plug."

"And what? You think I had something to do with her springing to life?"

"Maybe not you, but Roman or someone knows something."

"I don't even like him," he said. "We haven't spoken in weeks. And what could we have possibly done anyway?"

"Voodoo. Mad scientist stuff. You tell me."

"Wow. Did you come up with those theories all by yourself?"

"Don't patronize me. I know what I saw, and it wasn't natural. Neither was half the crap I've seen in the last few days."

"You're really serious about this," he said.

"Yes."

"You should leave."

I didn't think I'd ever seen anyone look so disappointed. Being an outsider all your life forces a girl to pay attention. To know people's motives—before they did sometimes—in order to stay one step ahead of fools looking to stir up drama. My BS meter was almost never wrong. If his medallion did cause Victoria's resurrection, Ethan legitimately didn't know about it.

"All of this is connected," I told him. "I don't know exactly how. Maybe Roman did something to that necklace you gave me."

"You know, I thought you were different," he said. "Turns out you're just like the rest of the assholes in town."

"No, I'm not," I told him. "And I'm not crazy either. Look around your compound. Talk to your friends. Somebody there has to know what's going on."

"Get out of my house." He opened his front door and nudged me down the front steps.

"So you're just going to throw me out when I need your help?"

He slammed the door shut.

"Fine." I turned and began walking back home.

Bastard. As always, I had to handle this myself. I reached the entrance to the farmer's market field, which led back to Main Street. Seconds later, I was in tourist shops central.

"You know, he shouldn't treat you like that," somebody said from behind.

I spun around to find Tara with her hands shoved in the pockets of her puffy jacket.

"Were you eavesdropping on us?" I asked.

"It's not my fault if people shout." She walked up to me. "If you still need help finding out what happened to Victoria, Im-way our-yay irl-gay."

I'm your girl.

Yes, the fact that I even considered working with a twelve-year-old spy was a testament to my desperation, but what other options did I have? If I didn't figure out what happened to Victoria soon—well, I didn't want to think about that.

"What do you know?" I asked.

20

I ARRIVED AT LUCIDO'S that afternoon, relieved to find the restaurant already buzzing with the lunch rush. Ceramic plates clinked in back, while the sizzle of grilled chicken and red pepper marinara wafted out each time the kitchen doors opened. Christian had gone home sick, and my eight-table section had me teetering on the edge of beautiful insanity, taking orders, running food, filling drinks, ignoring rudeness, and clearing dishes.

Take my tip, thank you very much.

Now repeat.

The never-ending chaos filled my brain with precious white noise, bright and loud enough to drown out the living nightmare that had become my life. After seven hours of non-stop action, every muscle in my body ached. If I could only make it through the rest of my shift without some new disaster looming, karma and I would be square.

"Nina." I walked up to the hostess stand. "Slow down seating me. I can barely keep up."

She nodded just as the front doors opened. Ethan stood in the entrance, wearing a frayed army surplus jacket, jeans, and black Doc Martins. Customers in the restaurant lobby parted from him. This was just perfect.

Apparently, everyone in North Hills knew that survival clothing meant the Awakeners, and most of these people probably recognized the leader's son.

Ethan shook snow from his jacket and pulled down his hoodie. A well-dressed elderly couple next to him looked horrified, as though he'd tried to flick dandruff on them. He walked up to me. Then I saw the cuts on his face, the blood drips down the front of his jacket.

I reached out for his swollen, bruised cheek. "What the hell?"

Raw skin wrapped down around his chin. He flinched his head back, and I pulled my hand away. What was I thinking, trying to touch him like that? His wounds just looked so painful.

"We need to talk," he said.

"If this is about Tara—"

"It's not, although she's about as subtle as a rhino in a nursery. If you wanted information, you should have come to me."

"You threw me out of your trailer, remember?" I couldn't believe his nerve. "And another thing, don't ever compare me to the other people in this town. I wouldn't have come to you if I wasn't certain that something was going on at your church."

"You caught me by surprise," he said. "I'm ready to talk now."

"Yeah, well, my shift ends at nine. Come back in forty-five minutes."

"This can't wait."

I glanced back at the owner, Bob Lucido, the lordiest bible-thump in all of Jesus-Ville and a greasy pervert too. He stood with his huge body squished behind the hostess stand, rubbing up against the help. He should have been more concerned about his cholesterol instead of giving me the stink eye.

"My boss isn't fond of you guys," I told Ethan. "And I really can't afford to lose my job. You need to come back later."

"There isn't time. I'm leaving town tonight, but I had to warn you first."

"About what?"

He glanced nervously around the packed restaurant. "Is there a place we can be alone?"

"You're freaking me out," I said. "Is this about Victoria?"

"And you too."

One of the patrons at the bar said something about heathens. Great. The natives were agitated. Again. Now they had two freaks for the price of one. Cult-boy Ethan talking to Monique the Dreary. That was like pouring water on a grease fire for these people. I needed to get him out of here.

"I'll try to take a break," I told him. "Meet me in back of the restaurant in five minutes."

He nodded and walked out the front door. I dropped off two checks and waited for a lull in the seating action, which came quickly. I found Sarina marrying ketchup bottles in one of the hidden booths behind the bar, getting ready to go home for the night.

True, she was thirty-something, but even Lucido's trademark white button-up dress shirt, black pants, and green half apron couldn't put a damper on her perfect body. No matter how busy we got—and today had been insanely hectic—she seemed immune to this restaurant's nonsense. With her platinum blond pixie haircut, she always looked runway ready, as if this job was a minor inconvenience on her way to rockstar-ness.

"Sarina, can you watch my tables for a second?" I asked. "I need to take a break."

"He's cute," she said without looking up. "Yours?"

"You mean Ethan? No, we're friends." I thought about how he'd treated me in his trailer earlier. "Kind of."

"I'll bet those cult boys are real kinky in bed."

My cheeks burned. "You can quit."

"I'm just saying. If you don't want him, Miss Sarina could teach that boy to bark like a dog."

"You're scarring my brain," I told her. Now, I'd have to scrub the image of Ethan on all fours from my mind, complete with a spike collar and a rolled-up newspaper. "Can you watch my tables or not?"

"Whatever," she said with a wide grin. Then she closed her eyes and held the back of her hand against her forehead. "Miss Sarina sees filthy things in your future."

"Just keep an eye on my tables, please." I walked away before her perpetual dirty mind turned to plushies and Harley Quinn cosplay. Then I walked through the kitchen and pushed open the back exit door.

In the alley, Ethan stood near the building's brick wall, away from the dumpster. The fresh layer of snow under his feet had been trampled by his heavy pacing. He blew hot breath into his hands and looked up at me.

"You need to be more careful when you come into town," I said. "These people are still angry about Victoria's accident. They blame your church."

"They should."

"Come again?"

"There's no way to explain this to you. I need you to come with me back to the Awakeners grounds tonight. I have to show you something."

"Are you crazy? I am not going back there ever. Not ever. Not me."

"It's deserted right now."

"And that makes it less scary how?"

"I just mean that all of the members are in the town park until nine o'clock, in celebration of Victoria's miracle. This might be our only chance."

"Doesn't matter," I said. "I don't get off until ten. We're slammed, and I have to get back to work soon, or else Bob's 'Big Boy' Lucido in there will fire my butt."

"I think you're in danger," he said. "You weren't at our rally by accident. Justin and I gave Victoria the flier that day because my father wanted her to be there."

"You stalked her?" I took a step back. Hanging with him in this alley didn't seem so smart anymore.

"It's nothing like that. Carl Malakoff was close to signing a deal to kick us off our family's land. Some kind of imminent domain highway project, but it was really about getting rid of us. My father told me that he wanted Victoria to see that we weren't crazy."

"Well the car wreck sort of took care of that one," I said. "It *was* an accident, right?"

"I don't know. Not anymore."

"What do you mean, you don't know?"

"That's why I need you to come with me. Somebody else has to see what's going on."

"Quit being so damn cryptic and call the police if it's that bad." I realized fear had driven my dialect a little too ethnic, so I toned it down. "Sheriff Acosta will know what to do."

"You don't understand the lengths to which my father will go in the name of his cause. Truth and grace aren't the only things he's been stockpiling."

"Guns?"

"Seeds. Bunkers. Everything you can think of, and he's not going to leave that land without a fight. Monique, there are families with young children up there."

"He wouldn't hurt them, would he?"

"I don't know anymore. Half of our members left the congregation after Victoria's accident. My father is not the same."

"He did that to your face, didn't he?" I demanded.

"Of course not. He doesn't need to lift a finger when so many others are willing to do it for him."

"What happened?"

"We've been arguing non-stop. I left to clear my head last week. When I came back tonight, I saw what he'd been doing up there, and I confronted him."

"Does this have to do with your mother's necklace?" I asked.

"Who cares about that?" He seemed genuinely confused by the suggestion. "I just told you they have weapons. Lots of them, and that's just the beginning."

The hairs on my neck raised. I could tell he wasn't lying.

"What exactly did you see?" I asked.

"I don't even know what I was looking at. A shrine or something. Just come with me. It's safe. I promise I'll protect you."

"Uh huh. If I die handcuffed in a storm cellar somewhere, I'll haunt you forever and ever."

"I'd die before I let anyone hurt you," he said, and I believed him.

That's what worried me. *He gets killed, and then weird hill people impregnate me and feed me Rosemary's Baby juice until the spawn hatches from poor Monique's stomach.* Still, if this had something to do with Victoria's sickness, I had to go.

"Let me clear it with Sarina," I said. "She owes me."

"I'll wait for you here."

"I'm serious." I opened the back door. "I will haunt your ass."

He nodded. I walked inside and prepared myself to visit the last place I'd ever want to be caught after dark.

Thanks, karma.

21

W E DROVE DOWN THAT dark two-lane highway in silence. The unnatural fog grew thicker with each passing mile, until claws of mist appeared to grasp at the vehicle around every winding twist of the road. Ethan sat on the edge of the bench seat in his El Camino, leaning over the steering wheel to see.

What was I thinking coming up here? Robinsons knew better than to get caught up in these situations. Sky diving. Cliff jumping. Riding state fair rollercoasters. That type of behavior was fine for idiots with way too much free time and fool's luck. So how did I end up locked onto this train track? Victoria. She needed me more than ever.

Before the accident, her tantrums were a weekly annoyance. Now, her temper just might lead to a body count that would make a terrorist jealous. I had to know what was causing her condition so we could fix it. Those answers were somewhere on the cult's compound. I knew it, but time was running out before the members returned. We needed to hurry.

"It's eight-twenty," I said. "How much farther is it?"

"Don't worry." Ethan flipped on the windshield wipers to clear the spray droplets. "I wouldn't bring you up here if I couldn't protect you."

"Who's worried? I'm not worried, and I can take care of myself."

"My car is older than both of us put together." He glanced at me. "You're about to yank the door panel off."

"Sorry." I put my hands in my lap.

"It's fine. We're here anyway." He pulled off the highway near the sheer face of the obsidian cliff, across the street from the compound. "None of the members should be back until at least ten-thirty."

"What do you mean *should*?"

"Just trust me. This won't take long."

We got out of the car into complete darkness. No civilization, streetlights, moon, or stars. No forest chirps either. Just an eerie dead calm. I turned on the flashlight app on my phone, which barely lit the mist a few feet ahead of us.

We crossed the road and walked down the steep gravel driveway, past the barbed gate with the NO TRESPASSING sign. Patchy snow and rock debris crunched underfoot. I grabbed the back of Ethan's jacket sleeve and held him close enough to smell his scent of pine wood chips and some kind of spice. Something skittered in the underbrush. I clinched his jacket tighter.

We reached the center of the clearing where the church members had been spray-painting their crazy signs. A shadow of some new contraption loomed overhead, but I couldn't see anything except a few welded pieces of rebar.

"Wait here." Ethan turned to me. "I've got to switch on the lights."

"Uh uh. You are *not* leaving me here by myself." I shined my phone light in his face, which made his blue eyes unnaturally bright. "Got it, lemur boy?"

"The switch is right there." He pointed about five feet away to a mass on the ground.

"Then we go together."

We walked over. He leaned down and flipped a large toggle switch. A dozen floodlights snapped on around the clearing. Immersed in the veil of fog, the lights beamed like mini-nuke explosions, frozen in time at the detonation point. Then I saw it.

"Jeez-us." I stared up at the contraption in the center, which towered over us.

I immediately understood why Ethan needed me to see this in person. Since I'd been here last, they'd cut down more trees and expanded the circular clearing. Dead center, a massive lattice of welded steel—at least eighty feet tall—had been erected in the shape of a human torso with its hands on its skeletal head, as if it were screaming in pain.

Haphazardly attached to every nook and crevice, a slew of electronic devices formed the sculpture's lumpy black skin. Television monitors, phones, speakers, X-boxes, computers, and printers. Even an elliptical workout machine had been integrated. This thing was disturbing on levels that I might have appreciated in a museum, but here in the forest, it was out-of-your-freaking-mind nuts.

"What the heck is that thing?" I demanded. "The hands alone are bigger than me."

"The Awakeners are planning another rally next Friday."

"This doesn't even make sense. When I tried to get in touch with you, your dad told me that he hated technology."

"He plans to light this on fire as a protest."

"Burning Man's psychotic cousin." I tried to wrap my head around the scale of the project. "You left less than a week ago. When did they have time to build this without you seeing it?"

"You have to believe me that I didn't know," he said, and I realized my statement sounded like an accusation. "We have almost three hundred acres out here. Sixty families. Engineers. Artists. When we put our minds together—"

"I believe you," I told him. "I didn't mean it that way."

"Good." He looked down at a two-inch thick electrical cable on the ground. It was connected to the sculpture like an explosives fuse. The wire led back to a podium on a stage at the edge of the clearing. "The statue isn't the worst part."

"There's more?"

He walked over, hopped up onstage, and hit a different power switch. All the machines sprang to life, churning and spinning. Dozens of motors whirred. Blenders shrieked. Alarm clocks rang. Their noise bled over the top of metal bands and hip-hop and country music coming from several stereo speakers attached inside the sculpture. The symphony of randomness sounded like somebody was torturing the giant machine man, who was screeching his dying breaths.

Then the monitors flicked on and my blood turned to ice. At least a hundred different TV screens had been attached to the sculpture's skin. Every monitor broadcast some different picture of Victoria. Her middle school yearbook photo. The news story from the previous night. I was even on one of the monitors too. Somebody had secretly videotaped me at school! A graphic appeared over the top of every video and picture. One sentence, in all caps.

DEATH IS JUST THE BEGINNING.

"Turn it off," I told Ethan. "We need to leave."

"I have to show you our gun storage first." He killed the power to the machines, leaving only the ghostly glow of the floodlights.

"Don't worry. I believe you." I stepped back toward the gravel driveway. "Every bit of it. I believe you."

"But they won't. Whatever I have to say, the police will dismiss."

"Then I'll go to the sheriff's station tonight," I told him.

"And say what?" he asked. "None of what you've seen is illegal."

"Bull. Stalking high school kids has got to be against the law."

"You don't understand." He stepped down from the stage.

"I know these people. Contrary to public opinion, Awakeners are not toothless hillbillies, Monique. We don't even allow members to join who aren't top professionals in their field. My father, advanced mathematics, MIT. Daryl and Sarah Jennings are nuclear engineers. Jim Walker used to teach psychology at Harvard."

"What does that have to do with anything?"

"It means that we have to be smart. If we go to the police with this, my father will bring out some shrink to tell them that I'm making it up because I'm dealing with mommy issues."

"He'd use her memory against you like that?" I asked.

"For his cause, you're damn right he would."

"But we have proof. The videos on the screens."

"He'll switch those out before the police even mobilize. Amber Comstock lives out in the valley quadrant of our land."

"You mean Deputy Comstock?"

"That's why I needed you to come with me. I need an outsider to witness everything. This is probably our last chance to see the compound deserted before the rally."

I turned away from him to catch my racing heart. I didn't know what I expected to find out here. Salem-brand witchcraft, maybe. A cow sacrifice. Something logical to explain Victoria's condition and the voice that she'd talked to while in her coma, but this was far worse.

North Hills, a speck of a town with one main street that dead-ended at a cemetery—literally and figuratively—had its own Ted Kaczynski. Except this Unabomber was now fixated on maybe the deadliest weapon I'd ever witnessed. My best friend, Victoria.

No matter what, I had to stop him, but I couldn't do it alone. Ethan was my best shot. Could I trust him? He *had* taken a huge risk bringing me here, to work against his own stepfather, no less.

"Fine," I said. "We'll go to see the guns, but first fire up the statue again. I'm going to shoot some video proof with my phone. Then we'll film the guns."

"Okay." He looked relieved to have a plan. "Thank you."

"Don't thank me yet. You're going to have to come back here tomorrow and pretend to make up with your father."

"Are you out of your mind? What for?"

"It's the only way to keep him from being suspicious." And it was the only way to figure out exactly what Ethan's sicko father had done to Victoria. "That's the deal."

"Fine." He nodded. "We'll do it your way for now."

"Good." Now it was time for my leap of faith. "Turn on the machine man again. Next we'll video the guns. Then we need to go someplace private to talk about Victoria. I need to fill you in on some things before we go any farther."

22

FTER WITNESSING BURNING MAN-ZILLA, the Awakeners' gun storage seemed almost quaint. I videotaped every inch of the bomb shelter, which was meticulously lined with assault rifles, bulletproof vests, and crates of ammunition. Because that's what any post-apocalyptic church really needed. More testosterone. When we had enough proof of illegal activity, I grabbed Ethan's jacket sleeve.

"We've got what we need," I told him. "Let's go."

He nodded, and we hurried back through the compound. Our footsteps in the crunchy snow cut the silence of the dark fog. We jogged up the gravel driveway hill, crossed the road, and reached his El Camino.

"What's the plan now?" he asked.

"Victoria's house. I need to go there and warn her."

"Can't you just call?"

"I don't get reception out here." I checked my phone. Still no bars. "She hasn't been answering all day anyway."

"Don't worry." He unlocked my car door. "I don't think my father would hurt her or anything."

"I'm not worried for her."

"What do you mean?"

"Nothing." I wasn't sure what to say about Victoria's condition.

In the past week, she had come back from the dead. Then she decimated a forest of wildlife to regain her sight, just in time to become a television news celebrity. If Ethan's father struck a match too close to her, the entire town might actually ignite.

Ahead on the stretch of road, headlights turned the corner and barreled toward us. Had the parishioners come back early? Tires screeched as the car slid to a halt just ten feet away. The fog swallowed all light, except those high beams. The engine revved. Ethan stepped between me and the vehicle. The driver wrenched open his door. I knew that creak of metal on metal. It was our truck.

"Monique," my dad called out. His footsteps moved toward us.

"Dad," I said. "What are you doing here?"

"Get in the vehicle." His silhouette stood steady in front of the headlights. The barrel of his rifle hung over one forearm, pointed at the ground.

"Are you crazy?" I asked. What did he expect to do with that pathetic rusted thing against an armed militia? "Put that away."

"I told you to get in the car," he said. "We're going home now."

"Don't treat me like I'm ten."

"No, he's right," Ethan said. "You should go with him."

"What about Victoria?"

"She can wait until morning." Ethan stared at me with wide eyes, and I realized the other members would be back soon. Then he lowered his voice and said, "I'll find you tomorrow."

"Like hell you will," Dad said. "Monique, get your ass over here now."

"Fine." I walked to the passenger side of our truck.

Dad got inside with me and slammed the door.

"What the hell are you doing up here?" he demanded.

"I could ask you the same thing." I clicked on my seatbelt. "How did you even know where I was? Were you following me?"

"I went into town to see you at work, only to find out from the owner that my daughter had left early with one of the cult people. Now I'm going to ask again, and this time you'd better answer. What are you doing up here?"

What could I tell him? He already wanted to move us to a new city. If he knew about the statue, the guns, or the videos of Victoria and me, he'd be packed by morning. Not to mention the stroke he'd probably have, most likely stemming from those pulsing rage veins in his temples.

"You need to calm down," I told him.

"Don't tell me how to be."

"Ethan wants to quit the church." Technically not a lie. "He asked for my help."

"I don't give a damn about him. I've been calling you for the last hour, but you weren't picking up. I must've left a hundred messages."

"My phone gets no service up here. I'm sorry."

"Not sorry enough." He pointed across the street, where the guardrail still lay twisted down the ravine that bordered the highway. "Your best friend almost died right over there."

"I didn't mean to scare you." I glanced around. No other cars were coming down the road. Yet. "Now can we go? I have to see Victoria tonight."

"Like hell you do. You're grounded."

Please. He wanted to ground me, but what could he do? Stop me from working? Take away my right to read? There was nothing sadder than a parent with nothing left to take away.

"Let me get this straight," I said. "You want to ground me for trying to help someone."

"I've never even heard of this guy Ethan. He's at least eighteen."

"That's only a few years older than me," I said. "Not that

you'd notice, but I don't drink from Sippy cups anymore either."

"Don't give me that. You're only fifteen-years old."

"For another month. Considering our circumstances, I think I've earned the right to be treated like an adult."

"I don't care what you think you've earned. When it comes to our family, I only have one concern. To keep you safe."

"Really? Protecting me is your first concern. I begged you for years to watch what you eat, and look where that got us. You almost killed yourself."

"What does that have to do with this?"

"You never listen to me, just like you're not listening now." I pointed through the windshield at Ethan's car. "He won't drive away until we do. If his father finds out that he's planning to leave the church, who knows what will happen? Can we leave now?"

Dad shoved the Ford in drive, chirped the tires as he flipped a U-ey, and began winding home down Pickens Highway. We drove in angry silence. Maybe I'd gone too far, but I was tired of dancing on eggshells for him. We had serious problems. The sooner he realized that I wasn't a child, the better off we'd both be.

I reached forward and scanned through the FM stations, but up here we couldn't get anything but AM talk radio. Immediately, Dad reached forward and turned it down.

"Just so you know, I have a will," he said. "If anything happened to me, Randal and Cecilia will take care of you."

"Uncle Randy has never thought about anyone but himself. They'll dump me in foster care before the ink dries on your death certificate. Sleep on that one and tell me I'm lying."

"I know I screwed up," he said. "But that doesn't give you the right to hang around with those hill people."

"And I screwed up tonight too," I told him. "But that doesn't mean you can ground me like a child. I work. I get good grades."

"What, you think that makes you an adult? That you can go off wherever and whenever you want?"

"That's not what I said."

"Hell, you probably think that you don't need me at all either."

"Of course I need you." I tried to hold back my tears. "Every minute of every day, but you're not there."

"What are you talking about now?"

"Don't you know that we're drowning here? And instead of dealing with our money situation, you want to crack down on me for every little infraction."

"Don't tell me I'm not dealing with it. I had three job interviews today."

"We owe more than seventy-thousand dollars in credit cards alone, Dad."

"What do you want me to do?" he roared and swerved slightly, but I couldn't think about anything but his heart. "I'm not Victoria's father, who wipes his ass with hundreds."

"Nobody's asking for that." I tried to calm my voice.

"Then what?"

"Declare bankruptcy. That's what it's for."

"I told you." He pointed at me and flared his nostrils. "Robinsons pay their bills."

"Who are these Robinsons that you keep referring to?" I glanced around the truck's cab. "I don't see them, and I sure as hell didn't see them in the hospital when you were sick either. But when Aunt Sheila needed bail for her DWI, the one she got with her kids in the car by the way, oh, she came a-knocking. So who are you trying to impress?"

"We aren't deadbeats who sponge off the system. I won't live like that."

"Nobody thinks that of you," I said. "Nobody would dare, but they just might think that you're too stubborn sometimes. Just like when you ignored my warnings that butter and gravy weren't food groups."

"I haven't been ignoring any of our money problems. Why do you think I want to move? I've been trying to tell you this city isn't going to work. I know another person in this family who doesn't listen too good either."

"No, I heard you, but I told *you* that Victoria needs me right now. Tonight, as a matter of fact, and I don't care about you grounding me. I need you to cut me some slack and drive me over to her house."

"What's so damn important that it can't wait until morning?"

"This is where I need you to trust me," I told him. "I'm not throwing keggers. It's serious."

"This better not be about that guy."

"Ethan's not the problem here."

"He is for me. I don't want you to see him anymore."

"You don't get to dictate who my friends are." I couldn't hide my irritation if I wanted to.

"Do you want to go over to your friend's house or not?" he asked. I didn't give him the satisfaction of an answer. "Have it your way."

He turned off the highway toward our house. Didn't matter. The minute he fell asleep tonight, I'd sneak out. When a potentially psychotic preacher from the hills fixates on your best friend, you warn her, even if your stubborn mule of a father is too obstinate to get out of his own way, let alone yours.

23

AS PREDICTED, GRUMPS ROBINSON passed out in his recliner within fifteen minutes of us arriving home that night, exhausted from his futile mission to control my life. Once his symphony of snores began, I covered him with a blanket and grabbed the car keys. Victoria needed to be warned about Roman Santo's deranged statue, sculpture, whatever that monstrosity was, and she'd picked a pretty lousy time to avoid my calls.

Quietly, I crept outside. Then I got into our truck, pushed in the clutch, and coasted down the driveway. Déjà vu swept over me. My mother. In that dream, she'd left us that night, just like this. Car in neutral, headlights off. I pushed it away. That never happened, no matter how empty the hollowness in my chest felt. Why did it feel so real?

Once I'd coasted to safety, I started the car and drove off. Minutes later, I parked down the street from Victoria's wrought iron fence so Carl and Lita wouldn't hear the ridiculous rumble of our gas-choked clunker. I killed the headlights. Victoria's house was bathed in darkness. It was only 10:06 p.m. Had the Malakoffs gone to bed already?

Once again, I snuck into her house. The frigid temperature inside seemed colder than the walk-in freezer at work. I tiptoed upstairs and found Victoria's bedroom empty. Then I moved back down into the kitchen to look for a note or some kind of clue to where they went.

A soft bell chimed behind me and something scraped. I spun around, but I could barely see anything in the dining room. Idiots in horror movies just loved to holler out people's names while rushing into scary dark rooms. Not me. Time to go. I started for the doorway.

A shadow walked into the kitchen's entrance. Another chime sounded.

"The police are on their way." I snatched a knife from the cutlery set on the kitchen island in the center of the room.

"Jesus, Monique." Ghost light from the street lamps outside filtered through the windows and striped Lita's face. She held her hand over her heart. "You scared me to death. What are you doing here?"

"I could ask you the same thing."

"This is my house."

"Then why are you creeping around like a thief in the freezing dark?" I asked. "And nobody's here. Why are we whispering?"

"I'm just picking up my mother's antique clock," she said in her regular voice. "Do you want to put your weapon down? I don't know how useful that would be anyway."

I realized that I'd accidentally grabbed the dull knife sharpener.

"Sorry." I put it back in the block.

"We already talked about this. You're not supposed to sneak in here."

"This couldn't wait." I reached for the dimmer control to turn up the kitchen lights.

"No." She sounded way too intense. "Leave them off."

"What is going on? Where is Victoria? I have to speak with her tonight."

"She's in New York with her father." The clock Lita carried, encased in its glass dome, clanged again in her arms. She set it on the marble chopping block in the center of the room. "They went to see some specialists about her scars from the accident."

"Why aren't you with them, and why isn't she returning my calls?"

She paused. I wanted to tell her about the statue, but I couldn't. She'd inform my dad, and we'd be packed to leave by morning.

"I don't know how to say this, but I suppose you're going to find out soon enough anyway," she said. "I filed for divorce yesterday."

"Oh." I tried to pretend like I felt her emotional pain, but even in this dim light, I could see faint bruises on her neck. "I'm sorry."

She walked over and touched my shoulder. "This has nothing to do with you or Victoria."

"I didn't think it did."

Awkward. What did she expect me to do? Eat ice cream with her? Watch Massengill commercials and reminisce? Carl was a douchebag. Besides, that just wasn't me. I didn't like anyone harassing me when life hurt, even Victoria. In fact, my most hellish purgatory had been Dad's hospital stay, where a line of strangers wanted to hug me and touch me and pet me, oh George. *Honey, you can save the fake concern for the Facebook feed where it belongs. Better yet, stay at home and keep it to yourself.*

"You're doing the right thing," I told her.

"This has been escalating for a while."

"Considering what he did, it's overdue."

"I know," she said. "But that means Queen Lita, no more."

"Yeah." I always cringed, thinking of low points in my own behavior. "I never really apologized for calling you that name. It was stupid."

"No, you and Victoria saw what I refused to. I sat here on my high throne, turning a blind eye to all of the terrible things Carl did to this town because he never directed his anger and greed at me. It was a lie. This life. My marriage. Everything."

"Not everything," I told her, taken aback. She'd never really spoken to me as an adult before. I probably represented a lack of options. *I'm guessing Persephone didn't have many girlfriends left after she married Hades either.* "It wasn't a lie for Victoria and me."

"That's sweet, but you don't have to spare my feelings. She's never approved of me."

"That's not true," I told her.

"How could she? I was only twenty-one when I married her father."

"You just don't understand her. We're best friends, and if she doesn't tell me that she hates my guts twice before lunch, something's wrong. And she's ten times worse when we don't speak for an entire day. When is she coming back?"

"Monique, it's really important that you listen to me now. You have to promise that you won't sneak in here ever again." I nodded, so she gently grabbed my wrist. "This isn't a game."

"I promise." I pulled my hand back. "I only came here because Victoria's not answering her phone, and now her voice mailbox is full."

"Carl changed her number this morning because of what happened with the television station."

"He really is crazy if he thinks he can keep me away from her."

"Let me finish," she said. "You need to stay away from this house altogether. Not even if she invites you over during the day."

"I can't do that. She's my best friend."

"I didn't ask you not to be friends. Once she's back in school, you'll see her every day. When things cool down, and they will—"

"That could be months. Or years."

"Monique, he blames you for all of this."

"What is going on here?" I demanded. "Ever since Victoria's accident, everyone seems to have lost their damn minds."

"It was a traumatic event for this town," she said.

"I don't care. Earlier tonight, my dad drove out to the Black Hills with his shotgun to confront the cult people. Your husband nearly killed you."

"That's my point," she said. "Carl is dangerous, more so after I leave. I have no clue of what he would do to you."

"He doesn't know that you're divorcing him yet, does he? That's why you don't want the lights on."

"I never know who he has watching this place. I'm only here to pick up my mother's clock while he's in the city." She looked disgusted. "He can have all this."

"So you're not even going to say goodbye to Victoria?"

"Eventually, but you saw what happened in the bathroom upstairs. Just my being here makes it worse."

"She'll be alone here with that psycho."

"He flipped out because of us, Monique. Not her. Besides, I convinced him yesterday to hire security to protect her. I handpicked the guard, and Jim knows that she is his first priority."

"Good," I said. Victoria wouldn't be pleased, but so what? An armed guard could help protect her from Roman's cult too. "Is the guard with them now?"

"He starts tomorrow. Just trust me on this. Go to the Oakville Fair with her next weekend. See her at school, but don't come over here. If you set Carl off this time, I won't be here to talk him down."

"Fine," I told her. "But I want her new number."

"I can do that." She pulled out her phone and sent me a text. "Just remember what I said."

"I will."

"Good." She grabbed my cheeks and then hugged me. "I'm heading to the airport now. Call if you need anything. Even just to talk."

"Okay."

"Do you need a ride home?"

"Nope," I told her. "Dad was being a pig head, so I took his truck."

She laughed, straightened her face, and said, "I suppose that's not funny."

"Yes, it is."

"I'll miss you." She wrapped me in a snake coil hug, and I realized just how much I did care about her. She'd snuck us into wildly inappropriate horror movies and even knew how to braid *my* hair. She'd always thought of Victoria first, no matter how difficult my friend could be and, for lack of options, she'd been the only mother I'd ever really witnessed in action.

"Okay." She pulled away and picked up her clock. "I know you'll find your way out. Let Victoria know that I'll be back soon to explain everything."

"I will."

Then she opened the sliding glass door to the backyard and left me in the kitchen. Right then, life in this town seemed colder, and I felt more alone than ever. Maybe she would come back one day. No, something told me that she never would.

Biological or not, once a mother left, she was gone for good.

24

I FINALLY REACHED VICTORIA on the phone the next morning. The call should have calmed my nerves, but it only made things worse. Carl must have been eavesdropping or something. At least I hoped that's why Victoria rushed me off the phone before I could warn her about Roman and his disgusting statue. This was getting ridiculous. Victoria's life was in danger, and here I was, playing games with her father. A grown-ass man.

Not to mention the fact that Sheriff Acosta still hadn't gotten back to me about the videos of the bunker that I had emailed him last night. Despite what Ethan thought, even if North Hills PD was as useless as everyone claimed, the sheriff and my dad were friends. He would at least listen to me. If he didn't contact me by the end of school today, I'd go down to the station and make him listen.

Until then, I had one laser-focused mission. Convince Victoria—ruler of the adrenaline junkies—to stay safe at home until Ethan and I could figure out how to deal with the Awakener threat.

Early Monday morning, I headed out for school early. Yes, I'd promised Lita that I wouldn't enter Malakoff Manor. No one said anything about the land around it though.

I turned down the frosted bike path that crisscrossed Victoria's neighborhood and reached the pond directly behind her estate. In the dawn's dim light, frozen tree bramble and stalks of dead swamp grass appeared to claw through the water's brittle ice skin. I pulled out my phone to call her.

A twig snapped behind me. I spun and found her just feet away, dressed only in her Billie Holiday T-shirt nightie.

"Jesus, ninja-girl." I grabbed my chest. "What are you doing, creeping up on me like that?"

She hunched forward on the balls of her bare feet, glaring at me. Her matted hair looked as though she'd just gotten out of bed. She must have seen me walking down the path behind her house and rushed outside.

"Victoria, next time you come out to meet me in the freezing cold, at least grab some slippers," I said, but she still didn't answer me, so I snapped my fingers. "Hello?"

"You need to go," she said quietly. "It's not safe anymore."

"I know." I took off my gray coat and tried to hand it to her. "That's why I came here."

"I told you to leave." She shoved the jacket back in my face. "You can't be near me."

"What is going on with you?"

An animal ran across some brush to our left. Victoria's muscles tensed. She searched the forest line beyond the water. Was something watching us from the trees? I hadn't seen her act this detached since the night in her bedroom when she almost went back into her coma. The night her touch had almost killed me as well. My god. She hadn't come out here to meet me. I'd accidentally stumbled on what she'd already been doing.

"You're hunting," I said. "Just like the birds the other night."

"I don't have a choice," she snapped at me and then scratched at the back of her hand with tweaker intensity. "There isn't much time. I have to be ready."

"For what? Two days ago, you killed half the forest life to get *ready* for my expulsion hearing."

"I'm going back to school today," she said.

"Are you out of your mind?"

"Don't try to stop me. I already have a press conference in front of the school at ten."

"Do you even understand the danger we're in?" I threw up my hands. "What am I saying? Of course you don't. You rushed me off the phone before I could warn you. I snuck out to the Awakeners compound on Saturday. Roman Santo and his church freaks built a two-story monument shrine that's dedicated to you."

"So what? I've got bigger problems than that."

"No, you don't," I told her. "They've also got a rally planned in your honor next Friday, and it probably involves our ritual virgin sacrifices. This isn't me being me. It's serious."

"If they're so dangerous, why did you wait an entire day to warn me?"

"Your dad changed your phone number to keep us apart."

The look on her face made me fear for Carl's life. "He did what?"

"That isn't the worst part. The church has been secretly filming you. They've got monitors everywhere with your picture that say 'death is just the beginning.' I need you to stay inside. Don't go anywhere until we figure out what to do with them."

"I can't," she said. "I have to go back to school today."

"Why? Principal Rademacher isn't going to care. I can bring your homework to you."

"I'm dying," she said softly and pulled on her own wrist, looking as though she might jump out of her own skin. "My body hurts, Monique. The animals aren't enough. Each rush lifts me, but the darkness is always there, waiting to swallow me back down."

"Take a hit from me again." I rolled up my sleeve.

"No." She pushed my arm away. "It's too hard to stop with you."

"We'll be more careful this time."

"You don't get it," she said. "I nearly killed you, and even that wasn't enough. At school, there are fifteen hundred students. All those people brushing up against me. I could make it so quick that they'd never know the difference."

"If you're worried about hurting me, what makes you think that you can stop yourself with the other kids?"

"You're not like the rest of them. You're more alive." She inspected my head and hair with predatory eyes. "Everything in this field is barely more than shadow, but you shine differently. With them, I can stop myself."

"You don't know that."

"I do."

"Then prove it. If you want to go to school, show me that you won't accidentally murder everyone there."

"You don't know what you're asking."

"What if you kill somebody? We have to know for sure whether you can control this thing."

I stepped toward her and held out my arm again. With my other hand in my coat pocket, I secretly flipped off the cap to my pepper spray keychain.

Can't fault a girl for being smart.

"Do it," I told her. "I can handle myself."

She snatched my wrist, and my arm weakened. Then my shoulder went numb.

"Okay, that's enough," I said, but she dug harder, until her nails bit into my skin. White spots appeared in my vision, and the world began to glow. "Victoria, stop it."

I almost let her have a face full of chemicals, but she finally let go.

"That wasn't—too bad," I said, but I swooned.

"I need more. A lot more. I have to go to school today."

"What about Roman and the Awakeners?"

"Please," she said. I could already see the change in her demeanor from that little bit of energy that she'd taken from me. "What exactly do you think those primates can do to me now? I have to go to school."

She was right. I didn't have enough energy to sustain her, and who knew what the long-term effects of her feedings were? What if I only had so much youth? I refused to be an old crone before my sixteenth birthday. At least if she was at school, I could keep an eye on her.

"If we do this," I said. "You can't leave my side. We don't even know what you are yet."

"Then we'll find out."

"That won't be easy," I told her. "I googled energy-sucker to find out about your condition. Only one term came up that fits. Psychic vampire."

"Really?" She looked excited. I thought for sure she would have dismissed it. "What did you learn?"

"Other than the fact that the blogger earned her doctorate with a degree in Internet moron? Nothing."

"I'm not so sure," she said. "I feel dead."

"If you are one of those, you're some kind of mega-vamp. That only makes going back to school worse. What if you lose your temper?"

"I won't." She shook her head.

"You have to promise that if I ask you not to do it with somebody, you won't. And never out of anger. You can't do it to Alexis Hall, no matter how much that bitch deserves it."

"Why would I bother to step on an ant?"

"Then I'm with you," I told her.

She smiled. I wanted to hug her, but I didn't dare. Yes, part of my motives were selfish. To walk down the halls of

North Hills High, past the stunned faces of all those who had written us off, only to find that we didn't break so easily. Could there be better justice? Not in this world, honey.

"Get ready for school," I said. "I'll meet you there. I want to stand next to you for your big announcement."

25

I HURRIED TO SCHOOL that morning, strangely hopeful. We understood Victoria's condition, a least a little bit. Psychic vampire, aura-sucker, whatever's clever. She needed energy to live. Assuming her hunger didn't get worse, we now had a plan to feed her without hurting anyone. I just hoped that today would go smoothly.

I wasn't foolish enough to expect the student body to give her a slow-clap standing ovation for returning from death. Not in this town, given its generational wealth, which bred a certain inferiority complex. I mean, half of the families here owned yachts and summer homes, but it was never enough. Victoria's art exposed the lie. Her gift couldn't be bought or taught. They couldn't bestow it to their clone offspring either. Some things were still beyond their control, and most families here quietly hated her for it.

Add to that the stress of North Hills High, a pulsing throb of teen drama, which behaved like a living organism itself, feeding off of the psychic energy of its students. That meant we had thousands of potential disasters today. I needed to run interference, Gandhi-style. Redirect anyone who aimed to needle Victoria or spark her temper, at least until she learned how to master this thing. I had been deflecting these fools since grade school, so bring it on.

I turned onto Main Street. Several cars honked in the distance. My stomach couldn't have sunk harder if I had leapt from a bridge.

Directly ahead, traffic was backed up as far as I could see. Three, no four news vans had parked in front of the school with their satellite masts raised. Maybe a hundred kids hovered out by the front steps, obviously searching for a chance to be on TV. Several idiots wearing Guy Fawkes masks stood behind the reporters giving the two-finger salute.

I pulled out my phone to warn Victoria. There was no way she could come here today. Her line went straight to voicemail, and there wasn't time to get back to her house to stop her from coming to school.

"Monique," a woman said.

I turned. The reporter Amber Gonzalez walked toward me. With her brunette hair pulled underneath a white knit beret, she strayed far around the dirt-crusted snow bank that lined the street, clearly trying to keep her fur-collared jacket clean.

"Do you have a second to talk?" she asked. With her microphone cable, she dragged her hunched cameraman behind like an unwanted pet.

"I don't have time," I told her. "Victoria will be here soon, and she needs me."

"This won't take long."

"How about after school?"

"That will be too late." She looked concerned. "I want to give you a chance to answer some of the rumors before we run our piece tonight."

"What are you talking about?" I glanced back at the mob, which seemed to grow by the second. I didn't need to guess who had been spreading rumors. Alexis Hall had probably been working overtime. "I didn't push my best friend into traffic. That's just idiotic."

"Monique, I've seen this kind of thing before. When you avoid the situation, it only gets worse. Let me tell your side of the story. Most people have a short attention span. Give them what they want, and they'll get bored."

She had a point. I checked my watch. Victoria wouldn't arrive for another half-hour, and I really wanted Amber to be gone when she did.

"Where do you want to do this?" I asked.

"Here is fine." She turned back and motioned to her grizzled companion, who hoisted his camera over one shoulder. Then she said to him, "Make sure you keep me framed in the shot. I don't want the network cutting me out of this story."

"We're rolling," the cameraman said.

"Monique," Amber said somberly into her microphone. "I know your life has been turned upside down since the accident that nearly took your best friend's life."

"It's been rough, but we can handle it."

"I can only imagine your pain. This morning, how did you feel when you saw her wandering in the hills behind her house?"

"Who told you that?"

"Concerned neighbors reported seeing her several times, half-naked."

"And? She's been through a lot. Last time I checked, sleepwalking's not a crime."

"Of course not," she said. "Obviously after what she's been through, some strange behavior is to be expected."

"She just needs space," I said. "That's all, and this attention isn't helping with her recovery."

"Forgive me, but I have to ask. Our station has gotten dozens of calls. Have you heard that almost every pet in her neighborhood went missing shortly after she came back from the hospital?"

I had to get her away from that line of questioning.

"She can barely see," I told Amber. "Are you insinuating that she's kidnapping pets?"

"I don't think she did, but you were spotted with her too. Just this morning, in fact."

"I should've known better than to trust you."

"Monique, please understand." She lowered the microphone slightly. "I have to ask these questions. Denying accusations outright on camera can stop the rumors in their tracks, but you have to admit, the situation looks bad."

"What situation?"

"We found the trash bags stuffed with mutilated animals behind your house. Did you girls have anything to do with that?"

"This interview is over."

I should have never brought those disgusting things back with me, but how could I know that Amber would go dumpster diving? I felt like we had been Facebook-raped for our private data, and I wasn't about to inadvertently give her more. I turned to leave.

"We're just trying to get to the bottom of the story." She grabbed my shoulder. Her cameraman stepped forward. "We want to help you."

"Don't pretend that you care. How long have you been spying on me?"

"So that *was* you who put the animals there?"

"I didn't hurt them," I told her. "Don't make me sue you to prove it."

"Our goal here isn't to smear you, but this town has been rocked, and the people are concerned about you. Especially considering that your mother was admitted for treatment on two separate occasions."

Son-of-a-bitch. I should have known this was coming.

"I don't even remember the woman." I tried to keep my voice from shaking. "Thankfully, she didn't take everything when she disappeared. She did leave a box of old horror movies in the attic. I have those instead of photo albums to fill in the blanks, so unless you want to know which *Nightmare on Elm Street* is the best, I can't help you."

"That must've been rough for you."

"What does she have to do with any of this?" I asked.

"You may not know this, but mental illness can be hereditary."

"You're unbelievable. Now I'm crazy too. Anything else you want to throw on the pile?"

"Look at the facts. Half of the student body claims that you pushed Victoria into traffic that day."

"If by half, you mean Alexis Hall, she wasn't even there."

"Other students have said that you worship Satan, and that you sacrificed those animals."

"You should be ashamed of yourself, Amber," I told her. "I know I'm different, and I honestly don't care what you or anyone else says about me, but you're supposed to be a professional."

"The people of this community have a right to know if they're in danger. Somebody is responsible for this, and I think you know who it is."

Hopefully, she didn't see my shock that she'd gotten so close to the truth. Right idea. Wrong culprit. Instead of chasing me, she needed to spend some quality time with that psycho Roman up in the hills. That would give her something constructive to do.

Actually, that wasn't the worst idea I'd ever had. Even Sheriff Acosta had to play by the rules, but trash-picker Jane here had no problems with breaking them. I couldn't let her put this story on the news. Luckily, I had a better one.

"Turn off the camera," I said.

"What for?"

"I'll tell you what's going on, but you're not going to air your story. It's all BS anyway."

"Sorry, but we have a deadline to meet."

"That's the deal. If I give you the real story, you have to promise not to run it until Victoria is out of danger."

Her twinkly brown eyes shined brighter. She clearly couldn't wait to destroy anything in her path. Me, Victoria, baby seals, or kittens. Didn't matter. So what if I couldn't trust her? She wanted to nail someone for all of this. How about Roman Santo? I couldn't think of a more deserving recipient.

"This better be legit." She turned to her partner. "Shut it off."

He lowered the camera.

"I'm not stupid," I told him. "Turn it off for real."

"Do it," she said.

He finally powered down the camera.

"Don't worry about it," I said. "I have a video that will put whatever you've filmed to shame."

"Did you shoot it yourself?" Amber bristled with excitement. Clearly, home movies were catnip for reporter trash. "What is it?"

"What do you know about the Awakeners Church?" I asked.

"Enough."

"No, you don't," I told her, and her eyes nearly popped out. "Look into them however you can, but don't go up there. It's not safe."

"Got it."

"Call me when you know everything about them. When I'm convinced you're telling the right story, I'll send you a video that will curl your toes."

She was already racing away, dragging her cameraman on that microphone cable leash before I could finish the sentence.

Now I just needed to intercept Victoria before she arrived into this mess. I turned as her black sedan pulled up to the school. She'd arrived a half-hour early! The other reporters moved toward her, which agitated a crowd that tensed and constricted around her vehicle. Nitroglycerin, meet Mr. Fuse.

I raced forward into the mob, shoving people aside. I didn't want to think about what would happen if I didn't reach her first. At this time tomorrow, North Hills High might not be a school anymore. It just might be a national tragedy.

26

IN A FULL-BLOWN PANIC, I shoved my way through the swarm of people that surrounded Victoria's limo sedan and reached the rear passenger door. Through the tinted glass, I could barely see her. What was she thinking pulling up here like this? I searched the sea of nondescript faces. Were any of them Awakeners? Who could tell? It wasn't as if I could see anything in this mess.

I knocked on the glass, expecting her to crack the window. Instead, the driver door burst open. A middle-aged thug wearing a black leather jacket got out and raced around the vehicle.

"We ain't in Hollywood," he said in a Boston Southie accent. Then he shoved down a reporter's camera lens. "Snap that thing this way again, and I'm going to ruin your chances of having children."

"You have to get her out of here," I said and pushed over to him.

"Step away from the vehicle or else," he said.

"I'm here to help you."

"Don't make me say it again." He shoved a finger in my face. His breath smelled like he'd been chewing rotten rose petals. "I mean it, sister."

"Fine." I backed up.

Lita told me she had handpicked security. How could we possibly turn down the volume out here with this asshole running around? He opened the rear door, and Victoria stood on shaking legs.

"Use me for energy if you have to," I shouted over the ruckus, which surged louder. "You can't stay here."

"No." She leaned on the open car door and took several deep breaths, looking as though she was about to drop from exhaustion. "We're not leaving."

"It's too dangerous."

"I told you to back up." Her security guard shoved me with his beer belly, allowing an older brunette to slip past both of us.

"Bless you, darling." She grabbed Victoria's cheeks.

The woman's arms jerked and fell to her sides. She opened and clinched her hands several times, clearly trying to work out needles of muscle sleep, but her tears of joy never wavered.

One of the twits from the computer hacker group Anonymous grabbed Victoria's hand next. Immediately, he pulled up his Guy Fawkes mask, swooned, and then pinched the bridge of his nose. Victoria stood straighter, shoulders back. Then she raised her head and faced the barrage of flashing cameras.

I ducked down and let the crowd deal with her guard. With a final push underneath everyone, I found myself in front of her. I reached back, snatched the elbow of her leopard jacket, and pulled her through a flurry of gropers' outstretched hands, which all snapped back as they touched her. We slipped through those butterheads like a white-hot energy-sucking knife. Up the front brick steps, I yanked her, until we raced into the safety of the school.

Victoria's security guy pulled the doors shut behind us and began to hold the people back. Other faculty members stepped in and helped him regulate.

"Jeez-us, they're out of their minds." I turned around and froze.

Inside, the mood shifted instantly. As we walked down the hallway, students shrank from us, hugging their lockers on either side, glaring with edgy eyes. They must have sensed that a predator had been released into their population.

"What are you bitches looking at?" Victoria said. "Haven't you ever seen a fucking miracle before?"

"Victoria Malakoff." I grabbed her jacket and pulled her into the deserted chemistry lab. I slammed the door shut behind us. "What were you thinking coming here like that?"

"That was..." She began pacing. "I don't know how to say it without sounding like a blonde, but it was awesome. Inspiring of my awe. My skin, it's still tingling." She rubbed her hands together and visibly shivered. "I think I just touched God's muff. We have to go back outside."

"No. That was insanely dangerous, even for you."

"Shhh." She turned her head to the side and moved her hair. "Do you hear that buzzing sound? It's faint, but it's been driving me nuts since I arrived."

"Victoria, there's no buzzing noise."

"Don't tell me you can't hear that."

"There's no noise," I said firmly. "I need you to focus for a second."

"Quit worrying," she said. "You saw it for yourself. I have it under control."

"What if they figure out what you're doing?"

"You're right. Too close to home. Where can we find more people?" She rattled off, almost too fast to comprehend. "Have you ever been to a sports game?"

"No."

"Of course, you haven't. Stupid question. We've both seen the videos though. There must be fifty thousand people at those things."

"Victoria, grab the reigns," I told her. "You're orbiting Jupiter, and we're lucky half of those people outside aren't dead."

"Why do you always have to be like that? Don't you see? It worked."

"For how long?"

"I don't know, a day. Two." She grabbed a flint lighter for the Bunsen burners that someone had left out and repeatedly squeezed the handle. The cup sprayed a shower of sparks. "Anyway, it worked. Who cares?"

"I do. Your dad was supposed to hire competent security. What's with *My Cousin Vinnie* out there?"

"Well, I wanted Kevin Stromsky, but my father *Carl* said he doesn't do this kind of work. Besides, I like Sentinel Meatfingers more anyway."

"That's his name?"

"Gave it to him this morning," she said.

"He nearly got you mauled to death. This is a school, not a boxing match."

"Boxing match? I bet that would be a packed sporting event. Think of the testosterone. Ooh, I know. What about India? Those people are stacked on top of each other like Oreos. A billion in the pack. We have to go there, promise."

"Listen to me." I grabbed her shoulders. "Do you know what happens when engines rev too hard for too long?"

"Yeah," she said. "Fast, fast, go, fun."

"No, they pop, and then they don't ever run again, so dial it back. Do you even remember this morning out in the field?"

"What about it?"

"Why didn't you tell me that you were hunting the neighborhood pets?" I demanded. "That reporter Amber knows about the animals now."

"So what?" she said. "Don't you get it? I never have to hurt anything again. I never really thought coming to school like this would work. It was my last chance."

"You're still in danger from the church."

"Please. I can handle L. Ron Hubbard and his lackeys."

"What about—"

"Quit it," she said. "You punch everything in life like a worry clock. Time to go to work. Dad's gotta take his meds. When is our next class? Don't want to be late."

"Somebody has to be responsible."

"Just where has that gotten anyone? One day, you're sailing along, and then bam." She slapped the desk. "Some asshole on an icy road knocks you into hell. Is that fair?"

"Of course not," I said.

"That's right, it isn't." She glared up at the ceiling. "You listening, jerk-off? So instead of taking care of everyone else, let's ditch today."

"Victoria, you're all over the place. You just came back to school."

"I already did what I came here to do. Now let's have some fun for once."

"I can't leave. Principal Rademacher already wants to kick me out."

"Stop being so linear." She grabbed my arm and pulled me over to the window. Several police cars had arrived to deal with the mob, which now filled the courtyard. "They're probably going to cancel school anyway."

"Maybe."

"You're a goddess for this moment, but the clock's ticking, Nefer-titty. We have a chauffeur who will smash anyone's shins if we like, and I have this." She whipped out a credit card from her purse and waved it in front of me. "What do you want to do with the rest of your life?"

"I don't know."

"Well, figure it out." She began tapping her foot, and I noticed her five-inch heels.

In the chaos, I hadn't really paid attention to her outfit. The leopard bolero jacket, black skirt, and pendant choker looked as if a stylist had dressed her. Even her new haircut had been sprayed, crumpled, and meticulously sculpted to frame her face. She'd always had her quirky cool style, but death had turned her into a flipping runway model, and it scared me.

Though she refused to acknowledge it, a divide had always existed between us. For the first time, I watched it widen. Between the snapping cameras, clothing, and people yelling her name, my crystal ball cleared.

Her brilliant future involved New York skyline parties and art galleries, whereas I'd probably be slinging pasta to snobs and granny blue-hairs until the grave. That was fine. What type of person wouldn't want her best friend to escape this town? When the day came for her to leave, I'd hide my pain so well that God himself wouldn't notice. Just like I hid it then. Still, if that were my fate, I didn't want to regret this moment.

"Where are we going?" I asked.

"Anywhere." She whistled and twirled. "Everywhere. First we have to shop though."

"For what?"

"Girlie, a pea coat and jeans is not an outfit. It's a cry for help, and my heart is just too big to let that go. Now grab your shit." She squeezed the flint lighter into another spray of sparks. "We're going to set this world on fire."

27

GIVEN THE SECURITY LOCKDOWN, ditching class wasn't as easy as I'd hoped. Heading back through the mob outside obviously wasn't safe. To make matters worse, Victoria's brush with forty people had her acting as though her heart now magically pumped Red Bull instead of blood. Just looking at her made me jittery. We couldn't risk any other confrontations, which meant we needed to stay out of sight and move quickly.

With the front and rear entrances blocked, we had one chance of escape without being noticed. Unfortunately, it also happened to be the worst place on campus to avoid drama. The girls' locker room. If we could just get through there, the football field was a straight shot, and then we'd be home free on Jenson Avenue, where Victoria's new security guard would be waiting with our ride.

We snuck into the darkened gym. Meager light spilled through the doorway behind us, revealing a pallet of paint cans, two-by-fours, and North Hills Beaver propaganda, which had been set out for the Winter Formal on Friday.

I reached back to grab Victoria's elbow.

"I'm fine." She crept forward and peeked around the extended bleachers, which were normally collapsed against the wall. "There goes that freaking buzz noise again. It's louder here."

I listened, intently this time.

"I'm sorry," I told her. "I just don't hear it. Now, it's too dark in here. I can't see a thing."

"I can," she said.

"Seriously?"

"Especially with you vibrating and splashing like white-hot chrome." She looked around the side of my face, then at my neck as if studying a sculpture.

"Do you want to quit having a sexual experience with my aura?" I whispered. "I am not on the freaking menu, so pay attention. Can you see?"

"You're extremely bright. Everything else looks like a dark bedroom with a nightlight on."

"Good, because I need you to guide me. The bell will ring soon. If we don't make it out by then, we'll be trapped until lunch."

"Then let's go." She grabbed my hand and led me effortlessly through the thick darkness.

We raced the back way into the lit girls' locker room, down the farthest, most hidden row, past a few early birds getting ready for second period gym. At the end of the aisle, we turned the corner, and I froze. Queen of the class hive, Alexis Hall blocked our exit. Why me? Why now? If there was one person who I didn't want to run into today, here she was, primping in front of a full-length mirror.

On either side of her, stood two of her worker drones, Kaci Laci—yeah, her actual name—and Jessica "the Garbage Disposal" Flynn, who Victoria nicknamed last year for her taste in men.

Keeping Alexis and Victoria apart had been my daily mission even before the accident, but if we wanted to get out and avoid the mob, this was our best shot.

"Who are they?" Victoria asked. "I just see a bunch of swirling light."

"It's Alexis," I said quietly. "Stay behind me and keep moving. We'll be outside before they recognize us."

"I'm not scurrying for anyone. We can handle the slut patrol."

"You promised never to do anything to her and never out of anger," I told Victoria. "I'll handle this."

She reluctantly nodded, so I started down the aisle with her in tow.

The second we reached Alexis, she saw us, stepped over the center bench seat, and blocked our path. She wore a cinched volleyball jersey and a pair of yoga pants that snugged her dainty girl parts so tight, I swore I could see her uterus. In contrast, both of her minions were probably men in their past lives.

"Excuse me." I tried to step around the three girls, but they didn't move. "Alexis, do we have to do this now?"

"We need to talk."

"Why? You just want to create drama, for whatever reason, so call me names behind my back or do it to my face later, but I have to go."

"I don't need to lower myself to name calling. You know what you are," she said. Her drones giggled. Victoria bristled in my peripheral view. "Besides, I'd never have to speak to you again if you didn't blow me off in the library. You were supposed to show up to study with me last Thursday after school."

"I've been busy," I said. With work and freakish cult statues. Not to mention the reporter that she'd probably sicced on me this morning. "I don't have time to pretend-study with you."

"Yeah, well that's not good enough for my mother. She expects you out there on Wednesday to set up too."

"She still wants me to help you with the Winter Formal? I've got bigger concerns."

"So I've heard, and what do you know? Here she is." Alexis held her hand over her chest. "I heard what happened, Victoria. That you're blind now. How awful for you, sweetie."

"It could have been worse." Victoria stared at her like a wolf that had spotted an injured fawn in the dark woods. "I could have been born without any vision."

"How will you do your little art projects now?"

"You'll have to be my inspiration," she said flatly. "It's one thing to get honors in school with so much money, but to do it without any talent or brains, well, that's something else altogether."

Alexis's eyes widened. She clearly couldn't believe blindness hadn't taught her lowly sophomore nemesis humility.

"I know you've fooled everyone into thinking you're something special," Alexis said. "But we both know better, don't we?"

"Alexis, just drop it." I tried to lower the temperature. "You're a junior. Why do you even care about us?"

"Somehow, it's been determined that it's my job to rescue the hopeless. My grade got dinged when you didn't show up."

"I'm not trying to get you in trouble," I told her. "I'll make it to the next study hall on Thursday."

"See that you do. All valedictorians at North Hills have graduated Magna Cum Laude, and I won't have some loser screwing up my GPA."

"Why stop there?" Victoria said. "When you're already on a path to graduate magna cum-dumpster."

"Excuse me?" Alexis said.

"It's a real honor, and a fitting title for such an innovative working girl."

"Listen, biyatch, talk all you want, but I saw you this morning, crossing my yard in your panties. I know what you did to those birds, and I'm going to make sure everyone else knows too."

"You should be careful," Victoria said. The quiet tone of her voice scared me. "I know a secret about you as well."

She glared at me. "I don't care about bra-stuffing videos that you two lesbos saved from grade school."

"I'm not going to post it," I told her.

"Go ahead. Put your video of me on Youtube. It'll only give the horned toads here a reason to go blind, just like your friend there."

"You don't understand," Victoria said. "This secret is so much bigger than some video."

"I can't wait to hear all about it."

"Come here for a minute," Victoria said. "I'll show you."

I grabbed her arm and lowered it. "You promised."

"Calm down. I've got this." Victoria pushed past me and said to Alexis, "The truth is, I'm not blind, *sweetie*. I can see people's auras now."

"Don't tell her that," I said.

"Ooh, look at the Swami girl here." Alexis laughed, and her girls followed suit.

"I don't know why," Victoria continued. "But everyone is a different color. See, Monique is chrome. Kaci and your other friend here are both shades of green, but Alexis, love, you are yellow. Bright and shiny." Then she held one shush-finger over her own lips, pointed at Alexis's belly, and said, "Purple. What could possibly be cooking in there?"

Alexis Hall, a girl whose impressive chiseled smirk never cracked, even when Jason Kendall dumped her at lunch in front of the entire school, visibly recoiled. That, in turn, agitated her drones.

"You are both so dead," Alexis said. "I'm going to make sure everyone knows about you Satan-worshipping freaks."

"I can't tell how far along you are," Victoria said. "I don't have those powers, but I do think you're heading for a date with a vacuum cleaner. That is, if you want to beat me next year for valedictorian."

"Shut it," I said to her. "You're not helping." Then I turned to Alexis. "This ends now. We're leaving, and every one of us is going to forget this moment. Got it?"

Before anyone could answer, and while Alexis's minions still tried to figure out how their master had been bested, I grabbed Victoria and shoved my way past the others.

"This isn't over," Alexis called down the hallway.

"Not by a mile." Victoria opened the locker room door, and we raced outside.

Coach Sweeny stood on the other side. Shit. Busted.

"You two come with me." He lowered his clipboard. "To the office. Now."

28

I KNEW MY SCHOOL CAREER dangled on a ledge as Coach Sweeny escorted Victoria and me into the principal's office. For one thing, even Rademacher's do-gooder secretary glared at us like lepers at a clambake when we walked through the door.

Beware the day they change their mind.

I didn't know why I couldn't shake that thought. It didn't even apply to this situation. Nana Robinson had quilted the saying, framed it, and hung it on our living room wall. She'd deliberately left off the first lines of the poem, which read something about Negroes being sweet and meek, humble and kind. Mr. Langston Hughes wouldn't mind the omission, she'd said once. No point in scaring our white guests.

Maybe that's why the image of that quilt wouldn't leave my brain. The faculty and student body at North Hills High were a wealthy breed, who didn't seem to fear anything. They tolerated me, the grain of sand in their white oyster shell. Rich folks loved a pet pearl project. That's precisely why I laid my gloom on a bit thick some days. They needed to know that they didn't own me, and they sure as heck couldn't change me.

Except this time, I'd pushed it too far. I could feel it in the secretary's heat lamp stare, which warmed my cheeks. I'd broken too many of their rules, and the staff here had already *changed their minds* about me. If I could just get through today, I'd never even show up late again. Ever. I just needed to convince the school of that fact.

Behind us, Coach Sweeny cleared his throat to announce our presence.

"I want those two in my office," a deep voice said. I turned to find Principal Rademacher holding a hand over the mouthpiece of his cellphone. Then he covered his ear with two fingers and turned away. "Yes, Mrs. Carter, the school is perfectly safe." Pause. "You have to under—this isn't any normal circumstance. The crowd will disperse by lunch. Believe me, we're doing everything possible."

Coach Sweeny nudged my shoulder and escorted us into the principal's office. Then he went back out and closed the door behind him, leaving us alone in the room.

"When Rademacher comes in, let me do the talking." I sat in the far chair.

"Please, I think I can handle a high-school bureaucrat." Victoria walked around his desk, picked up the picture frame of his wife, and traced her finger across the glass. "Do you think they still do it?"

"Quit," I whispered. "He's going to come in any minute."

"Big deal." She opened his lower desk drawer and began rifling through his things.

"Victoria, they already have ten reasons to kick me out," I said. "Don't give them eleven."

"I just want to see if—jackpot." She grabbed a handful of the school's assorted freebie condoms from his drawer and stuffed them in her jacket pockets like restaurant mints.

"What are you planning to do with those?" I asked. "Build a raft?"

"I already died a virgin once." She closed the drawer, moved back around the desk, and plopped down in the chair next to me. "I won't be making that mistake again."

"Slut it up with the basketball team if you want, but when Rademacher comes in here, I'll handle it, okay?"

"Relax. He's not going to do anything stupid, or else he'll have to deal with me."

"No. Absolutely not."

"What are you so afraid of? Not that you'd notice, but I deserve Vampire of the Year award for not dropping Alexis where she stood."

"You're not taking this seriously." I picked up a condom from the floor and stuffed it in her pocket. "That's what I'm afraid of."

"Have it your way." She crossed her legs, pulled her black skirt to her knees, and placed her hands in her lap. "I won't say a word."

Great. I knew where this was going.

"If he asks you questions," I said. "Answer him."

She shook her head and grunted, as if her lips were glued together.

"What are you, ten?" I demanded.

The door opened. Rademacher stormed inside, and I sat up straight. I'd never seen him without a suit coat. That armpit dampness on his blue dress shirt didn't bode well for us. Even his wispy comb-over seemed to have thinned considerably since he'd tried to kick me out of school at my expulsion hearing.

He put on his steel-framed glasses and sat at his desk. "Do you two have any idea of the problems this stunt out front caused today?"

I found a glimmer of hope. He was stressed about the mob. Did he even know that we were trying to ditch? Now that I thought about it, Coach Sweeny had only grunted a few words when he found us. *You two, come with me.*

"We're sorry about the people out front," I told him. "They were already here when we showed up."

"Of course, Miss Robinson."

"It's not our fault," I said.

"It never is." He picked up the phone receiver and stared

at Victoria. "Call your father. He hasn't been answering, and we need him to pick you up now. You are not to come back to school until this nonsense you girls created quiets down."

Victoria didn't look at him. She just stared through the frosted window over his shoulder.

"I'm not playing games with you," he said loud enough to be heard in the next county.

"Just do it," I told her.

"As for you." He turned to me, smiling like a snake that had just been fed. "I wondered how long it would be until you finally went too far. You've got until the end of the day to clear out your locker."

"What?" I demanded. "How is this my fault?"

"It's one thing to make a habit of skipping school, but now you're getting in the way of other students' educations. I won't have these disruptions."

"I didn't tell those idiots outside to come. They were here when I showed up."

"That's what happens when you call in the press. Now you get to lay in the bed of your making."

"You mean lie," I told him.

"I'm really going to miss you," he said. "You can call your father when she's done. Have him pick you up."

"But—"

"Protest all you want," he said. "I've got a meeting with the board after this. You're gone, and I implore Miss Malakoff here take notes about your departure, or she'll be next."

My chest felt crushed. Nothing I said or did would change his mind. That much was clear. Dad would move us now. How would I see Victoria? How would she function at school?

"I think this has gone on long enough." Victoria finally broke her silence. She turned to face him. "Don't you, Phil?"

"Keep talking if you want to end up with your friend."

"I don't think you understand what's going on here, Phil."

"Victoria, don't," I said.

"Take this phone and shut your mouth." He shoved the landline receiver toward her. "Call your father now, or else you can clear out your locker as well."

"Victoria," I told her. "We'll figure something else out."

She snatched his fingers, pinching them to the phone.

"Let go of my hand." He tried to pull away, but her grip must have been too tight. Then he gasped for breath. "What are you doing to me? Stop."

His eyes glazed over, so I stood and reached over to pull her hand back.

"Sit down, Monique," she said.

My legs buckled, and I fell back into my chair. Christ, what was going on? She hadn't even touched me.

"Stop doing that," I said. "You'll kill him."

"Not if I push the other way," she told me.

"What does that even mean?" I demanded.

"Taking energy is one thing, but if I have a little extra like I do now, I can always push it back the other way. Isn't that right, Phil?"

Rademacher and Victoria began to sway in sync, like a snake charmer and cobra. Victoria still crushed his hand against the phone's receiver. I swore I could hear his finger bones popping. Then she let go, yet he still swayed, blinking lazily, holding the phone up. I sat frozen too. I could move most of my body, but I was too stunned watching the scene unfold.

"You love pushing students around like a big man." She glared at him with those fiery green eyes. "Because you're so limp at home, I'm guessing."

"No," he said.

"Oh, yes." She leaned in. "That's why Mrs. Rademacher pickled your balls and put them on her mantle. That's why you can't get it up anymore, isn't it? You're just a sad little monkey doll now, beating his tambourine." She started clapping. "Dance, monkey, dance."

"No." He seemed to be fighting her, or at least trying to. "That's—not—true."

"Monique Robinson is a hero." Her voice turned deadly serious. "Say it."

"She's a hero." A sliver of drool leaked from the side of his mouth.

"That's right," she said. "Now say it and mean it this time, with your whole heart."

"She's a hero." A giant tear of awe spilled down his cheek. "God bless her."

"You will give her whatever she wants. Got it?"

"Yes." He nodded. "Anything."

"Good." She seemed ready to let it go. Then she stopped and turned back. "Actually, while you're at it, I need you to switch my second period to Mrs. Carter's class. That way I can take American History with Monique too."

"I'll do it now." He couldn't have seemed happier.

"Excellent." She leaned over the desk, grabbed his tie, and wiped the drool off his cheek. "Now I want you to forget everything that happened here."

He nodded. She glanced at me, and suddenly, my body worked again. She went to leave, and her legs wobbled. She immediately turned to me.

She held out her hand. "Give me a hit."

"Hell no," I told her. "Haven't you had enough for the day?"

"Quit being stingy," she said, and I could see that she was out of breath. "I've never tried that before, and it's not exactly easy to change that asshole's mind."

I glanced at Principal Rademacher, who still sat with a stupid look on his face. Reluctantly, I held out my wrist. She snatched it just long enough to leave a pinkish hue over my vision, and I had to admit that I was scared. The energy thing went both ways. I couldn't even begin to contemplate all the implications there.

"Okay," she said. "Let's go, hooker. I don't know how long his daze will last."

I stood slowly, almost unable to process what had just happened. Right in front of me, she'd literally brainwashed the most hardheaded man on earth.

That image of Nana's quilt popped back into my head, except this time, I knew exactly what my unconscious brain had been trying to tell me. It was a warning that had nothing to do with ethnicity, the faculty, or me getting booted from school.

Langston Hughes had it right, but his poem didn't only apply to people of color. Until this point, I'd seen Victoria repeatedly force her primal instincts into check, mostly for my sake.

Beware the day she changed her mind.

29

STRAIGHTJACKETED, GAGGED, AND tagged. That's how I felt as I sat through third period English Lit. In front of the blackboard, Mr. Dawson emphatically defended the affair between Romeo and Juliet. Any other day, I would have raised my hand to inform him that Shakespeare's *love* story was actually a tale of impending kiddie porn gone wrong, but I couldn't concentrate.

Victoria's display of mind control in Rademacher's office still had me freaked out. She hadn't just used her new gift on him. My legs and arms had been useless to stop her, and she hadn't even been physically touching either of us at the time.

To make matters worse, we had been caught ditching. I wasn't about to try again, so here I was, stuck in class, watching helplessly through the windows as new picketers arrived and dispersed into the swelling crowd down on the street. They carried signs with identical words painted on them.

Death is just the beginning.

The Awakeners had arrived. What else could possibly go wrong today? At least Sheriff Acosta was down on the street, shoving back bystanders when they got too close to the campus. Why didn't he make the Awakeners leave? Better yet, why hadn't he done anything about the video I'd emailed him?

The break bell rang, giving me exactly ten minutes to convince him to do his job. I grabbed my backpack, hurried through the quad, and approached the short brick wall in front of the school. None of the church people seemed to have noticed me. Yet.

"Sheriff Acosta," I called out.

He glanced back, whispered something to his deputy, and motioned me over to his police vehicle. When I got there, he pulled up the yellow caution tape so I could pass.

How he'd gotten elected sheriff in our WASP-filled Pennsylvania community was beyond me. He was a third-generation Mexican Texan—at least according to his TV commercial. Maybe the ad, featuring him in his trademark snakeskin boots kicking pedophiles' butts into the gas chamber, convinced these voters. In any case, he belonged in North Hills about as much as I did.

"How's the old man?" he asked in a mesh of accents. Was southern-drawl Spanglish a thing?

"Stronger," I told him.

"That's good." He lifted his black cowboy hat just enough to wipe strands of his peppered hair back underneath. "Make sure he comes by to see me when he's feeling better."

"I will."

"Well, this shit storm out here ain't gonna let up anytime soon." He grabbed a roadwork sawhorse from the back of his SUV and leaned it against the bumper. "You've got five minutes. What's going on?"

"The Awakeners Church is here."

"Yep. Roman Santo and his flock never let an opportunity go to waste."

"Did you watch the video from their compound that I emailed you?"

"Sure did. Just not sure what you want me to do about that blurred, shaky mess."

"Arrest them," I told him. "I don't know. Shut them down."

"And what do you suppose the charges would be?"

"Um, they're stockpiling weapons." I didn't mean to come across so snarky.

"They sure are. Lots of them." He reached back into the vehicle, this time pulling out a stack of orange cones. Then he slammed the rear door shut. "This is America. Everyone has a God-given second amendment right."

"Those guns can't be legal though."

"They invite me up there twice a year to go shooting. I've inspected their bomb shelter just last month, and it's on the level."

"Then what about that statue?" I asked. "There's got to be some kind of stalker law."

"Look, Monique, I get it. Roman and his cronies are weirdoes, and they're about as useful as a pallet full of dented cans, but they don't mean anyone harm."

"Are you serious? Look at their signs," I spoke too loudly, so I quieted my voice. "Death is just the beginning."

"I don't care if they spray-paint their peckers and dance around bonfires. So far as I know, they've never hurt anyone. There's nothing I can do."

"Well, sorry to take up your precious time," I said. "I hope you remember this conversation when you find my head on a stick."

"Come on." He chuckled. "Don't be like that."

"This isn't funny."

"No, it's really not, but you two girls weren't scared of the publicity Wednesday night when you pulled that stunt on the news. Now look at this mess. Every one of my deputies is on overtime."

"If I could make all this go away, I would."

"That's real nice, except I was parked across the street this morning when Malakoff's daughter showed up here in a limo like it was a pick whip party."

"We didn't ask these people to come." I pointed to a wheelchair-bound old man, carrying his oxygen tank on his lap. In his right hand, he held a pole staff with a peace symbol welded onto the end of it.

"What?" he said. "Now you've got a problem with Gandalf the Grey over there?"

"In case you haven't noticed, they're nuts."

"I know they are, so you better listen good. That church is just a small piece of the problem you girls are creating. If you keep tickling this hornet's nest, you're gonna get stung."

"Can't you go to the Awakeners compound? Just go look for yourself."

"Why?" he asked. "I've already seen the crazy shit they pull. It's not going to change my mind."

"Why are you protecting them?" I demanded.

"That's it." He slammed the sawhorse down, and I stepped back from the look in his eye. "I was hoping we could do this the easy way, but some people don't listen too good."

"I'm not lying," I told him. "We're in danger."

"Do you know what the judge will say the moment I show your video in court? First words. What were you doing on their private property, young lady?" When I didn't answer, he added, "Well, who brought you up there?"

What could I say? I'd promised Ethan I'd never tell anyone about what he'd done. Especially not one of Dad's friends, who also happened to be the sheriff.

"I went alone," I said. "Someone at work told me about the statue."

"You know what that's called, right? Trespassing, and considering the amount of trouble you've been in lately, you're probably looking at a juvenile sentence if you don't watch your step."

"I haven't done anything wrong."

"Ditching school. Driving alone up to those hills with only a learner's permit." He grabbed a finger for each talking point. "The accident with your friend. Now you've got reporters sniffing around, talking about dead animals. Get this straight. I haven't been protecting Roman. I've been trying to keep your ungrateful ass out of trouble because if your daddy found out about any of this, he'd probably end up in the ground."

God, I wanted to let him have it, but I stopped. The weight of his words squeezed my chest. He was right. I pressed my lips together to stop them from shaking.

"Monique." His craggy face softened. "It's not that bad."

"I'm fine."

"You need to listen for once. There are a lot of stupid people in this town with too much free time and money. They've got nothing better to do than stir up nonsense for my boys and me. You don't have that luxury."

"I know."

"Your best friend is the worst offender."

"Okay," I told him. "I get it."

"Good," he said. "Because I can't keep covering. You're already breaking about a dozen age-related labor laws by waiting tables down at Lucido's. You really can't afford to have anyone looking into you too closely. You get me?" He picked up the cones. "Go on back to school now. When the day is finished, come find me, and I'll make sure you girls get home safe."

As I turned to leave, I knew he was right. We had to stay out of the spotlight, but no matter what I did, the situation always seemed to escalate. I began walking back to class.

Something moved behind the bushes that bordered the sidewalk. Was that Roman Santo? It was. How long had he been standing there, eavesdropping on our conversation? I pretended that I didn't see him and hurried toward the building.

I opened the front doors to the school and glanced back. This time, he stood inside of the police perimeter, just down the stairs from me. With both hands shoved in the pockets of his tweed jacket, he glared at me like I'd just pissed on his bible.

Sheriff Acosta stood with his back to us, completely oblivious. I raced inside the school and slammed the door shut behind me. Through the glass, Roman just stood there, smiling.

We were so dead.

30

AYBE I'D BEEN TOO AFRAID for too long, but something inside of me snapped the moment Roman Santo hopped across that police line. There was no mistaking the look in his eye. He wanted to hurt me and everyone I loved. That much was clear, but he'd gone too far this time. I wasn't afraid anymore. At least not like before. Victoria had been trying to tell me what to do about the church all along.

Let them come for me, she'd said, but I'd been too worried about her to listen.

Not anymore though. For all I cared, Roman and his flock could chant naked and live out their end-of-the-world bomb-shelter fantasies in private, but if that bastard wanted war, he'd picked the wrong chica.

My best friend was one bad mofo mind-controlling psychic vampire with a short temper. So why were we the ones hiding like fugitives? Roman was long overdue for his meeting with Victoria Malakoff, version 2.0. A nice handshake between them would set him straight, preferably in a public place. Like right outside this school, where he just happened to be now.

The lunch bell rang, followed by the squeaking, laughing, chipper ruckus of the student herd rushing toward their tater-tot trough. I waited long after everyone left class before heading out into the hallway. Now to find Victoria.

"Monique, hold up."

I turned and saw Ethan rush toward me, wearing his trademark frayed army jacket, jeans, and black boots. Was he out of his mind coming here? And what was the purpose of the backpack? Camouflage? If so, his attempt to blend in amongst the students was about as useless as tiger stripes in the inner city.

"I've been looking for you everywhere," he said.

"Are you crazy?" I glanced around to see if anyone had noticed him. So far, the hall stragglers seemed far too absorbed gazing into their mirrors and shooting selfies. I pulled him into the nook created by the end of a locker row. "You can't come here dressed like that. How did you get inside anyway?"

"Do I embarrass you or something?" he asked.

"That might be the stupidest thing I've ever heard."

"Well, that's how it seems."

"They've locked down the school, genius. All of the seniors are stuck on campus, and the only thing these knuckle draggers love more than throwing feces is pummeling anyone who is different. Your jacket is a dead giveaway for the church. Hand it over."

Reluctantly, he unbuttoned his coat. Underneath, he wore a fitted navy thermal long sleeve. Passable, especially considering his muscled body. His dark, shoulder-length hair was sufficiently unkempt too. Hopefully, the 'roid freaks wouldn't view the cuts on his chin from the fight he'd had with his stepfather as a call to arms. I yanked the store tags off his crisp Jansport, loosened the straps, and put the jacket inside his bag. Then I zipped it shut and handed it back to him.

"If you're going to come inside the school," I told him. "Only wear your backpack on one shoulder."

"You know that's insane, right?"

"I have no clue why it's important to these morons. It just is."

"You're wearing yours on both shoulders."

"I'm a girl," I told him. Sure, making him follow social dogma when I refused was hypocritical, but my bad attitude didn't put me in physical danger. Besides, a lopsided book weight combined with my breasts made my back hurt sometimes. He started to protest, so I held up my hand. "Don't overthink it. Today, you're visiting the *Planet of the Apes*, Dian Fossey. Now, what are you doing here?"

"You wanted me to bury the hatchet with my father," Ethan said. "Well, he had me enroll at school to watch over you and Victoria."

"He had you sign up just to spy on us?" I thought of those school videos of me that the church had uploaded on Burning Man-Zilla. "How many other spies does he have here?"

"I don't know, but I'm supposed to convince you both to go to the ceremony in Victoria's honor on Friday."

"That's never going to happen," I said. "And aren't you a little old to be in high school?"

"I'm seventeen."

"Really?" I'd never bothered to ask his age. Still, his lack of baby fat and serious demeanor shouldn't have thrown me that much. I probably wouldn't have even bothered to check his ID at Lucido's. In any case, it didn't matter. "You can't stay here. The other students will figure out who your father is, and then it won't be pretty. Trust me."

"I can handle myself."

"Clearly."

"That's not fair. These high school rules are idiotic," he sounded flustered. No argument there. "At least now we can talk every day without worrying about who's watching. I think Roman really is losing it."

"He won't quit, will he?" I asked.

"Victoria is his white whale. She always has been. He's convinced the world will end soon, so he collects members like action figures to fill specific human roles for his reconstruction. He wants you too."

"He's got a funny way of showing it," I told him. "He threatened me."

"What did he say?"

"Nothing, really. He just stared at me like he wanted to chop me up."

"Fear is one of his tactics," Ethan said.

"Well, I'm not backing down anymore. I want you to tell your father to meet us after school today."

"That's a bad idea," he said. "This thing will blow over. I promise, but you have to stay away from him."

"We tried that."

"Monique, he's never been this reckless before."

Neither had I, but megalomaniacal cult leaders who let children dip their hands into butcher's blood for signs, who constructed giant shrine altars and secretly videotaped me had a way of testing my common sense. It was time to change the script.

"Just set up the meeting," I told him.

"I don't like this."

"I don't care. Set it up." I stepped out of the cove into the hallway. "Now, I have to go find Victoria. I think it's time Captain Ahab got a taste of exactly who he's been chasing."

***

As Ethan took off down the stairs to find his father, I hurried in the opposite direction, eager to meet up with Victoria. I hadn't seen her since she'd turned Principal Rademacher into a breathing meat puppet this morning. At least then, she'd shown some control. I hadn't heard any cryptic PA announcements or ambulance sirens during the last two classes either. That was a good sign. If she could handle getting through the school day without incident, we had only one problem left, which I intended to fix right now.

Yeah, I knew unleashing her on Roman Santo was dangerous. So what? He'd been using her resurrection to increase his hold over the Awakeners congregation, and he wasn't going to let go of that bone without a fight. Nana Robinson always told me some folks enjoyed learning the hard way. What a coincidence. The new and improved Monique Robinson spoke *hard-way* fluently. As long as Victoria didn't accidentally kill the creep, I was cool. Now, I just needed to arrange their meeting.

Most of the students had already made their way to the cafeteria by the time I arrived. The scent of boiled hamburger patties drowned in ranch dressing assaulted me. No wonder the Barbies didn't need to work at their eating disorders here.

I spotted Victoria, sitting at the central table, where the Neanderthal football team—a powerhouse of higher brain function and date rape—normally ate. What was this? Some kind of *Twilight Zone*? In place of the jocks, the special needs kids surrounded her in that prime cafeteria real estate.

Furthermore, a perimeter of empty tables created a buffer between them and the rest of the students, who milled around the outskirts of the room, stealing angry glances at Victoria like hyenas who'd just had their kill stolen. I walked over and sat across the table from her.

"How did everything go today?" I asked. Without looking up, she continued to draw on a sketchpad, shielding my view of her art with the flip fold cover. "Victoria? Hello? We have to talk."

She held out her open hand and said, "Blue."

Ronnie Numark pushed forward the joystick on his Stephen Hawking wheelchair and handed her a magic marker. She snatched it and began drawing feverishly.

"You better not be feeding off them," I told her. "Or controlling them. That would be perverse, even for you."

"We're not supposed to be sitting here," Ronnie said to her. "It makes the other kids mad at us."

"Who cares what those bitches think?" she replied in a voice far too crass for her black runway model outfit. "This is my school now. Prison rules. This table exists only for me and my close friends."

From the way she spoke, I knew she was purposely excluding me from said group of friends.

"I haven't seen you in two hours," I said. "What could I have possibly done to piss you off this time?"

"Orange." She handed the blue back to Ronnie. That's when I noticed every kid at the table held a different colored pen. Without looking up from her drawing, Victoria snapped her fingers and said, "Orange."

Lisa with the headgear stood and ran over to Pete Washington, who sat with his back to us, head down, wearing the same Dodger hat that his father had given him. Lisa took the orange marker from his hand and handed it to Victoria.

"They're not your slaves," I told her.

"I can't see the colors." She pulled off the cap and began drawing. "They're helping me, which is more than I can say for you."

"I don't know what I did, but you need to get past it. We're in danger, and I need you."

"If it was so important, why did you leave me hanging?" she said. "I waited by your locker for ten minutes after the lunch bell rang. No Monique."

"Seriously? All of this because I was late."

"It's my first day back. My real friends were here for me."
She motioned to everyone around the table. "Where were
you?"

"I got caught up," I told her, but she still continued to
draw. "Would you stop what you're doing for a second?
Roman Santo is outside."

"I'm finished now." She stabbed the marker down on the
page. "Pete, look over here."

His head sunk lower. She better not have done anything to
make him act this way.

"Don't ignore me," she said. "You know I can make you
turn around if I want to."

I stood up and shoved my chair back. "Victoria Malakoff."

"Look at me, Pete," she said. "Or else."

"I swear if you dance him around like Rademacher," I told
her. "We really won't be friends anymore."

He finally turned to the rest of the table with that same sad
face he had the other day, when those bastards had tripped
him in the hallway.

"Now, Pete." She glanced at the students all around us and
said loudly, "If any of these limp dicks call you Grendel again,
you show them this picture." She tore her drawing out of the
sketchpad and slammed it down on the table. "This is who
you are."

I was taken aback. I didn't know why I thought that the
loss of her regular vision would destroy her artistic gift. If
anything, death magnified her talent. Thousands of dots
showed a purple figure, who seemed to glow and sizzled with
electricity in a dark room, as if he was composed of pure
energy. The person's aura formed magnetic pole lines around
his body, but there was no mistaking Pete's face, his eyes. She
even matched the style to the comic books that Pete carried
in his arms every day.

This must have been how she saw the world now, and I was jealous in a good way. I would have gladly traded my own vision for her new sight. I felt terrible for thinking the worst of her. Pete hugged the picture to his chest and wrinkled it. Then his lip quivered.

"What's wrong," I asked him.

"They're going to ruin it."

"Who will?" Victoria asked.

"The other kids," he said.

"If anyone even breathes on this picture, you come see me." Victoria's eyes burned. "They'll never make fun of you again, Peter Washington. I promise. You're a goddamn superhero. Now act like it."

He slowly nodded, and then he smiled through his wet eyes.

Screw her artistic talent. No matter how inspiring her work had always been, I'd never been as proud of her as I was at that moment.

"Now." She turned to me. "Someone owes me an apology. I wonder who that might be."

What could I do? She was right.

"I'm sorry I thought you'd hurt Pete," I told her.

"And?"

"You can save the attitude. I'm not sorry I was late for lunch. Roman Santo threatened me out in front of the school just now."

"He did what?" she demanded. Good. This was the girl I wanted that crazy-ass cult guru to meet. "Is he still out there now?"

I nodded. "I told his son Ethan to set up a meeting with you. I want him to learn some respect."

"That's not funny." She began to fidget. "Don't kid around with me. Not like that."

"No lectures, I promise. Let him have it. All of it." She jumped out of her seat and hugged me so tightly that I couldn't breathe. "Just don't kill him."

"I promise he'll limp away," she said.

"You're supposed to meet him after school."

She grabbed her jacket from the back of her chair. "Nope."

"What?" I asked. "Now?"

"Can you think of a better time to catch him off guard?"

I thought about the reporters outside and the unruly crowd. The gossipers and the dead animals. I thought of all the wonderful things that old Monique would have twisted in the wind over, and I threw them under the bus.

"Lunch is almost over," I told her, "but we can still make it if we jet."

She nodded, blocked her ears with two fingers, and wiggled them around as if trying to relieve altitude pressure.

"Are you okay?" I asked.

"I'm fine. It's just that stupid buzzing noise. It's driving me nuts."

As usual, I heard nothing except the solemn murmurs of the students around us.

"We can always do this later," I told her.

"Oh no," she said. "You're not taking this one away from me."

"Okay. Let's go then."

Minutes later, Victoria and I walked out the side cafeteria door. With the police and faculty distracted by the growing mob, we reached the school's front steps with ease. Even from here, I could see the crazies bunched together with their own kind. Apparently, attention whores, PETA dingbats, and your garden-variety racists feared catching cooties from each other as much as they loved their causes.

Roman Santo stood dead center of the insanity. He'd

clearly dressed up for the part. With his brown hair parted on the left, trimmed beard, and tweed jacket, he might have passed for a college professor. That is, if it weren't for those deep eye sockets and that seven-mile POW stare. He carried a taut leash, which strained against the force of the biggest wolf that I'd ever seen. That monster could have held its own during the Jurassic period.

"Maybe this isn't such a good idea," I told Victoria.

"Boo," she said. "You promised to let me have my fun with this guy."

"Look at the dog. You'll never get close enough to touch him with that thing around."

"Says you." Despite her five-inch heels and tight black skirt, she picked up her pace down the front steps.

Ahead, Roman Santo began walking toward us with his dozen disciples in tow. Not good. Immovable object, meet unstoppable force. I was pretty sure the Big Bang started this way.

"Victoria, listen to me. I know you can handle yourself, but this situation is too chaotic. That's why I wanted to wait until after school."

"Don't vaj-out on me now. You promised."

"Just don't do anything unless we have no other choice," I told her.

"Fine." She stopped at the two-foot brick wall that separated us from the crowd out front. "After all the hype, I've been dying to hear what he has to say for himself anyway."

To our left, a sculpted hedge provided some privacy from the police and other onlookers. Roman approached us from the other side of the wall and yanked the wolf, cinching its windpipe tighter. The behemoth whined just above a hoarse whisper. Jeez-us. Its blue eyes glowed like chips of glacier ice.

I—like any other sane person—stepped back from its gaping jaw. Not Victoria. She stood just feet from the thing.

"Are you trying to scare us with the dog or something?" Victoria was never one for subtlety. "Because if that thing comes after me or Monique, it won't end well for you. I promise."

"My apologies." Roman's smile was so creepy that I half-expected a serpent tongue to flick through his cracked lips. "Some people in town don't want to hear the truth. Darwin here was meant as a deterrent for them. Not you." He kneeled down and began to pet the dog. "Weren't you, girl?"

"Get rid of it if you want to talk," I told him.

He glanced up at me slowly, paused, and then motioned to one of his followers. An older, curly haired woman stepped forward, and I realized every Awakener here today was female. Some of the women wore T-shirts and mom jeans, while others wore designer suits. I felt a chill. Not all of his followers lived up in the hills. These women could be anyone or everyone. Just how far did Roman's reach extend?

Without breaking eye contact, he handed the leash to his minion, who fed the behemoth a treat of raw steak. Or human flesh. Who knew what those sickos did up in the hills for funsies? Then the woman slithered back into the crowd.

"Now," Victoria said. "I hear you've been harassing my friend."

"That wasn't my intent. I just wanted to talk earlier today."

"No," I told him. "You tried to scare me, and it didn't work."

"You misunderstood. I wanted to give you this." He pulled out a folded blue flier from his coat pocket and handed it to me. "We're having a celebration on our compound next Friday in honor of Victoria's miracle. We were hoping you both could attend."

"Sorry, I've got a big dance that night." It might have been the stupidest thing I'd ever said, but Mrs. Hall had made it clear. I needed to be there. "We won't be able to make it."

"Monique," he said. "I know you have reservations about our teachings."

"I don't have reservations. I want nothing to do with you, so I'm asking nicely. Please leave us alone."

"We just want you and Victoria to hear us out. That's all."

"Don't pretend this has anything to do with me," I told him. "You want her to fill a role for your end-of-the-world fantasy, and you'll tolerate me as long as I can help get her onboard."

"It's troubling to me that you don't know your own worth." His voice was calm and even. He stared directly into my eyes.

"Do *not* try to hypnotize me, Rasputin," I told him. "I'm not that easy."

I don't know why I felt so bold, except that I stood next to Victoria now, a psychic vampire, who was already itching for a fight. His disciples looked horrified.

"You've got me wrong, Monique," he said in a quiet voice. "I sent my son Ethan to ask both of you girls to join us at the rally the night of the accident. You've been an outsider your entire life. You don't belong with these people any more than Victoria does."

"I get it," I told him. "Where would the Vatican be without Michelangelo? I still don't see what I bring to your table."

"What good is a civilization built on knowledge without the strength, wisdom, and heart to guide it?"

Right then, I knew how Roman Santo converted so many supposed geniuses to his cause. Find the emptiness in a person's life. Throw in some ego strokes—and voila, mind zombies by the dozens.

"Sorry," I told him. "I'm not a joiner."

"That was your big pitch?" Victoria seemed legitimately let down. "After all I've heard about you, I expected more."

Ouch. That one made me feel bad for him.

"You want the real truth?" he said. "I can give you that."

"I'm waiting," she said. "And don't bullshit me. I can see when people lie to me these days."

"Fair enough. I've run the calculations, over and over and over, and I wish I could find a different result. Our society is a house of cards. The structural Ponzi scheme of this entire civilization, which is based on infinite resources, will collapse."

"So what?" she said.

"So, these flowery neighborhoods won't slip into gradual disarray once this world hits its zenith, either. The subsequent nadir point will be brutal. A world population of billions will fall to five hundred million. It will be one of the largest extinction events of a single species in earth's history."

"Excellent," she said. "Less people clogging up my path every day."

"It's not a joke." He pointed to the people out front. "They'll trample the bones of their own children into the mud when the food shortages start. The only question is, will you be one of them?"

"And they claim I'm disturbed," I said.

"We want both of you with us. The Awakeners represent the best chance to rebuild."

Victoria glanced over his shoulder at his collection of glassy-eyed followers.

"If you say so," she said.

"So, will you both come out on Friday?" he asked.

Staring into his wild eyes as he spoke, I knew only two things. First, he really didn't want me to join his cult. I was a means to an end, and I would probably be Darwin snacks the minute I outlived my usefulness. Second, as I suspected, he would never leave us alone without a fight. So be it. No one could say that I didn't try for peace.

"Promise us right now that if we come up there on Friday," I told him, "no one will hurt us."

"I personally guarantee your safety."

"Okay." I shoved out my hand to shake on it, which he did. Then I glanced at Victoria. Most days, we didn't need to speak to communicate.

Let him have it, I told her with my eyes.

She looked positively giddy. Roman moved over to her, and they shook hands too. Although I could appreciate parts of his crazy, and although his theories would have made an excellent movie, it was time to teach the jerk some manners. Victoria squeezed his hand harder.

She snapped her arm away as though he'd stabbed her with a needle. Then she wiped her hand on her leopard jacket and stepped back.

"What is it?" I asked.

She glanced over her shoulder. "I have to get back to class."

"Are you okay?" Roman said. "Do you need a doctor?"

"She's fine." I pulled her back.

"Let's just go," she snipped at me.

We turned and began walking away.

"Come out Friday," Roman said. "You won't regret it."

As I glanced back, I saw him still smiling at us as we entered the school.

31

ICTORIA DIDN'T SPEAK MUCH after her encounter with Roman, and I couldn't blame her. How could I have been so incredibly stupid? We had no clue of what we were dealing with. We didn't even know whether the Awakeners cult had brought Victoria back from the dead, but that didn't matter to me. Like a general playing with his new tank, I'd sent her into harm's way, to do what exactly? Teach Roman a lesson? She was a person. My best friend. Not a weapon.

Sure, people acted crazy when fear took over, but Robinsons didn't have that kind of leeway. We had to work ten times harder for the same respect and be ten times smarter than other people as well.

With my brain finally functioning as it was intended, I could only think of one person who could help us now. As much as I hated the idea of involving adults, this was the time. Now, I just needed to convince Victoria of that.

After the final bell rang, I met her at her locker. With circles under her haunted eyes, she still looked shaken. The other students kept a serious distance when passing us in the hallway.

"How are you doing?" I asked her.

"Fine." She quietly ruffled through her locker without looking in my direction.

"We need to talk about what happened."

"There's nothing to say."

"You don't look so good." I pulled up my jacket sleeve and held out my wrist. "Do you need a bump or something?"

"Will you fucking listen for once?" She slammed her locker. Everyone in the hallway stopped and stared at us. "I already told you that I'm fine."

"Sorry for trying to help."

She pinched the bridge of her nose with a shaking hand. "I just want to get out of here, okay?"

"That's fine," I told her. "Let's just go."

She nodded, pulled out her phone, and texted her driver. Minutes later, we hurried out of the back of the school into her limo.

"Where to?" Victoria's driver called back through the lowered partition window. I didn't think it possible, but his stench of sausage breath and garlic sweat had gotten worse.

"Take me home," she said.

"I can't go to your house," I told her. "Not with your father there. I know you want to be by yourself, but we need to talk."

"Can't it wait?"

"After what happened today, there are things you need to know."

"I don't want to be around people right now," she said. "They disgust me. I feel like I'm crawling out of my skin."

"I know the perfect place. We'll be alone." I turned to her bodyguard. "Take us to Roosevelt Gardens."

Victoria nodded at him. Two blocks later, we pulled up to the town's only cemetery. We got out and walked far past the newest headstones, to a section so decrepit that grave robbing here would probably be considered archeology.

All around, charred, dead bramble spread everywhere, digging its snow-frosted claws into the granite statues and headstones, smothering the last standing mausoleum, which looked seconds away from implosion under the strain.

To lighten the mood, I stopped in front of Jelilah's tomb.

It read:

Here lies Jelilah Bronson,
Mother to Loretta Swanson,
One night alone, she spooked the sheep,
A grit-filled hoof, kicked in her teeth,
So now she sleeps beneath the ground, son.

That headstone never failed to get a rise out of Victoria, until today.

Every single thing in this clearing was dead. In contrast, not fifty feet away, the forest seemed eager to devour this pocket of decay back into the earth. The pine-scented breeze, chilled by shade, seemed to calm Victoria. She sat on the boulder in front of the headstone.

I knew she wanted space, so I gave it to her. After a few moments, she finally looked up at me and asked, "Why are we here?"

There was no easy way to do this, so I jumped right in, explaining everything that she'd missed while recovering. To her credit, she didn't interrupt as I told her about my visions of spiders that came out of her eye sockets, how she'd awakened screaming from her coma, the church's sculpture that had been dedicated to her, their arsenal, and finally about Ethan's pendant, which she still wore around her neck. Just going back over the details left me exhausted. She didn't respond.

"Well," I told her. "Say something."

"So how big did you say that sculpture was that the Awakeners made for me?" She casually dug a dull stick into the char residue from the chiseled words on Jelilah's tombstone.

"Don't play this off," I told her. "I hate it when you do that."

"What do you want me to say?"

"Something big is about to happen. We both know it, and I'm scared. What happened with Roman today?" I asked, and she looked at the ground. "Victoria, I can't help if I don't know what's going on."

"My textbooks are useless." She began picking mud off of her heels with the stick. "Chemistry and English, all of them. I can see the book's shape and the pages, but not the printed words. I guess that means television's out. Movies too. In order to draw Pete today, I had to push hard enough into the paper so I could see the grooves."

"What does that have to do with Roman?"

"Just hear me out. My vision is different now. It's always on, like a light bulb with no switch. Even if I'm turned away from you." She closed her eyes. "I can still see you."

I lifted my arm and flashed her the hippie sign for peace.

"You're holding up two fingers," she said.

"Damn."

"It's not just that." She looked up at me. "Right now, you feel guilty about what happened with Roman. I can see your shame pouring out of you like a purple flood of energy that colors everything around you, and you're always fifty times brighter than any other person I've seen. Whatever you feel, I do too after I feed on you. Doesn't matter if its anger or fear or happiness, I feel those too. It's like that with other people, but more so from you."

"What did you feel from Roman?"

"Nothing."

"I saw how you reacted," I told her. "Something happened out there."

"You don't understand. He was nothingness. Barely more than a shadow when I first saw him, and that's why I wasn't scared, but I should have been. He feels nothing. Not even hate."

"You mean like a psychopath or something?"

"No, psychos have emotions, I think," she said. "He was worse. Like a black hole, draining every bit of life around him. If I hadn't pulled away, I would have gotten lost in that vacuum."

"Victoria, this has gone too far. We have to do something. Tell someone."

"Who?" she asked. "No one will understand. It's only you and me now."

"That's not entirely true." Here it was. The part she was going to hate, but I'd gone over it a million times in my head. I knew of only one person scarier than Roman Santo, and the two men were already natural enemies before Victoria's accident. "We have to tell your father."

"That's the stupidest thing I've ever heard."

"I don't like the idea either, but we don't have a choice."

"He only makes things worse."

"Sheriff Acosta already said the police couldn't help us. The church hasn't broken any laws yet, but your dad doesn't care about that."

"I can't even believe we're having this discussion," she said. "You should know better."

"Victoria, these aren't just a few guns. The cult has stockpiled an arsenal, and they're after you. If Ethan's necklace brought you back to life, who knows what other power or control they have over you?"

"Please." She took off the necklace and threw it on a patch of snow. "I was only wearing this stupid thing because I thought you gave it to me."

"What are you doing?" I snatched it off the ground.

"Calm down," she said. "If I needed it to live, I'm guessing it would glow or something. See." She waved her arms around. "I'm fine without their voodoo-child necklace, so can we forget the talk about my father?"

Did that mean the medallion wasn't responsible for her condition? The minute it touched her hand that night in the hospital, the electricity flickered, and she'd screamed herself awake. That couldn't be a coincidence. I wrapped it up and tucked it in my coat pocket. If the medallion wasn't responsible for waking her up, what had?

"I know your father is a jerk," I told her, "but he can help us with the church. What if Roman comes after you?"

"Then I'll deal with him then."

"Victoria—"

"Do you remember Jenson's Tire?"

"You mean the empty warehouse off Old Moon Road? Yeah, so what?"

"It wasn't always deserted. We used to own it. The day my father dismantled the company, he brought me to work with him. He said he wanted to show me how a Malakoff handles business. I sat on the couch in his office while he fired most of the staff that day."

"That's awful. How old were you?"

"I don't know, eleven." She stared absently at the crumbling, decapitated statue of a child next to us. Its stone head lay half-buried under the crunchy snowfall below. "Most people took it well that day, but the last man—he was older. I'll never forget the way he carried his Steeler's hat, which he kept pinching between his fingers as he begged for any work. I pleaded with my father to keep the man on his payroll, so Daddy gave me a choice. If I chose to hire the man for a different position in his company, we'd have to cancel our trip to Cambodia later that month."

I remembered that year, and how jealous I'd been when they left on that vacation. Victoria, the girl who had everything, or so I'd thought back then. How could I have been so blind?

"That wasn't your fault," I told her. "He was a prick for putting a little girl in that position."

"The man's name was Joe Gutiérrez."

"Phillip's father?" I didn't mean to speak so loudly.

"Two days after we got back from the resort, Mr. Gutiérrez jumped from the Tenor Bridge," she said. "It was for insurance money or something like that. My father made sure to leave the Gazette story open to the right page at breakfast the next morning."

"Why didn't you ever tell me about this?" I demanded.

"Because I couldn't bear for you to look at me the way you are now. The rest of us aren't good like you are, Monique."

"That's BS, and you know it."

"I'll tell you what I know. When I was in my coma, underneath everything, I *knew* why I was being tortured. It was punishment for who I am."

"Quit saying that."

"The children of monsters are monsters too, Monique, even if we don't want to be. And somebody else always pays for our crimes."

"Victoria, I am so sorry that happened, but it's not your fault."

"Either way, I don't care. I'll die before I ever ask my father for anything again."

I sat down next to her on the boulder and put my arm around her. "Okay."

"Just don't leave me," she said.

"Never."

That's when I noticed her crying, which shook my core. Maybe it was her savant nature or her warrior spirit that always seemed detached, but until now, she usually only cried tears of rage.

"Let's go home," I said. "We'll figure something else out. I have a few ideas."

We stood and walked back to her limo. If karma had any sense of justice, Carl Malakoff would get his one day. I just hoped that I'd be around to see it. Until then, we needed to be careful. The Awakeners were coming for my best friend, and with or without Carl, we needed to be ready when they did.

32

I TRIED NOT TO LET VICTORIA see my mood, but after hearing about what her own father had put her through, my imagination turned dark during our silent ride back to town. Flaying and waterboarding. Creative use of meat hooks. All those punishments seemed way too lenient, considering his crimes.

Who was I kidding, though? Carl Malakoff and Roman Santo felt nothing for the people they hurt. Me? I made Dad hold a funeral service for the raccoon that he accidentally hit with his truck. When it came to ruthlessness, I just couldn't compete, and with the Awakeners rally scheduled in three days, we were running out of time.

As angry as I felt, I could think of only one solution to our situation. Cure Victoria. Problem was, my vast Hollywood-horror-movie knowledge turned out to be as useful as the Pope's swollen balls. I was an amateur when it came to actual psychic phenomenon. I needed a pro, so instead of heading home after the cemetery, I made Victoria's driver take me to downtown. After I gave her an energy bump that left my vision clouded orange, I had her driver drop me off in the town square. Caddy-corner to the intersection, the neon sign for *Psychics and Nails* flickered.

Yeah, maybe involving Sarina might not be the smartest move, especially considering her position as head honcho of the town's gossip mill, but she knew about this stuff. I didn't. Case closed.

I began to head over. With most of the seasonal mom-and-pop stores closed until spring, the downtown square at dusk left me with an apocalyptic chill, as if Jesus had just vacuumed up his followers.

Something hissed behind me. I spun and stared down the barrel of a dark alley. At the far end, a can rattled, followed by a wind gust.

"If anyone's following me." I pulled out my keys. "I've been hoping for a chance to use my pepper spray."

About five feet away, Tara peeked out from behind a stack of pallets. Her messy hair framed her flushed cheeks.

"What are you doing, hiding back there like a serial killer?" I demanded.

"Looking for you," she whispered and glanced around. "I didn't want anyone to see me."

"It's getting late. Your parents are probably worried."

"I've-way ot-gay omething-say—"

"Skip the Pig Latin, Tara," I said. "What's going on?"

"I found something." As she wheeled her bike out, those same purple sneakers with the haphazard charms clicked and shooshed. "From the way Mr. Santo was acting, I think it's important."

"I told you not to spy on that man." I thought for sure Ethan had put a stop to her nonsense. "It's way too dangerous."

"You're welcome." She jutted out her chin. "I have been waiting outside your work for an hour, you know, because *somebody* never gave me her home address."

"Come with me." I glanced at the older couple across the street, who seemed to have magically appeared. Roman had people everywhere, even in town. "We've got to get inside."

"Not until you apologize."

"From the bottom of my rotting, wretched soul," I told her. "I'm sorry."

"Apology accepted," she said. Whatever butt-hurt feelings she had clearly vanished instantly.

"It's not safe for us in the open," I said. "That shop across the street will close in five minutes, and I need to talk to Sarina. After that, show me what you found and go straight home, okay?"

"Deal."

We hurried over to *Psychics and Nails*. Tara set the kickstand on her bike, and we went inside. Above the door, the dingy, brass bell clanged. To our left, a gas fireplace warmed my face. A strong whiff of cinnamon almost masked the scent of acrylic.

"What are we doing here?" Tara picked up a bottle of cuticle remover on the counter, which sat just behind a box of smudges. "Is this about Victoria coming back from the dead?"

"Just be quiet and let me do the talking."

"I'll be with you momentarily." Sarina played up her breathy, fake Southern accent. Then she shoved aside the curtains that led to the back rooms, saw me, and said, "Shit, Monique. Why didn't you say something? I thought you were a real customer."

"We are real customers," Tara told her.

"I don't see real money, honey." As usual, Sarina's thick eyeliner made her eyes seem anime-large. Random pink spikes highlighted her platinum pixie haircut now. One side of her head had been shaved down to stubble, giving her black feather earring room to shine.

Tara pulled out a twenty-dollar bill and set it on the counter as though it were gold bullion. Then she said, "We need your psychic powers to help with something I found."

"Put the money away," I told her. "We're not here for that."

"How cute." Sarina glanced at me with a forced smile. "You picked up a stray."

"I am not a stray. You would think a real psychic would know that."

"It's kind of a nasty little thing, don't you think, Monique," Sarina said. "What are you feeding it?"

"My name is Tara Elizabeth Ann Michelle Mossri, and I demand to speak to your manager."

"You'd better tell your little hell minion to behave." Sarina snatched Tara's wrist, flipped it over, and began tracing the lifelines on her palm. "Or I just might have to put a hex on her."

Tara shrugged. "I dare you to try."

"Don't say I didn't warn you, little bird. A loveless marriage for you, it is."

"Tara, chill out," I said. "Sarina, we need to talk."

"What? You need to switch shifts at Lucido's or something? You didn't have to come into the shop for that."

"Tell me everything you know about psychic vampires."

"Why does it always have to be danger and gloom with you?" She clicked her tongue. "I know. Why don't we discuss your future with that rugged piece of man-candy you brought into the restaurant a few days ago?"

"You mean Ethan, don't you?" Tara's eyes lit up.

"So, Mr. Mysterious does have a name." Sarina winked at me. "I see lots of sex in your future."

"That's what I told her," Tara chimed in. "They should do it everywhere."

"Good thinking," Sarina said. "I'll bet that boy speaks fluent cunnilingual."

"She's only twelve." My cheeks warmed. "Take it down a notch."

"Fine, sourpuss. I'm just saying, if it were me, I'd ride that bull all the way to Pamplona."

"Can you help me with my problem or not?" I demanded.

"Come on back. I'm almost finished cleaning for the night anyway."

We followed her behind the front desk, down the hallway, past rows of framed headshots of D-list celebrities. All of them signed. At the end, we reached the individual mani-pedi stations.

"The moment you showed up." Sarina began packing her supplies to close. "I knew I was going to have nightmares tonight, so you might as well get to it. What do you want to know?"

"Psychic vampires," I said. "Have you dealt with one?"

"You mean besides every loser I've ever dated?"

"I'm serious."

"So am I," she said. "Gunner the Drummer was definitely an energy vamp."

"What happened with him?"

"Well, after he puked on my couch, he couldn't be bothered to clean it up. Instead, that drunken genius turned the cushions over and slept with my roommate that very night. Fucker." She glanced over at Tara. "Don't ever date a musician, honey."

"Sarina," I said. "This is serious."

"What's the big deal? Most people are energy sucks in one form or another. Mothers, politicians, needy friends..." She glared at me extra-long for effect. "These days, it seems everyone has a mind-draining agenda."

"You don't get it," I told her. "I'm not talking garden-variety here. How do you deal with a hardcore mega-type psychic vampire?"

"Um, you leave them the hell alone," she said.

"There's got to be some kind of cure. Some way to stop it. This doesn't just happen for no reason."

"Why do you care about this stuff so much?" She paused

mid-thought. "Oh my god. You're talking about Victoria, aren't you?"

"No." I fought the urge to race from the store right then.

"It makes sense. She's the one who's been killing all the animals."

"Do *not* tell anyone about this," I said. "Promise me."

"Never," she said, and I could tell she meant it. "I love that girl."

"I think the Awakeners did something to bring her back from the dead."

Tara, who'd already overheard some of this info outside Ethan's trailer at the farmer's market, didn't bat an eye. Instead, she asked, "Can you help us?"

"Honey, if you need me to read Victoria's palm, give her a little woo-woo show, I can, but this is way out of my league. What type of energy is she feeding on? Life force, sexual, what?"

"Victoria told me that she can see what I'm feeling." I thought about that dream I'd had of my mother leaving. "Maybe she's feeding off my memories too."

"She's a soul eater?" Sarina spit out the words as though they meant pedophile.

"I don't know. Maybe," I said. "She told me my energy is way brighter than anyone else's."

"Of course, it would be." She sounded somber. "Soul mates can generate big Universe power between them."

"You got it wrong. We're not gay."

"That's a misconception. A kindred spirit can be any person you feel drawn to. Your souls travel through lifetimes together. Monique, you're in danger. Eventually, animals won't be enough for her. Has she been feeding off of you?"

"Just a little," I told her.

"Son-of-a-bitch. What is wrong with you?"

"Victoria would never hurt me."

"The girl you knew wouldn't hurt you. She's different now. Everything else, this world and everyone in it, is a twinkling bitty star in a big black sky, and you're a supernova, dancing around right next to her."

"I can handle myself," I told her. "Roman Santo did this to her. Can it be reversed?"

"I don't know, maybe. What did he do to her?"

"That's why I came to you. That man is beyond dangerous."

"I think you're right," Tara spoke softly, which was so out of character for her, I stopped to listen.

"What do you mean?" I asked.

"I tried to show you earlier." She pulled out some kind of cloth from her jacket pocket, unfolded it, and produced a nylon string.

I glanced down and saw dozens of laminated passes hanging from it. All of them had pictures of Amber Gonzalez from Action News 7. They were her press badges that I'd seen around her neck just before I'd told her to check out the Awakeners.

"I found them on the compound," Tara said. "Can you use your psychic gift with these?"

Sarina picked up the badges and began flipping through them. Suddenly, she threw them back on the counter in front her, as if the plastic had burned her fingers.

"You both need to go," she said.

"Where?" I asked.

"To the police."

"Did you have a vision?" Tara asked. "Did you see Amber somewhere?"

"No," Sarina pointed. "That ID right there is covered in blood."

"What?" I glanced down and realized she was right. "Tara, where did you get these?"

"I didn't know it was blood." Her face bleached of all color. "You have to believe me."

I grabbed her shoulder. "Where exactly did you get these?"

"In the main office. I overheard the camp elders talking. Mr. Blackstone set it on Mr. Santo's desk and said the problem had been dealt with."

"Monique," Sarina said. "Please tell me you're not going to try to deal with this on your own."

"Not this time." I wrapped up the laminate passes in the cloth again and put them in my coat pocket. "Tara, come with me. We're going to see Sheriff Acosta." I glanced at Sarina. "Turn off the security alarm so we can leave through the back exit. I don't want anyone knowing we were here."

She nodded and led us down the hallway to the back door.

She keyed in the security code on the pad. "You know where my apartment is if you need somewhere to crash until this blows over."

Then she unlocked the door, and Tara walked outside.

I turned back and said, "Roman is dangerous. Leave your phone on. I might need to call you and don't go anywhere alone. Just in case."

"Monique," Tara called from outside.

"I have to go," I told Sarina, who hugged me.

"Stay safe, honey," she said.

I went out into the dark alley. The smooth knob-less door clicked shut behind me.

I'd never been so scared, but there was something else hiding below the surface too. Hope. For the first time since this nightmare began, the tides shifted in our favor. We finally had the proof we needed to lock that jerk Roman Santo away for good. On his day of sentencing, oh, I was going to be sitting front and center. Electric chair, lethal injection. Hell, I didn't care if they shoved him off a building.

"Tara?" I glanced around the alley. "Where are you? We have to hurry."

That's when I saw the shadow looming next to the fence a few feet away.

"Hello, Monique." Roman stepped into the dim moonlight.

Then one of his followers appeared to my left. And two more to my right. Then another, until the alley was blocked off from all angles.

33

AS ROMAN EMERGED FROM THE shadows, that massive gray wolf-beast Darwin stalked beside him. Four Awakeners closed in slowly from every direction as well. Then all at once, as if communicating telepathically, they stopped moving. The chilled wind seemed to pause with them. Even the insects quit dancing near the flickering street light above. Roman's followers gazed at him, clearly waiting for orders.

I couldn't outrun them all. Sheriff Acosta might be our only hope now, if I could just live long enough to get him the evidence of Amber's murder.

"We've been looking for you," Roman said.

"I don't have time to talk." I started walking down the alley in the opposite direction.

"I think you'll reconsider when you hear what I have to say," he called out.

Two of his men, dressed in jeans and what looked like home-sewn brown leather bomber jackets, stepped into my path.

"You want to tell your gorillas to move?" I slipped my hand into my coat pocket, flicked off the lid of my pepper spray, and turned to face Roman. "My dad is waiting for me at Lucido's."

"No, he's not." He walked up to me. Though he stood in a lit area now, shadows draped across his bearded cheeks and pooled in his eye sockets. I could smell the wood smoke on his jacket from here. "Your father had a job interview in Philadelphia with Van Houghton Construction today. He won't be back until seven."

"What are you doing, stalking us?"

"You've given me no choice," he said. "I learned many lessons watching my wife wither away, while machines pumped industrial waste into her frail body. Do you want to know the biggest one?"

"No, but I'm pretty sure that you're going to tell me anyway," I blurted, and his eyes narrowed. Shit. *When psychos talk about their dead wives, shut your stupid mouth, Monique.* His silence felt like a noose around my neck, so I said, "What did you learn?"

"Never underestimate any threat. Not when family's involved."

"How am I a threat to you or Ethan?"

"That's not the family I'm referring to." He glanced at his followers, and then over at the only female, a brunette with thin features, whose eyes were spaced too closely together. She smiled back at him with the intensity of a person who would gladly rush headfirst into a wood chipper at his command.

"I'm not a threat to these people either," I told him.

"Maybe not yet, but even the deadliest cancers begin as single cells, undetectable. Liver, skin—marrow. They bury themselves deep in the bone, whispering their lies, and they multiply. Do you understand what I am saying?"

"Of course, I do. I'm not an idiot. Next, you're going to tell me that you have to stamp out these threats before it's too late, right? Well, you don't need to. If you wanted to scare me, mission accomplished."

"Our goal isn't to frighten you."

"Right. That's why you ambushed me with four goons in an alley."

"I had to find a place where we could speak alone," he said. "So you could understand the weight of my words.

Make no mistake. I won't have anyone, even Victoria's best friend, poisoning our youngest members' minds."

"If you're talking about Tara, I ran into her by accident."

"Do not lie to me," he said in a low growl, and my heart raced. "It's demeaning. Now, you know what we want, and we're not leaving until we get it."

I glanced around, but there was no path for escape. The way I saw it, I had only two options. I give him the evidence. He gets away with Amber's murder, but maybe Monique lives through the night. Or, I hit him in the face with a shot of pepper spray. His band of merry nutcrackers proceeds to stomp me senseless, only to find that same evidence in my pocket seconds later. Then Roman straps poor Monique to one of his bonfires and gets away with double-murder.

Not much of a choice.

"Fine." I pulled the badges out of my pocket, shoved them forward, and prayed Sheriff Acosta would listen to reason, even without proof. "Just so you know, it wasn't Tara's fault. She doesn't even know what this means."

Roman glanced down at Amber's bloody press passes. Then he turned and smiled at his followers, who smirked too.

"You should take those to the police where they belong." He nudged my wrist back toward me with hands far too soft for a survivalist gun nut. "It's evidence."

"You'll never let me do that."

"Sure, we will. Isn't that right, girl?" He kneeled and scratched Darwin's scruff. The massive wolf beast with the blue eyes leaned against his leg. "Monique, trespassers get lost in our hills all the time. The river currents are dangerous. The ledges are steep. Some nosy people never find their way out again. I'm afraid that's what happened to your reporter friend."

"So you didn't hurt her?"

"Of course not," he said.

Right then, I was positive he'd killed Amber, but that didn't matter. I wasn't going to let him know that because I sure as hell didn't want to end up alongside her.

"I'm sorry," I told him.

"Water under the bridge, but just to be clear, I won't have this conversation again."

"Can I go now?"

"We're not finished quite yet," he said. "We came here tonight to make sure Victoria attends her celebration on Friday. You need to convince her to come with you."

"She doesn't listen to me or anyone else for that matter," I told him.

"Believe me," he said. "She's going to want to be there for this. We both know that she doesn't belong down here in town anymore, especially now that these new abilities of hers are manifesting. She needs to be with us, where she will be free to fly."

How the hell did he find out about Victoria? Not from Tara just now. She hadn't been outside alone with him long enough to say anything. Maybe he could have pieced it together. Victoria had tried to feed from him at school. With all that had happened in town, Sarina didn't need much help figuring out our secret. More likely, though, Roman knew because he was responsible for Victoria's condition.

"What did you do to her?" I demanded.

"There you go again, placing blame." He petted Darwin's back and nodded at his minions, who began to disperse. "If you want answers, make sure Victoria comes with you on Friday. I promise, we have the best and the brightest minds. If anyone can help her sort this out, we can."

Then he turned and disappeared into the darkness from where he'd come.

***

After I was positive the Awakeners had actually left, I hurried across town with the evidence Tara had given me. Did Roman really think I'd roll over and bring Victoria to his rally because he threatened me? Stupid man. And if he *had* changed her into a psychic vampire, why would I ever bring her near him again? Instead, I had a better idea. Sheriff Acosta needed to see that monster for who he really was.

Seconds later, I arrived at the police station and walked inside. North Hills wasn't exactly a hub of criminal activity, so slipping past the desk clerk wasn't difficult. Down the back hallway, I found the sheriff in his office at his desk, hunting-and-pecking his computer keyboard with his back to me. A matted ring formed in his gray hair where his cowboy hat had been.

Inside, the scent of leather and faint cigar smoke filled the room. Quietly, I closed the door behind me. Sheriff Acosta squeaked around in his swivel chair and glanced up at me with his reading glasses lowered on his nose. He took them off.

"Before you say anything," I told him. "Just know, I'm not stupid enough to play games with you or do anything to put you in a bad position."

"And yet, here you are." He leaned forward in his chair. "I'm sure this is going to be good. Out with it."

"Roman Santo killed Amber Gonzalez."

He looked surprised, and then he seemed to catch himself. "What makes you think that?" he asked.

"These were found on the Awakeners compound." I pulled out the press badges and set them on his desk. He picked up the passes and studied them. "You'll have to check, but I'm pretty sure that's her blood."

"Jesus-H-Christ-in-a-bucket-of-popcorn," he mumbled,

and then he looked up at me. "Didn't I tell you to leave those people alone? What part of that didn't you understand?"

"Roman came after me," I told him.

"Go out to my truck and sit there until I'm finished." He grabbed his car keys and tossed them to me. "Now."

"I wouldn't make up something like this."

"Monique, you can either walk out of this building of your own accord, or you can do it in bracelets." He jingled the handcuffs on his belt. "Make your decision."

"Fine." I turned and stormed out of his office.

"Don't you even think about running off either," he said. "You'd better be waiting when I get out there."

I walked out the back entrance, through the dark gravel parking lot. Then I remote-unlocked his truck and got into the passenger seat.

How could anyone be so blind? I mean, I'd all but hand-wrapped Roman and put a bow on him. A little gratitude would be nice for once, but instead, I was made out to be the bad guy in all of this yet again. Not to mention the fact that our lives were at stake, and the one person hired by the state of Pennsylvania to protect us—with my tax dollars, no less—was a pigheaded mule. How could I expect anything else from one of Dad's friends?

The driver's door opened, and Sheriff Acosta stepped up into the cab. He took off his hat, set it on the dashboard, and began to rub his temples. Tension poured from him and filled the quiet, frigid truck cab.

When the silence became uncomfortable, I said, "I'm not lying to you."

"Monique, you're a big girl now, so I'm going to treat you like one. Leave those fucking people alone."

"You're supposed to protect us." I knew my mouth would only make things worse, but screw him. He had one job. If he didn't do it, who would? "Whether you choose to listen or not, Roman and his cult crazies murdered Amber Gonzalez."

"You bet your ass, they did," Sheriff Acosta said.

"So what? Now you believe me?"

"I can spot a liar at twenty yards in a shit storm. I believed you earlier today when we spoke at your school."

"Then why have you been treating me like an attention whore?" I demanded.

"Because you're too blind to pay attention to your surroundings. Back at North Hills High, you failed to notice Mr. Santo eavesdropping on our entire conversation."

"You saw him there?"

"I see everything," he said. "You girls have no damned clue of what you've stepped in. Amber Gonzalez wasn't Santo's first ride at the fair. So tell me. What exactly do you hope to gain by pissing him off?"

"I want him to leave us alone," I said.

"He has spies everywhere. Maybe even in my own office, so don't go shooting off your mouth and ruining my investigation. You're getting in the way. Let us handle it."

"I wish I could, but that jerk trapped me tonight in an alley," I told him. "With four of his mind zombies, and he threatened me."

"Maybe if you weren't out collecting evidence, he wouldn't have come for you."

"I didn't ask Tara to do that." I threw up my hands. "She just went off on her own, but since you have evidence now, what's the problem?"

His gray mustache twitched as though he wanted to unleash a Fukushima blast of fury on me. Then he stared through the front windshield.

"Monique, I'm going to make this simple for you." He reached for a pack of Marlboro's in his shirt pocket, lit up, and then lowered his window a crack. "Busting bad guys is my job. One day, if you want to go through the police academy, you'll get a glowing recommendation from me, but this has nothing to do with you."

"Like hell it doesn't."

"From now on, you go to school and then straight home until this blows over. It's bigger than you think."

"But—"

"I'm serious now. If I catch you anywhere near that compound or those people, so help me, I'll be on you faster than flies on shit."

"What if he tries to kidnap us? Can't you lock him up?"

"Santo doesn't just collect followers with fancy degrees." He picked something out of his teeth, probably tobacco. Then he made some weird click noise with his tongue. "They have money and influence too. Why do you think he wants Malakoff's daughter?"

"That's exactly my point. Whatever we do, he keeps coming. Just arrest him. You have the evidence."

"Without Miss Gonzalez's body, your evidence won't matter. Besides, if anyone from my office breathes in his direction, I get a call from my donors first. Next comes a message from the mayor himself, and it goes all the way up the food chain. That's why we take our time and build a proper case first before we go kicking in doors. You can't take them on, so quit trying."

"I'm not. That's why I came to you."

"Well good, but the situation is under control," he said, but I could tell from his level of frustration that it really wasn't. "That man out there is playing the long game. Chess, not tic-tac-toe, and he'll sacrifice every player on his board. You, me, and all of his followers, including the children, you feel me?"

"What are you going to do?" I asked.

"Trust me, Santo is going spend the next fifty years trying to figure out how he got taken down by a good old boy Mexican from the Texas border, so don't screw this up."

"I'm supposed to go to a dance this Friday," I said.

"You go to school. You go to work, and then you go home. No exceptions."

"But Mrs. Hall is making me go."

"What am I? Speaking French? School. Work. Home. That's it. If she has a problem with that, send her over my way, and I'll scare up some sense for her."

"Fine." Actually, I felt relieved. Her plan to transform me with dances and cake into a vapid little princess had just been squashed by the biggest bully in the county. "I'll make sure Victoria doesn't go either."

"I'll take you home." He started the car. "And not a word of this to your old man. I know him. He'll head right up into those hills with his ratty-ass shotgun, and he'll make things worse. I promise you that."

"He won't be home until later."

"If you run into any trouble, call me first. Make sure Malakoff's daughter does the same. This is no time for one of her stunts."

"I know," I told him.

He pulled out of the parking lot. School. Work. Home. For once in my life, I could get behind an adult's bossy orders. I just prayed I could convince Victoria to do the same.

34

I ARRIVED AT SCHOOL Thursday morning a hot mess. My frizzed hair only responded to a scrunchie. My brain was scattered, which only made sense. During the events of the last few days, I'd probably ingested enough no-bite fingernail polish to cause toxic shock syndrome. And sleep? Not likely with Roman and his bunch slinking around.

It wasn't just the looming Winter Formal or the Awakeners rally that had me on edge—both scheduled for tomorrow night. Nor was it Victoria's never-ending radio silence. At least I'd see her at school today. No, this uneasiness ran deeper, and it had been growing steadily with each passing day.

Sunlight spliced through the trees to a concert of chirping birds. In the distance, a gas-powered weed whacker hacked and chawed on monkey grass or something. I knew what that meant.

Brace yourself, Monique.

Springtime had arrived early. Ugh. Not only did I have to find a way to convince Victoria to stay home tomorrow night, but now I also had to do it while contending with unbridled displays of female prancing and bitchery. The school's hallways would become a battlefield of headlocks and guys shoving each other into lockers to prove to females...what exactly? A promising future of domestic abuse?

Normally, I'd dress in black to signify my mourning period that would last this entire season, but I couldn't afford to stand out more than usual. Instead, I wore my jeans with the ripped knees and a gray mesh sweater over my tank top.

I reached the school's rear parking lot and prepared myself for the nightmarish hellscape of geeks, lip-gloss sluts, joiners, and jocks that had already formed.

In the center of the madness, Tim Donnelley threw Derek Jones a football between the parked cars. A spatter of doe-eyed freshman girls frolicked around them, desperately trying to out-giggle their competition, until the shrill bursts threatened to pop the blood vessels in my eyes.

Even an ABC Pest Exterminator van had set up shop. Two men in HAZMAT suits dug through their equipment. The school's basement probably had another springtime rat infestation. As I walked past Mindy Cohen, her group of Alexis Hall suck-ups shot me dirty looks.

Yeah, definitely rats.

I spotted Ethan alongside one of the special education extension trailers that lined the school's parking lot.

"Monique." He walked over to me. "I've been looking for you."

What could I say? The guy learned quickly. He'd already adopted the other students' styles. Wearing a gray V-neck with the sleeves pulled up, jeans, black boots, and a belt, he went from prepper to prepster in record time.

"Have you seen Victoria?" I asked.

"No, but she needs to be warned." He pulled me into a cove away from the other students. "I think the members are out in force looking for her."

"Already?"

"The plan changed for some reason," he said. "They were supposed to approach her tomorrow night, but when I woke up, the camp was deserted. I think they know something is going on with me."

"They might," I told him. "Tara was trying to collect evidence, and your father caught her."

"Are you kidding me?" he demanded.

"I tried to stop her. In case you haven't noticed, she doesn't listen very well."

"I know." He nodded. "I'm not accusing you of anything."

"Maybe I should have done more. I didn't know what she had planned. Can you check on her today or something? I'm worried."

"I'll handle that later—"

A football whizzed by just inches from my head and wedged underneath a Lexus on the far side of me. Derek Jones, the only other black face in school, walked up to us. He belonged in a commercial for a modeling agency, especially with that light skin—even lighter than me. Like every other athlete douchebag, he strutted his blue-and-white letterman jacket like a magic cape.

"Monique, help me out." He snapped his fingers. "Get me the ball."

"What, are your arms broken or something?" That jerk had barely spoken two words to me ever. All of a sudden, he was acting like we were long lost bourgeois *Jacks and Jills.* "Get it your damn self."

"See," he said. "There goes your problem right there."

"Yeah, what's that?"

"Those tits and that good hair would have taken you all the way to the top, if it wasn't for that personality."

"Well, asshole, your big mouth and walnut brain are about as handy as a used condom."

"Like I said, a man tries to pay you a compliment, and you immediately turn bitch."

"Hey," Ethan said. "Just back off."

Derek stepped closer and pushed Ethan's shoulder. "Are you going to make me?"

I realized too late that Ethan had been his target all along. At six-four, that Goliath Derek towered over almost everyone in school, and shepherd boy Ethan certainly hadn't brought his sling.

"Nobody here wants you around, Derek." I tried to step between them. "Just go back to your cave."

"I wish I could, but your boyfriend here has got a problem with me."

"I don't want any trouble." Ethan held his palms up. "Seriously."

"Then you should learn to keep that mouth shut." Derek tried to shove him again, harder this time, but Ethan slapped his hand away.

Derek swung. Ethan stepped to the side, grabbed Derek's balled fist, and twisted it behind his back. Then Ethan yanked upward, kicked the back of Derek's knee, and slammed his face against the grill of the Lexus behind them.

"Shit." I searched the parking lot. It happened so quickly that none of the students had noticed yet. Even Derek's football buddy Tim Donnelly seemed preoccupied with his freshman entourage. For now.

"Ethan, we need to get out of here." I grabbed his shoulder gently.

He leaned over Derek's ear and said, "I could break your arm in two places. Instead, I'm going to let you up. No one has seen anything. It's our secret, so let's do this quietly."

Ethan let go and stepped back. Derek pushed off the hood of the car. Two hundred plus pounds of twitching muscle and adrenaline rage sprang up to face us. He clearly contemplated whether to tear both our heads from our necks or to stomp our faces into the curb.

"You're dead," he said.

"I've studied my whole life for this." Ethan spoke quickly,

which seemed to pause the moment. "Krav Maga. Brazilian kickboxing. I've trained just like you have for football, and I've seen you play. Number forty-three. Derek Jones. Do you really want to put your college future in jeopardy over someone as insignificant as I am?"

"Listen to him," I said. "You're not an idiot, most of the time, so quit acting like one."

He glanced at me. Then he straightened his letterman jacket. Ethan nudged me, turned, and we started to walk away.

"That was amazing," I said when we'd made it about ten paces. "I had no idea you were like a Bruce Lee ninja or something. I thought for sure you'd end up a stain on the concrete."

"Whatever you do." Ethan barely glanced in my direction. "Don't look back. I got lucky."

"Um, I saw what just happened. That was not luck."

"Word of advice," he said. "Before you get into a bare-knuckled brawl, make sure your shoes are tied."

"Come again?"

"That monster could crush the snot out of me with one hand if he really wanted, but he tripped." Ethan picked up his pace. "Let's not give him a chance to figure that out."

I didn't know if it was true or not, but I liked him even more for saying it. Still, something was bothering me.

"Do you really go to our football games?" I asked, a little disappointed in him.

"A bunch of grown men in tights, chasing a ball around on a field?" He smirked. "What's not to love?"

"Then what was all that school pride crap? You knew things about Derek."

"Any man who wears his own name and number on his jacket has got bigger problems than me," he said. "I just helped him figure that out."

I looked back. Derek had made his way over to his group of friends. He pointed in our direction. Tim Donnelly jumped off the hood of his Jeep and grabbed one of his other football goons around the neck in...wait for it. Yep, a headlock. They began heading toward us.

"I don't think Derek figured anything out," I said. "He's coming our way with backup this time."

Ethan opened the door to the school, and we hurried inside. "What's the plan?"

"You need to leave before the first bell rings," I told him. "Or else the teachers will stop you. Go check on Tara. I'll warn Victoria about the Awakeners."

"What about them?" He motioned outside behind us.

"Please. I've been dealing with those pinheads for years," I said, even though I had to admit Derek had never been so malicious. "They're not going to do anything to me."

"Okay. Just try to stay out of trouble."

Considering how the morning started, I wasn't sure if that was possible. Ethan turned and hurried out the front entrance.

In order to avoid Derek and his goons, I ducked into the girls' bathroom. The first bell would ring any time now. In the far right stall, I lowered the lid and sat down, grateful for the break. I mean, what the heck was going on?

Derek had never been a jerk to me. No, we weren't ever going to be best friends, but as the only other black kid in school, I gave him his respect, and he usually did the same. It wasn't just him, though. Principal Rademacher and Mrs. Hall. Even Mr. Doyle. Everyone seemed to have lost their damn minds.

That first day back after the accident, I remembered feeling a chill, as if something wicked had infected the school itself. Now, I was starting to think that something really had, using Victoria as its conduit. If we could get through these next two days, I knew things would calm down. Forty-eight hours. That was doable, and then there would be no dance to worry about. No rally, nothing.

The main bathroom door swung open. I pulled my backpack underneath my legs.

"Yeah, but did you take care of it?" a male voice asked.

"I came in here for a reason." I immediately recognized Alexis's voice. "To get away from you. That's what you want, isn't it?"

Through the hinge space in the stall door, I could see that she'd stopped in front of the sinks.

"What do you expect from me?" he asked. "I gave you the money."

This was exactly what I didn't need. A front-row seat to Alexis Hall's high school extortion tactics and narcissistic undertakings. If she saw me in here, things would only get worse. I stood, ready to leave as soon as the best opportunity presented itself.

"Get out of the girls' bathroom," she told him.

"I'm staying right here until you tell me if it's handled." Through the crack, I saw a hand touch her shoulder.

"Don't worry." She shrugged it away. "You're off the hook, douchebag. Just leave me alone."

"Look, we don't have to stop seeing each other. I just think taking a break for a while might be the best thing."

"Do whatever you want," she said in her sweetest voice. Underneath, I could hear her pain. "You were just a stupid mistake I've already moved on from."

"You don't have to be like that. It was an accident. I pulled out."

My god. Victoria had been right about her pregnancy. What was the money about then? An abortion? I fought the urge to peek and see who the father was.

Not your business, Monique.

And I needed to keep it that way. His footsteps moved toward the door.

"One more thing," she told him. "If you say anything about this to anyone, I promise the entire school will find out just how small you are."

"Why do you always have to be such a bitch?"

Seconds later, the door swung shut. I held my breath and waited for her to leave. Something metal snapped the mirror glass, and I realized it had cracked. Then I heard a sound that I didn't think possible. Alexis was crying.

Right then, I wished I could have been anywhere but there. No one deserved that hell, even her. Worse yet, no one deserved to have her mortal enemy listening in while it happened.

The bell rang, but she didn't leave. I couldn't miss class, not with Rademacher looking for my scalp. I waited another minute, but I knew she wasn't going to budge. There was only one way to do this. Rip off the Band-Aid.

I grabbed my bag, opened the stall door, and headed directly toward the exit. With my head down, I desperately tried to avoid eye contact, but I could feel her gaze burn into me from the mirror.

"This is just perfect," she said. I glanced over as she wiped her eyes. "If you tell anyone, I'll crucify you."

"Alexis, I would never do that to you."

I wish I had something better to say, but I didn't. A few platitudes came to mind. There are other fish in the sea and all that. Thing was, anglerfish's teeth were so large and sharp that they couldn't even close their mouths. Great whites were fish too. They lived in the sea. Okay, I just wasn't equipped for this.

"Are you going to be okay?" I asked.

"What is this?" she hissed at me. "Do you actually feel sorry for *me*?"

"I didn't mean to piss you off."

"Look at you," she said. "Loser. You're never going to be anything. You know that, right?"

"Whatever."

"Get out of here," she said.

Right then, I knew I should have been angry, but I felt sorry for her instead, and nothing she said could change my mind.

"If you ever need anything—"

"Get out," she shouted.

I walked out of the bathroom. Yeah, I wanted to hate her, but in that moment, her venomous bite just seemed like an exaggerated defense mechanism. I could understand that, more than I wanted to admit. I went to my locker. As I grabbed books for my first class, I knew only one thing. My fears weren't just some paranoid delusion. The school's energy had soured, and it had nothing to do with spring.

Since Victoria had come back from her coma, the other students had become darker. The faculty too, and not just toward me. I couldn't help but think that the voice from Victoria's coma was causing it.

This school began to feel like a damaged submarine, lying on the sea floor, slowly being crushed under the weight of an ocean of darkness above. I needed to make sure that Victoria and I weren't around if and when the school finally popped.

***

I made it through the next two periods without incident. Still no Victoria though. I went to her locker at first break to find her. Instead, Pete stood there by himself. As always, he sported the frayed Dodger's cap that his father had given him, except now he wore a blue jersey to match. I'd never seen him seem so excited.

"Victoria is looking for you," he said.

"Shhh." I glanced over the second floor railing just as Derek and his entourage stalked by below. As a sophomore, avoiding seniors was fairly easy, unless I ran into them during class break or lunch.

"What's going on?" I turned back to Pete. "Where is she?"

"It's a secret." He grabbed my arm. "She wants to show you something."

Not good. Victoria's last surprise had been the sign-burning rally the night she'd nearly died in my arms down a drainage ditch. I pushed that thought away. The Awakeners were actively searching for her. She needed to be warned, like right now.

"Take me to her," I said.

He pulled me along to the end of the hallway, down to the first floor, and over toward the abandoned cafeteria, which had been under construction since a grease fire in the kitchen had given the school administration the excuse they needed to build a state-of-the-art deli.

We crossed the final outdoor hallway with the enclosed rounded Plexiglas roof. Normally, the faculty locked the door at the end to deter nosy students, but now it was cracked open.

We went inside the dark and demolished cafeteria. Without thinking twice, Pete crossed two sawhorses that blocked our path. For the past few months, the construction crews had been here. Something must have sent them home. The smell of char still hung thick from that blaze. What was Victoria thinking bringing Pete to this place?

"We shouldn't be back here." I nudged him away from a

long pile of tile flooring debris, rusted nails, and broken glass. Even the connected oven and deep fryer that had caused the fire had been torn from the wall and placed in the rubble. "It's too dangerous."

"She's back there." He pointed to a door that led to the old kitchen.

That's when I noticed a strange drone noise, low and ominous, resonating from beyond the doorway. I didn't know why that sound filled me with such panic. I only knew that Pete didn't belong anywhere near here.

"I'll find Victoria. You go back to class," I told him, but he didn't seem convinced. "The bell is going to ring any minute. Your teachers will be worried if you're not there."

Reluctantly, he turned, glancing back once before he crossed beyond the sawhorses into the main school building. I snuck through the door into the kitchen, which had been stripped down to bare concrete and stud. Rays of speckled sunlight filtered through the trees outside, and then through the saw-dusted mini-windows that lined the ceiling.

That's when I saw Victoria. Wearing black heels and a charcoal gray sweater, she stood with her back to me on top of a massive piece of drywall that had been pried loose from the studs. A sticky, brown, glue-like substance covered it.

What the heck? Her clothing appeared to move and squirm in the dim light.

"Victoria." I crept forward. The low rumble drone grew louder, into a buzzing sound. Just beyond her, a honeycomb filled the interior of the exposed wall between its two-by-fours. "What are you doing down here?"

She turned to face me. Jesus. Dozens of bees crawled across her cheeks and her arms. They were in her hair too. I didn't dare make any sudden movements, not with her sting allergy.

"Took you long enough." She sounded detached. "I found the source of the buzz that's been driving me nuts. All this time, they've been back here, calling out for me."

"Move slowly." I stepped toward her. "We need to get you out of here."

"Don't be stupid." She shook her arms, and I froze. Several of the bees flew away, only to land on her again. "They won't hurt me. I'm their queen now."

"I'm sure they already have an insect queen."

"Not anymore." She held out one hand, which was covered in honey. She turned it over, admiring the bees that smothered her wrist as if they were diamonds. "Me and their old leader had a little disagreement on who runs this hive. Let's just say that in this circumstance, size did matter." She dropped a gigantic smooshed bug onto the floor in front of her. "Bitch didn't know who she was messing with."

"Victoria, what the hell is wrong with you?" I spoke softly. "Why are you acting so crazy? And what if they sting you?"

"They can't. I control them now."

"You don't know that."

"Of course I do. They aren't much different than people." She shook her entire body, and a massive swarm of thousands poured from the walls, flew up to the ceiling, and landed there. I wanted to run, but my legs felt jittery. She glanced up at them and said, "It takes a lot of my energy and focus to control them, but watch this."

All at once, the bees dropped and hovered closely together, forming a thin sheet of insects that floated a few feet above our heads. I stood in awe of its breathtaking, terrible beauty as waves rolled across the surface. She reached up into the swarm. Dozens of bees died on contact with her touch and dropped to the floor, but the rest hovered in place, leaving a wake of emptiness where her hand had been.

"Please just come with me," I said. "School is about to start. I have to talk to you before class. You're in danger."

"You haven't even seen the best part yet." She waved her hand, and the swarm shot over to the wall on the far side of us.

They landed and scurried until the bees packed in close. Then they began to arrange their wings at different angles, which reflected various waves of light. An image began to peer through the chaos. Eyes and nose and mouth. The horde's wings came into focus to reveal a portrait of me.

"I found my new canvas," she said. "And they're my paint."

"Please, stop this. Stop—" My stomach leapt into my throat, as if I were helplessly watching a toddler play with a loaded handgun.

I choked. Right then, I had to get out of there. I couldn't breathe, so I raced from the room out into the main cafeteria. My chest hurt.

"Quit being such a coward," she yelled from behind.

Desperately, I tried to take deep breaths, but I couldn't. I'd never felt so overwhelmed, lost in the middle of the storming ocean in the dead of night, with wave after merciless wave crushing me. Dad's heart attack. Victoria's accident. Alexis. The cult Nazis. Jesus Christ, for once in my miserable life, karma, could I just catch a break?

I put my hands on my knees for balance. Slowly, my breath came back to me, and I cried. I don't know why I lost control except that scene had been so perverse, so twisted, that I had no words.

That's not your friend in there.

I swore if that nagging voice in my head wouldn't be quiet, I would shut it up with drill-bit lobotomy. Victoria was hurting and lost. That's all, and she needed me more than ever.

A hand gently touched my shoulder from behind. Thank god. She must have come to her senses. I turned around and saw Pete standing behind me.

"Are you hurt?" he asked. "Did they sting you?"

"No," I whispered. "I'm okay."

"Only one stung me." He held up his muscles and showed me a puffy red mark on his bicep. "I'm tough, though. Want me to walk you back to class?"

"Just sit with me for a second." Even though I hated the idea of Pete in this place, I needed him right then. Everyone had their breaking point, I guess. Here was mine. He hugged me. In that moment, I'd never felt safer, and yet, I'd never felt so alone.

What could I do about Victoria? I felt her slipping away. How could I possibly reach anyone who'd strayed so far from reality, especially my best friend, who'd never been tethered there in the first place?

"Ho-lee shit." I instantly recognized Tim Donnelly's voice, and my skin crawled. I pushed Pete behind me as he walked into the cafeteria, swinging a two-by-four. Derek Jones and the other two goons from this morning followed on his heels. He turned to them and said, "I thought you said Robinson was banging one of those cult fags. Looks to me like she's been sucking Grendel off this whole time."

"Don't call him that," I shouted.

"Where is he?" Derek pushed his way to the front of the group, and they circled around us.

"Ethan's already gone. You're too late." I tried to shove my way past them, but they blocked my path. "Move."

"Say, Robinson, why don't you settle a bet?" Tim got in my face. "I think the reason you throw all that attitude at everyone, is that you secretly want us."

"Get out of our way," Pete shouted.

I turned to calm him. "It's okay."

Tim laughed. "Woo, looks like we've gotten Grendel worked up."

"Leave us alone." Pete clutched some piece of paper in his hand. He held it up to show them. It was the picture that Victoria had drawn of him as a superhero. "I'm not a Grendel anymore."

"What the fuck is this?" Tim started giggling insanely now. "We'd better be careful. It looks like Robinson has got some serious protection."

"Go away," Pete shouted. "Or you'll be sorry."

"I think I'll take my chances." Tim snatched the picture, tore it in half, and threw it on the ground.

"Hey," Derek said to Tim. "Quit being such a prick."

Pete's scream sounded far too manic. With his bulk, he accidentally shoved me aside and dove onto the ground for the shreds of paper. He scooped them up in his shaking hands. Then he glanced up with tears of rage in his eyes that terrified even me.

"Pete, calm down," I said. "She'll draw you another."

He leapt up and slapped Tim across his face hard.

"Hey, that hurt, you little punk." Tim shoved Pete, who tripped backward.

I could only watch in horror as he fell in slow motion. His head smacked the metal corner of the deep fryer. Then he collapsed to the floor with a sickening thud. I rushed down to his side.

"Fuck wad," Tim said. "He shouldn't have hit me."

Blood began pouring from a massive gash somewhere underneath Pete's skull. There was so much of it. What could I do? Apply pressure? I didn't dare touch him.

"Go get help," I shouted at them through my tears. "Go, you fucking losers."

Derek and the other two guys raced away. Tim just stared with his hands on his head.

"Robinson, you saw what happened," he said. "It was an accident. You have to tell them."

"Go to hell." I glanced up, and saw a shadow out of the corner of my eye. I turned.

Victoria stood just feet from me. Her body trembled. Several bees were still caught in her hair. She glared at Tim as though she had scissors pointing from her eyes.

"He hit me." Tim clearly sensed the danger. "It was an accident."

Victoria unleashed a scream worse than anything I'd ever heard. It reverberated through the dead cafeteria, feeding on itself until it didn't even sound human anymore.

"Tim, you idiot," I shouted. "Get out of here."

"I didn't mean to hurt him," he said.

The dark swarm erupted from the kitchen's doorway. Thousands of bees, maybe tens of thousands rose up to the ceiling, and the sunlight through the windows darkened. The bees flew directly to Victoria, swirled around her body, gathering their numbers. Then, she screamed again. With their purpose clear, they shot toward Tim.

"Run," I shouted, but he stood flat-footed, stunned by the spectacle.

The swarm descended upon him. The force of the impact of thousands of drones at once knocked him to the floor, and then, oh Jesus, the horde pushed him down like a giant fist. He rolled around as if he were on fire. The cyclone of bees roared over him like a convection current, rotating around to take more swipes.

"Victoria," I shouted over the hissing buzz. "Stop it."

I left Pete's side and raced over to her. Just one glance at the fury in her eyes, and I knew there would be no reasoning with her. I don't even think she could see me through her blood rage. I slapped her face. Her head snapped to the side and stopped with mechanical precision. Then she slowly glared at me.

"You're going to kill him." I glanced over my shoulder. Without her guidance, the swarm dispersed in every direction, leaving behind hundreds of stinger-less bees, stuck to Tim's face, skin, and jacket. Both of his eyes had already swollen shut. Bloody welts covered his face. Blindly, he slid away on his stomach across the floor, through dust and broken glass, with drool leaking from his lips. He pulled himself through the door on the far side of the cafeteria and closed it shut behind.

Victoria stepped toward me.

"You're not a murderer," I told her, but the ravenous look on her face said otherwise. "I won't let you kill him."

With a screech, she snatched both of my cheeks. The cafeteria began to vibrate. Victoria's arms and skin started glowing. Then her eyes seemed to explode in a white-hot spray of light that nearly crowded out the world entirely. My knees went numb. I collapsed and felt myself splash through the hard concrete below me into snow-blind nothingness.

***

A white flash blinds me, and I am choking on water. Victoria holds my hand as I stare upward at the steel beams of the ceiling. I lean on my side. My eyes sting with chlorine. The air smells like it too, and I feel like I'm going to throw up. A few of the other girls held me under too long. I don't think I've ever been more scared than in that moment when water went into my lungs.

"I knew we shouldn't have let her near this pool," a woman

*lifeguard says to one of her co-workers under her breath.
"Those people never teach their children to swim properly."*

*Funny thing about whispering. Someone is always listening,
and I've spent enough time around white folks to know what
she means by those people. It's one of two things. Poor or black,
maybe both. No matter how many times I tell myself that it
doesn't hurt, it really does. Dad says life is too short to let
stupid people ruin your day. He also says I shouldn't take any
shit from punks, but I'm too exhausted and waterlogged to be
mad about it.*

*"What did you just say?" Victoria stands up and faces the
woman. She is never too tired to be mad about it. Although she
just turned eleven last week, she gets in the woman's face.
"What do you mean, those people?"*

*"Oh, nothing, sweetie," the lifeguard says. Her tag shows
that her name is Jennifer. This indoor pool is always filled with
Jennifers.*

*"I only meant that all of our members already know how to
swim." The woman shifts uncomfortably.*

*"No, you meant black people," Victoria says too loudly. She
is causing a scene. Again, except this time, I don't want the
attention. I just want to go home.*

"It's okay," I tell her. "Let's just go watch Dead Girl."

*"That's ridiculous," Jennifer says. She is not backing down.
"She doesn't even look black."*

*"I didn't think you looked stupid," Victoria said.
"Apparently, we were both wrong. I want to talk to your boss."*

*Jennifer's coworker gives her a nervous glance. Everyone
knows who Victoria's father is, and most people are scared. He
even scares me. Jennifer is late to the party though. I don't
think she knows.*

Twenty minutes later, phone calls are made.

Jennifer cleans out her locker. Victoria smirks at her walk of shame out the front door, and I'm given a lifetime membership that I don't want to a pool that I don't like. I love Victoria, but sometimes, she doesn't understand that there are times when it's better not to fight.

Dad comes to pick us up. After hearing about what happened, he doesn't speak. He pulls to a stop. Just before he drops us off for a slumber party at Victoria's mansion, he gives me a hug, which I need, but I wouldn't tell him that. I don't know why Victoria always looks jealous when he hugs me.

"Don't get into trouble tonight," he says, and we nod. "I want both of my daughters to be safe."

Victoria beams, and we head up into her mansion. A flash of white light steals my vision.

***

I don't know how long I floated in that whiteness, dazed and lost. This throbbing headache seemed unfit for heaven, and the ring of tinnitus was too mundane for hell. That probably meant I wasn't dead, but I couldn't remember how I got here.

Finally, the brightness began to dim. Blurred shapes focused, and then I was staring out of a window at a hummingbird, which flew in place just beyond the glass. I sat up on a cot and touched the side of my throbbing forehead. That dream had been so real. Even now, I could taste the chlorine. I'd forgotten all about the day I almost drowned, and suddenly, that memory seemed more real than what I was experiencing now. I glanced over. Victoria sat in the chair next to me.

"What happened?" I asked her. "Where am I?"

"You hit your head when you fell," she said. Blue light surrounded her skin. I blinked rapidly, but she still glowed. "You don't remember the cafeteria?"

A wave of memories flooded over me, and I had trouble breathing. She reached for my hand. I flinched. This was the nurse's office. Victoria had fed from me, but this time she'd been violent and terrible. I felt violated. Sarina had tried to warn me this would happen.

She reached for my hand again. "It's okay."

I shoved myself back. "Stay away from me."

What was going on? I'd seen this glow in my sight every time she fed from me, but it had never been so vivid. Suddenly, I knew what it meant. Every time she took my energy, she somehow infected me. Dracula had to hit Lucy up like ten times before she finally turned. Did that mean I was on my way to being like her?

"I'm sorry," she said. "I don't know what happened."

"You attacked me. That's what."

"I screwed up, okay?" Her voice shook. "I don't remember much of it."

"What is going on with you?" I demanded. "I didn't even recognize you back there. One minute, you're acting like a crazy person with those bees. Then you nearly kill me in a rage. Now, you want to apologize?"

"It will never happen again," she said. "You have to forgive me. Please."

Then we sat in silence. Yeah, I could see that she was truly sorry, but what did that mean? No, it wasn't entirely her fault. It wasn't as if she'd spun out of control in a vacuum. If Tim Donnelly hadn't shown up, none of this would have happened. Oh my god.

"Pete," I said. "Is he okay?"

"I don't know. They rushed him to the hospital. I overheard Principal Rademacher in the office talking. He's calling this an unfortunate accident."

"Accident, my ass. Those jerks came after us. I need to tell

Rademacher what happened." I tried to sit up, but white spots still cluttered my vision.

"Trust me," she said. "Nothing you say will matter to them."

"What's wrong with you?" I asked. Her melancholy demeanor unnerved me. "Why are you acting like this?"

"Didn't you hear? Baseball season is starting up in two weeks, and North Hills High needs its star pitcher, Derek Jones."

"I'm going to put a stop to this."

"No, you're not," she said. "Because I am."

"Victoria—"

"Since I returned, I've spent most of my nights wondering what brought me back. Why was I allowed to escape death? All this time, I had no clue, but now I know what needs to be done."

"I'll make the school listen," I told her. "Those guys will get what they deserve."

"You're right about that." She stood and looked down at me. "The Winter Formal is tomorrow night. I know where and when the other three guys are going to be together next."

"You can't go to that dance. It's too dangerous."

"It doesn't matter what you say," she told me with the quiet fortitude of Mother Teresa. "I'm going to make them hurt for what they did to Pete, and nothing is going to change my mind."

"Pete wouldn't want that."

She walked out of the nurse's office just as my dad entered.

"What happened?" He rushed to my side, inspected the bandage on my head, and then hugged me.

"I'm okay," I told him, but he squeezed tighter.

"Who did this to you?" he demanded.

Over his shoulder, I saw Victoria in the hallway. I felt the overwhelming sadness in her eyes as she stared at us. The envy, just like she'd had that day at the pool. She looked so alone.

Then she turned and disappeared down the hallway.

35

I STAYED LATE INTO THE night with Pete in the hospital. I don't know what I expected to find there. Hope, maybe, or at least some good news. Anything to break this suffocating ache in my chest. If Victoria had stopped by, I might have had a chance to reason with her, but she never did. Perhaps that was for the best.

A few doors down, Tim Donnelly had been admitted for his bee stings too. Inside his room, balloons and get well cards spilled out into the hallway. Visitors poured in throughout the night. Football team members and family. Teachers. Everyone expected a full recovery.

In Pete's room, only his mother and I sat vigilant by his bedside. Though I tried, I couldn't shake the look on his face from my mind when Tim had torn up that picture of him. The hurt and sorrow. He'd suffered more than hundred lifetimes worth. Some burdens no one should have to bear, but Pete did it daily. He really was my superhero, but I don't think he would ever believe me if I told him that. The more things changed, the more they stayed the same, I guess. At least, he was going to be okay, the doctors thought, with a little time and physical therapy.

Later that night, I went home exhausted. First, I stayed up with Dad and watched *Loony Tunes* on one of our rabbit ears stations. When he'd calmed down from the day's events and finally went to bed, I called Ethan.

I couldn't do this alone anymore, and I needed his help, so I filled him in on everything. Victoria's psychic vampirism. The medallion. All of it. To his credit, he believed me, or at least he said that he did. At this point, that was good enough.

The next day at school was a blur. Everyone had heard about the bees, and everyone seemed scared, although they didn't exactly know what to be frightened of. For a second, I thought the administration might cancel the dance. That was just wishful thinking, though. A little pick-me-up good time normalcy was just what the student body needed after a tragic incident, at least according to Principal Rademacher.

I needed another chance to talk sense into Victoria, but she never showed up to school that day either. I don't know what she had planned. Nothing good. I only knew that if I didn't stop her tonight, she'd cross some line that couldn't be uncrossed, and I'd lose her forever.

During fifth period, with time running out until the Winter Formal, I typed into the computer station at the school's library. Every personal lead I'd followed to get to the bottom of her condition had proved fruitless, which left only one desperate option. The Internet.

For certain, no sane person should ever visit the dark recesses of the online community's imagination, but it wasn't as if I could WebMD her symptoms. After ten minutes, I needed a shower and a shot of Thorazine.

So what did I learn? Barely anything. At least according to legend, there were many types of energy suckers. Incubi were only males. X that out. Succubae drained people during sex. Victoria stole that pocketful of condoms for shock value, nothing more.

Other terms related to psychic vampires like biotic energy and emotional resonance came up. Actually, shielding could be useful—the act of protecting oneself from a psychic vampire—but I couldn't exactly teach all of the other students how to do that when I didn't really know how myself.

That meant curing her was the key, but despite the millions of anonymous online trolls, ready to ambush

Hindus, Facebook, socialism or capitalism, feminism, redneck reality stars, old ladies, handicapped children, or family values, the Internet finally decided to agree on one fact.

There was no cure for psychic vampirism. I refused to accept that. There had to be some way.

A hand touched my shoulder. I turned to find Ethan behind me. In this lighting, his blue eyes seemed brighter against his tan skin.

"What are you doing?" I pulled off my headphones and whispered, "You can't be in here. Derek and those assholes might still be looking for you."

"We need to talk," he said.

"Yeah, after school."

"This can't wait. We're running out of time."

He had a point. I glanced around the room. Everyone in the library study hall stopped and gawked at him like he was some lost transfer student who had yet to figure out that talking to me was social suicide. If they suspected he was the cult leader's son, we'd have a real problem.

Luckily, he wore a gray T-shirt, black jeans, and sneakers. Only his toned forearms, laced with scars, gave him away amidst this student body's crowd of soft hands and even softer brains. Faint remnants of the scabs from the fight he'd had with his father last week wrapped around his chin, reminding me of just how dangerous his father could be. And yet, Roman had nowhere near Victoria's destructive capability. Somehow, I had to reach her.

"Nothing online is making any sense," I told him. "What did you find out about Tara?"

"Somebody tipped off the members that Victoria will probably be at the dance tonight."

"Yeah, that someone might have been me in front of the school," I told him. Stupid, girl.

"Get her home tonight and stay there." He pulled one of the molded chairs from the pyramid stack behind us and set it next to my computer. "After the rally tonight, my father will calm down. I know it."

"Victoria has made it clear. She's going to that dance no matter what I say, so I have to be there to watch her."

"Then I'll be your date."

"Absolutely not," I told him. "Considering what happened with Derek, you'll only make things worse."

"Monique, there are twenty-three children under the age of eleven living on the ranch. Most days, it's my job to watch them. If she's as dangerous as you say, we can't let her anywhere near the compound."

"What are you talking about? Your father is just as dangerous."

"You're right, he is. More so even, which is why we need to work together to keep them apart. I'd go alone to the dance, but I didn't sign up. I can't get in without you."

"Can't you just find out what they did to her so we can reverse it? You've been back at the compound all week. Have you figured out who's responsible?"

"As far as I can tell, no one did anything to her."

"I watched her dance Principal Rademacher around like a marionette."

"Monique, these people have been my family since I was a kid," he said. "It wasn't them."

"Keep your voice down."

Some kids stole glances at us. Across the circular room, even the giant bronze statue of a girl seemed to disapprove from her pedestal perch with an open book in her lap. No one could be quiet or serious enough for this girl, whose haunted, off-center pupils looked as though she'd spent her summers at a reading camp in Auschwitz.

I stood and dragged Ethan to privacy between two aisles, next to the ancient remains of the Dewey Decimal card catalog system.

"No matter where we talk," he said. "The Awakeners are not responsible for her condition."

"What about this then?" I pulled out his medallion necklace from my jacket pocket.

"I told you. It belonged to my mother. That night in the hospital, I thought it might ease your pain if you held onto something real."

"The minute that I gave it to her, she woke up from her coma, shrieking." I couldn't shake the image of her broken-tooth smile. "This looks like a Native American trinket. Why is it covered with Latin writing?"

"That's not Latin," he said.

"What does it mean then?"

"How should I know? It's random symbol gibberish."

"I want to believe you," I told him. "But the minute it touched her fingers, she woke up. This writing means something."

"Turn it over," he said.

"Why?"

"Just do it."

I flipped it in my palm. He pulled back the black down feathers that were attached to the talisman's metal perimeter to reveal some text.

"Made in China," I read aloud. "I don't get it."

"My mother and I went to the Grand Canyon right after she was diagnosed. I bought it for her at a truck stop in New Mexico with my allowance."

"So what are you saying? The Indians put a hex on it?" Had the Awakeners tapped into some vein of evil that ran underneath this city? "This town's founder Chester North decimated the native tribes. That kind of bad mojo doesn't just dissipate."

"No," he said. "There were dozens of these necklaces on the rack. It's just a stupid souvenir that hung right underneath the stuffed head of a jackalope."

"Then maybe your mother's spirit is connected to it somehow."

"Listen to yourself. This is not a horror movie."

"Victoria used mind control on the principal last week," I told him. "She's sucking the energy out of every living thing that crosses her path, and it's slowly driving her insane. Quit acting as though I'm crazy to think this stuff."

"Monique, I believe you, but you're too close, and you're focusing on the wrong things."

"So what's your theory then, Mr. Smart Guy? Is Victoria cursed, or is she the test subject in a sick science project?"

"Have you ever heard of Occam's Razor?"

"Yeah, in chem lab maybe. What does that have to do with any of this?"

"It's a guiding scientific principle," he said. "Not just for chemists. All mathematicians, doctors, and physicists learn it. To put it in shorthand, it states that the simplest explanation for any event is usually the correct one."

Maybe it was the way the Awakeners lived, or it could have been his perpetual scent of weed, which gave me a contact high from here, but the way he slipped so easily into professor-speak shocked me. I guess it made sense. He had been surrounded and schooled by geniuses his entire life.

"So what's the simplest explanation for something that shouldn't exist?" I asked.

"I've known the families on our ranch forever. No one practices the dark arts, and the idea that someone is hiding a funded research lab is ludicrous. Besides, it goes against everything they believe."

"There has to be a reason for Victoria's condition."

"I think there is," he said. "My mother lived years past her diagnosis. Do you know what made the difference?"

"You told me it was the necklace."

"Not in that way." He looked down and began picking something from his fingernail, just like Dad did sometimes. "During her final days, I hid in the waiting room most of the time. In my eyes, the thing claiming to be my mother was a skeleton with skin stretched across it. Tubes were everywhere. She scared me."

"I get it." I couldn't forget how that pickup truck had mangled Victoria's body. "I hate hospitals too."

"Toward the end, she made me sit with her. Though it looked horribly painful, she sat up straight in her bed. She could barely breathe as she thanked me. She said that her little man had made her want to fight, which is why she lasted so long. Then she told me she was ready to go soon, and I shouldn't be sad when she did."

"I don't understand. What does she have to do with Victoria?"

"Don't you see, Monique? I don't think this necklace brought Victoria back any more than it helped my mother. There's no ancient evil or curse or reason for our pain in this world sometimes."

"I know what I saw. She woke up when your medallion touched her."

"When you touched her," he corrected me. "This has to do with you."

"I don't care what these fools in town say about me. I'm not some witch or Satan-worshipper."

"I don't think that's what happened. Just like my mother, you gave her a reason to come back, except somewhere along the way, it got twisted."

"If that were the case, other folks would come back from the dead all of the time."

"Victoria isn't other folks," he said. "She never has been. Everyone in this town has heard stories of her abilities since she was in preschool. I mean, when she was ten, the Catholic Church commissioned her for that fresco."

"That's different."

"Is it?" he asked. "Our brains develop new pathways when they're damaged. What if her mind rewired during her coma, and what if she turned just a fraction of that gift toward the task of getting back to you?"

"Anything would be possible," I said.

"These abilities might be some new consequence, or she could've magnified psychokinetic traits that are usually too subtle for others to notice. I'm not saying it's perfect, but the theory is a hell of lot better than ancient demons from the underworld."

"Says you." I didn't like his attitude. "While in her coma, Victoria told me that something had kept her trapped in nothingness."

"You mean sort of like being locked away in her own damaged mind?" he asked.

"No, she told me a different voice talked to her. It tortured her."

"What did that voice want from her?"

"To know where to find me," I told him.

"As amazing as you are, why would a demon, after years of solitude, want to find Monique Robinson from North Hills High?" My god. He was right. Then he said, "The human brain operates on levels that medical science barely understands. That voice could have been her subconscious mind or her unconscious urges. Just ask yourself, have you seen any demons running through town? I haven't. Or has it been—"

"Victoria," I said. "This whole time. It's only been her."

I felt a cold chill up my spine. All other explanations crumbled like sand the minute I picked at them, but this theory made sense on a gut level. Had I been deluding myself? A comforting demonic presence could be killed or extracted, at least according to every movie I'd seen, but the darker pieces of her personality, bubbling to the surface could never be removed.

"I don't think there is a cure for her condition," he said. "This is just who she is now. If we don't keep her away from my father tonight, we're going to have some serious problems."

"What can we do to stop them?"

"Nothing alone. There are too many forces at work here, so I'm your date for the dance tonight, whether you like it or not."

"Fine, but you have to deal with my dad."

"Good," he said. "I'll pick you up at eight."

36

EXPOSED. THAT'S HOW I FELT getting ready in front of my bedroom mirror that night. Not just because the black corset dress was strapless, leaving my girls a sneeze away from making an appearance. Nor was it because the steampunk skirt's pleated flare seemed longer on the website's model. No, my insecurity ran deeper than this outfit. What if I didn't fit in tonight? That thought worried me, but not for the reasons the other students might think. For all I cared, every bulimic pageant princess at the Winter Formal could duct-tape her belly flat and strut around in clown-face.

My concern was Victoria. Ethan had been right about her. No cure existed, which meant she had to learn to control her urges. That required time and patience. Two things we didn't have with Roman Santo lurking.

I pulled my curls back with a couple of barrettes, hit them with a shot of hairspray for wisp control, and grabbed my purse. Out in the living room, I found Dad snoring in his recliner. Even from here, I could smell his feet. One day soon when he wasn't paying attention, I'd burn those hole-ridden socks and that stupid *Rage Against the Machine* T-shirt with shotgun-carrying nuns.

"Dad," I said.

He scratched his nose with a snuffle. Then he glanced up and wiped the sleep from his eyes.

What a sad showing for an overprotective father. He'd left his rusted shell of a hunting rifle leaning against the fireplace, as if he'd gotten tired and lost interest in scaring Ethan away.

Or maybe, he'd correctly assessed that I'd be a spinster before anyone asked me out on a legitimate date.

"I'm leaving soon," I told him. "Don't stay out here all night, okay? Make sure you go to bed."

He grumbled something and started to lean on his side. Then he stopped and focused on my outfit.

"What?" I resisted the urge to simultaneously pull up my dress while stretching it down below my knees. "Is it horrible?"

He didn't answer. I knew it. Me at a Winter Formal? What a crock. No matter how much I tried to blend in, this would never work. I had to change. If I dressed like myself tonight, Alexis might take a few shots at me, but at least I wouldn't give her extra ammunition.

"Give me a second," I said. "I might be able to find another outfit."

He leaned his footrest forward and sat up. "Hold on."

"There isn't time."

I rushed back into my bedroom and began digging through my closet. Behind me, the door creaked open.

"Don't change your clothes," Dad said. "They're fine. You caught me by surprise. That's all."

"I get it. I know I don't belong at this dance. You don't have to pretend."

"Who says I'm pretending?" he bellowed.

"Me. Everyone. Just look around." I pointed at my bedroom walls, which were covered in classic horror movie posters. *Dark City. The Exorcist*, and *Ginger Snaps*. Even my favorite band poster featured Eva Marie from Dollhouse, sitting on a tile floor in a Catholic schoolgirl uniform with her knees locked, feet spread. She held the severed head of her guitar player in her lap. The caption read, *He Finally Gets Me*.

"So what?" he said. "You've got that dark Robinson blood. It makes you tough when everyone else is a punk. What does that have to with your clothing?"

"I don't know how to do this." I grabbed the ridiculously awkward dress and adjusted it. "Makeup. Hair. Any of it."

"Just calm down and listen for a second." He motioned to my bed, and I sat down. "Let me explain some things to you that you might not have considered. I'm not used to seeing you dressed like this. It's a lot for me to take in, especially since it seems like yesterday that I was hosing mud off your bare feet."

"Dad, I love you, but I'm not five anymore."

"Another thing," he continued. "I've *never* seen anyone look more beautiful than you do tonight."

My eyes welled up, so I blinked rapidly.

"I'm your daughter. You have to say that."

"Believe me, I would nail your door shut before I let any child of mine go outside looking like a street urchin." He kissed my forehead and hugged me. "I know you don't understand right now, but one day when you have children of your own, you'll know what this moment means."

"It's just a dance."

"No, it's not," he said. I didn't like the sadness in his voice. "I'm not too good at this sort of thing. I wish your mother would've been here for you tonight."

"I don't," I told him. "You're doing fine, Dad."

"Yeah, well, I appreciate you saying that anyway."

I thought about my dream that I'd had. How my mother had left us.

"I know you don't like to talk about it," I said. "But why did she leave us in the middle of the night? It was my birthday, I think. And Victoria was here, right?"

"You remember that?"

"So it is true."

"I don't think anyone will ever know why she left," he said. "It wasn't your fault, and it wasn't mine either. We tried to make it work, and it just didn't."

Down the street, I heard the faint rumble of Ethan's El Camino.

"I think my date's here."

"Like I told you, one day you'll understand." He pulled away and stood up. "I might as well go look this kid in the eye."

"Take it easy on him."

We walked out into the living room just as Ethan knocked on the screen door. I let him in. Wow, he wore a black suit, and he'd even combed his hair. I hadn't even considered the idea that he'd get dressed up.

Ethan looked at my dress with shock on his face. Was every man going to treat me like a leper?

"You better say something quick, son," Dad chimed in. "You don't want to piss off a Robinson. Trust me."

"You look amazing," Ethan said, and I could tell that he really meant it.

Then I noticed he had actually brought a corsage for our fake date. I guess appearances were important, in case the Awakeners saw us together or something.

"We're going now," I announced.

"Hold up." Dad walked over to Ethan. They shook hands. "I love only one person in this world. I want her home by midnight. You understand me?"

"Yes, sir," Ethan said.

"Are you sure?" Dad clearly wouldn't let go of his grip.

"Okay." I widened my eyes to tell him to tone it down. "He's sure."

"I just want the boy to understand that I work

construction. If anything happens, the concrete will dry before anyone reports him missing."

"Dad."

"You two have fun." He finally let go of Ethan's hand. "I mean it. Midnight."

I kissed Dad's cheek, and then Ethan and I headed out on what might have been the most elaborate faux date ever devised.

37

*T*HE MOMENT ETHAN AND I entered the hallway that led to the Winter Formal, I knew we were in trouble. It wasn't just the brainless dance beat, rattling the trophy cases that filled me with anxiety or the incredulous stares from every person we passed. Yes, Monique The Dreary had gotten dressed up and arrived at a school function with a date. Soak it in, folks, because this would be the last time. That wasn't why I was worried, though.

We didn't belong here. I knew it. The other students knew it too, which made them dangerous. Still, that didn't matter. Victoria's new power had twisted her personality. I had to find a way to reach her tonight before Roman or one of the other students did something stupid to ignite her rage.

"You deal with the Awakeners if they show up," I told Ethan. "I'll try to convince Victoria to leave early."

"Got it."

At the interior door to the gym, I stopped. Two six-foot candy cane props guarded the entrance to the dance. I glanced inside. The room looked as if it had been infected by a Willie Wonka herpes virus, which spread giant pink cotton candy sores throughout the gym. It didn't end there.

Massive chocolate bar replicas of Snickers, Hershey, and Reese's lined yellow brick pathways to the dance floor. The other students had all dressed in neon swirls with candy bracelets and necklaces. The girls' makeup covered every color in the Skittles rainbow.

Ethan gave me a can-you-believe-this-shit look. I kind of

liked his bad attitude, but I was more afraid than ever. Despite my allergic reaction to dances or any kind of Beaver school pride, this theme was impressive in scale and focus. Say what you want about Alexis Hall, but she wasn't weak when she put her mind to something. Victoria would not want to leave willingly.

We got into the line that formed inside the doors. Julie Chen sat at a plastic table, checking people in. Her white go-go dress barely covered her lady garden. Mini dots splattered her cheeks and her arms as well. Her black hair had been tied like a candy bag with crinkle plastic.

"Monique." She glanced up at us with a bubbly ASB president smile. "What are you doing here?"

"I go to this school too."

"Don't get me wrong. I'm glad you're joining us, but I don't have you on my list."

"Talk to Mrs. Hall," I told her. "She's the one who set this up."

"That's fine, but what are you?"

"Excuse me?"

"Kendra is dressed like a Jolly Rancher. Gina and the cheerleaders are the Sweet Tarts." She pointed back into the gymnasium. "Everyone picked a candy theme. What are you?"

"Diabetes," I told her. Her poor face froze in that chipper expression. After a few seconds, it was clear that I might have broken her.

"I can't let you in if you don't pick," she finally said with pep.

"Just put us down for dark chocolate."

"Oh, that's perfect." She tapped her pen twice and began writing it down. "Better than perfect. I love it."

"I knew you would."

Allowing her the stereotype was a minor annoyance that greased the wheels of this situation. Besides, my skin color had never been the problem at school. The students here liked safe things because they didn't force you to think. If I had been a two-pumps-and-a-bump, gangsta lean cliché, the other kids would probably love me as much as they did overachieving Asian Julie Chen here.

"And this is?" She glanced up at Ethan with flirty eyes and a flip of the hair.

"Monique's date," he said coldly.

I did a double take. This guy was scoring bonus points with me left and right. Did he think this was a real date? Yeah, right. Stupid thought.

Julie finished writing on a small piece of paper and dropped it into a raffle box on the table next to her.

"Well, Monique and her mysterious date, you're both officially entered for the King and Queen of Candy Land vote."

"My teeth can hardly wait." I grabbed Ethan, and we walked into my sugary nightmare.

"Do you see Victoria anywhere?" I asked.

"No," he said loudly over the music. Then he glanced around the room and nodded subtly to the left. "Jason Wheaton over there is one of our members. So is Lara Kingsley next to the stage. What's our plan?"

"Come with me." I grabbed his hand and pulled him away from the noise, through a set of double doors at the back of the gym that led to the main school building. We walked up the darkened stairwell to the platform between the first and second floor. Moonlight spilled through the tiled windows, splashing light across his face.

"Are we hiding now?" he asked.

"No, smart ass. That music was driving me nuts, and I didn't want to shout our plans at the world."

"So what are we doing?"

"You have to convince the other church members you saw to get out of here."

"I'll try," he said. "But I'm sure my father gave them strict instructions to watch Victoria."

"Lie to them. Say Roman changed his mind. Do whatever it takes."

"What about you?" he asked.

"When she arrives, I'll try to get her alone and convince her to leave this dance early."

"Is engaging her even smart?"

"What else can we do?"

"We just passed a fire alarm." He pointed to the bottom of the stairs. "Let's pull it and send everyone home. Or we could call in a bomb threat."

"No, don't do that." I didn't mean to sound so intense. "Any kind of panic might set her off."

"What exactly is she planning?"

"How should I know?" I told him. "Just deal with the Awakeners. I'll handle her, and make sure you keep your distance. She would've killed Tim yesterday if I hadn't stepped in. Her power grows every time she feeds, and these fools have gone and dressed themselves up as snack cakes. Promise me you'll stay away from her, no matter what."

"Fine, but only if you watch your back too."

"She's my best friend," I told him. "She won't hurt me."

"Don't take this the wrong way, but is she even the person you used to know anymore?"

"Yes," I told him "Or, she was at first, but something happened to her in the last week that changed everything."

"What could've done that?"

"That's what I'm going to find out."

"Just don't assume anything about your friendship. Power

does crazy things to people. I should know. My stepfather wasn't always like this."

I wanted to tell him that Roman Santo was a speck compared to the strength of Victoria and me. Best friends since kindergarten, inseparable since sixth grade, but I couldn't. Deep down, I knew he was right.

"I'll be careful," I told him.

"Then there's just one more thing. Considering the circumstances, I already know this will be one of the worst first dates in all of history. If I die tonight, I don't want to regret anything."

He put a rough hand on my cheek, and he kissed me. At first, the surprise of it left me with the urge to push him back, but his soft lips melted into mine. My stomach exploded in a shockwave of butterfly madness. His scent of soap and cinnamon musk washed over me, and I got lost in him. Then he pulled away too soon, leaving my muscles jittery and my brain dazed.

He stepped back and smiled slightly.

"Uh, that was..." I didn't know what to say. He *did* think this was a real date. "We should do that again. Soon, so don't get yourself killed, okay?"

"I don't plan on it. Now let's go."

We walked back downstairs to the door.

"Go in ahead of me," I told him. "When she arrives, I want to make sure she doesn't see you."

He nodded, opened the doors, and went back into the dance. I waited a few seconds and reached for the handle.

"He was right about one thing," Victoria called out from behind. I spun to see her draped in shadow down the hallway. She started walking toward me. "You shouldn't make assumptions about our friendship anymore."

38

AS VICTORIA WALKED DOWN the hallway, each click of her heels seemed to exude power. Her smoky eye shadow faded out to a reddish hue on her cheeks that matched her lipstick shade, Blood Rose. Two Japanese Sai-shaped letter openers crisscrossed the back of her head, holding a bun in place. Strings of wispy sideburns dangled on either side of her petite neck.

It didn't end there. Her makeup and hair flowed seamlessly with her dark, thin-strapped gown, which shimmered in iridescent shades of forest green with maroon highlights. Breathtaking didn't begin to describe her. Considering the hours it must have taken her to get ready, the odds of me convincing her to abandon her plan and leave early tonight plummeted, especially after she just caught me with Ethan. Still, I had to try to stop her or at least slow her down.

"Victoria, thank god you're here." I planted myself between her and the door that led back to the dance. "I've been trying to reach you all day. Where have you been?"

She walked up to me. "Busy."

Through the walls, the dance remix of Shirley Temple's *On The Good Ship Lollipop* shifted to a chaotic dub step beat. Still, she just glared with those accusing green eyes.

"I just want to talk," I told her.

"I think you've done enough talking for the night, don't you?"

"Why are you acting like this?"

"I don't know," she said. "It's not as if I caught my best

friend slinking around, talking shit about me with some deadbeat."

"Slinking around?" That didn't sound like Victoria at all. It sounded like her father.

"Don't try to deny it," she said. "I saw you with him. I heard everything."

"Good," I told her. "Then you know I wasn't talking bad about you. I'm worried. That's all."

"Maybe I don't want the details of my life broadcast to every sperm donor who wants to contribute to your cause."

"He's here to help us stop Roman, who has gone bat shit crazy, in case you were wondering."

"Just move. You're in my way."

"I don't know what you're planning," I said. "But I can't let you go in there."

"You really think you can stop me?" There was no mistaking the threat in her tone, which felt like a steel blade against my throat.

"No, but last week you were out chasing animals through the forest. This week, you put a kid in the hospital—"

"Screw Tim Donnelly and his football apes. After what they did to Pete, they're lucky I didn't bury them."

"Victoria, it's not your job to punish people. That's what jail is for."

"Are you kidding me right now? You know they're going to get off with a wrist slap for hurting Pete. And why do you care about the assholes at this school anyway? They treat you like the kitchen staff."

"I don't care about them," I told her. "This power is changing you, and not in a good way."

"According to who?"

"Kitchen staff. Deadbeat. Slinking. That sounds like your father talking."

"Don't you ever say that to me again." She brought her hand up just inches from my face. "Got it?"

"What are you going to do? Hurt *me* now?" I refused to flinch from her touch. "Go ahead, prove my point."

She tried to shove me aside. "Just get out of my way."

"I love you too much to do that." I stepped into her path. "I just want my friend back, like she used to be."

"Well, that girl died on the highway. There's only me now."

"That's not true. You were fine last week, and then you changed. Now you're acting like your dad. The one person you claim to despise most."

"Who cares if I sound like him?" She dismissed me with a look. "He won't be saying much anymore."

My heart raced. "What did you do?"

"He was the only person around besides my driver, and I needed a ride tonight."

"Is he alive?" I demanded.

"Relax. Daddy always said that a person's bite should match their bark, so I made him pull out his own teeth with pliers." Her smirk chilled my blood. "Now he can only whimper like a good boy."

"Have you lost your freaking mind?"

"Don't give me that. You know my father has blood on his hands." She motioned to the gym. "And these jerks tore open Pete's head. You want to know what I'm doing here? Tonight, justice will be served."

"Victoria, can't you see this power is taking control of you?"

"I *see* just fine thanks to my gift. Here in our school, the strong don't just prey on the weak. They try to break their souls, except tonight, oops, somebody changed the rules. For once, they're going to know how it feels."

"Hurting the students here won't solve anything. They're not all evil."

"After what they've done to you, how can you say that?"

"If our friendship means anything to you, if I mean anything to you, don't do this. Let's just leave."

She paused, and I knew that I'd reached her on some level.

"Please," I said. "For me."

"Fine, I'll leave right now, on one condition. Prove to me that they're worth saving."

"How can I do that?"

"Easy. We're going to play the game of lot."

"What the hell is that?"

"Abraham was set on a task to find one righteous person in the city in Sodom. When he couldn't, God destroyed it."

"You mean Lot from the Bible?" I couldn't believe it. Now she was quoting Old Testament references, just like her father.

"You're going to have to show me that these people can be redeemed," she said. "So we're going to walk through that gym right now. If we can make it to the parking lot without any of them demeaning you or treating you like trash, they'll have earned a second chance."

"That's insane. I can't stop them from being jerks."

"That's the deal," she said. "Entrance to exit. Prove to me that those people have more to contribute to this world than hate crimes and date rape cocktails. Otherwise..."

What could I do? Even if I wanted to stop her, Victoria could drop me in a second if she wanted. One straight shot through the gym and this nightmare could be over. That might be the best odds I could get to end the night safely.

"You can't talk to anyone or egg them on," I told her. "We walk straight out those doors, and we don't stop until we reach your house."

She made a zipping motion over her lips.

"Then let's go." I braced myself, turned, and opened the door to reveal a party that had doubled in size since I'd left. Standing room only. Worse than that, Alexis Hall stood just ten feet from us. She'd tanned and dressed in a yellow short dress with white lace fingerless elbow gloves. Her gorgeous Barbie outfit came complete with makeup, fabulous shoes, and a funky candy purse. Bitchy fake smile sold separately.

"It looks like you have your work cut out for you," Victoria whispered in my ear.

Then she plowed forward.

39

AS I FOLLOWED VICTORIA back into the dance, I knew we needed to move fast. Dawn Maxwell noticed us first. Her jaw actually dropped. After that, the vibe of the room changed. One by one, the other students began to glare at us as if we were carting a wheelbarrow full of dead Munchkins through their chipper Land of Oz. All the while, Alexis kept smiling at us.

Just one negative comment from any of these fools would be enough to set Victoria off. I grabbed her hand and started to pull her through the crowd.

"Monique." Alexis walked up with two of her senior minions. They stood between us and the exit. "I've been looking for you everywhere."

Maybe Victoria's sense of morality had gotten twisted, but she'd been right about one thing. The wealthiest, prettiest sharks in this school didn't just prey on the weak. They grouped together to devour anyone who didn't fit in, and I could feel a bleached slut feeding frenzy brewing.

"Don't worry, Alexis," I told her. "We're leaving right now."

"Why would you do that?" she asked. "You and Victoria both look so beautiful."

Yeah, anyway. Dark Victoria and me, the pseudo-steampunk girl, belonged here never.

"I'm not feeling well," I told her.

"You can't leave yet. We haven't even announced the King and Queen of Candy Land."

"I think you deserve to win," I told her without sarcasm.

Maybe this dance wasn't my thing, but it was impressive, and an ego stroke just might get rid of her. "Seriously, this place looks amazing."

"Well, yes, it does take a certain *artistic* eye to pull something like this off," she said. "But I've always had a gift for these things."

Victoria danced from heel to heel. She was clearly on the verge of popping.

"Entrance to exit," I leaned over and whispered to her. "That was the deal." Then I turned back to Alexis. "Good luck with everything tonight."

I tried to step past them.

"Don't go," one of her cheerleader minions said.

"Yeah, don't go yet," pinhead number two piped in. "Just stay a few minutes longer."

What the hell were they up to? Guilt by association was a mofo. Just talking to Monique the Dreary these days could destroy anyone's popularity. Speak with me long enough, and even Alexis Hall would be shunned, basted, and barbecued faster than a naked Wiccan at a Salem clambake. Whatever her stupid plan was, Victoria and I needed to be long gone before she launched it. Maybe I was going about this the wrong way.

"You know what," I told her. "You're right. We will stick around."

"I promise you won't be disappointed," she said with a gleam in her eye.

"We're going to get some air first." I grabbed Victoria's hand. "We'll be right back."

"Strange," she said. "That's exactly where we were going too."

Son of a bitch. Victoria stalked quietly beside me to the exit. She was clearly fuming, but true to her word, she didn't act out. Alexis and her girls followed close behind us. We reached the side door of the gym, opened it, and stepped outside. The freezing air in my lungs had never felt so good. I'd done it. We'd reached the exit.

That's when I saw Jake Cohen standing in front of us. When he wasn't lifting weights and guzzling creatine, he spent his days sexually harassing middle school girls. He nodded to Alexis and then backed away.

"Oh look." She pointed to a row of cars.

Under the glare from the football field's stadium lights, four more muscled douchebags wearing blue-and-white letterman jackets were huddled together around a vehicle. Tim Donnelly was probably still hospitalized from his bee stings, and Derek Jones wasn't here either, but I realized two of those guys had been the ones who attacked Pete and I in the cafeteria. Nuggets of breakaway glass scraped and crunched under their feet. Christ, that was Ethan's car!

"Don't mind them," Alexis said. "They're just taking out the trash."

At the sound of her voice, all four guys backed up to reveal Ethan. He'd been stripped naked in this freezing cold, laid out on his back, and tied with rope to the hood of his El Camino. Blood was smeared everywhere. His car door windows had been shattered.

"What have you done?" I shouted and charged over to him. I tried to shove the goons back, but they barely budged. "Get away from him, you idiots."

Bruises lined Ethan's ribcage, as if they'd kicked him repeatedly. His forehead and face had been beaten bloody. The misspelled words *Satons bitch* had been written in magic marker on his chest. I felt his neck for a pulse. He was still alive.

"Oh no, it looks as though nobody wants you here

anymore," Alexis said. "Or you, Victoria. Maybe you both should find a school more suited to tolerate your kind."

Then she and the rest of those assholes went back inside the dance. I untied the ropes on Ethan's hands.

"Victoria, help me," I said and put one of his arms around my neck. "We have to get him to a hospital now."

He clutched his ribs, which must have been broken. His bloody nose too. It poured like a spout over his chest.

"They came at me," he slurred with swollen cheeks. "From behind."

"It's okay," I said. "Save your energy."

I glanced up. Victoria stood in front of us. Her dress rippled in the cool breeze. Her chrome Sai hairpins gleamed in the light.

"I tried to warn you," she said. "They'll never learn."

"No." I pointed at her. "We made it outside. That was the deal."

"Sorry. That was their last chance."

She turned and walked back into the dance.

"Victoria, wait." I finally managed to get Ethan off the hood.

With his arm over my shoulder, I leaned him against his car, trying not to look at and touch his nakedness.

"Stop her," he told me.

"I'm not leaving you here."

"I've been through worse." His cough looked painful. He leaned down and spit out some blood. Then he picked up his torn clothing. "Go before it's too late. I'll get dressed and meet you inside."

"I'm not leaving you out here alone. What if you have internal bleeding?"

"I'm fine." When I didn't move, he said, "Just how long do you think she needs to murder every kid at that dance?"

He was right. I had to stop her. If Victoria killed anyone tonight, I'd never get back the girl I lost on that frozen highway.

"Here." I handed him my cell phone. "Get help."

Then I turned and ran for the door.

40

I RUSHED INSIDE THE GYM, but I couldn't find Victoria through the haze of the DJ mist and candy props. Adding to the confusion, dozens of Mylar helium balloons had just been released. Instead of racing up to the ceiling, they'd been weighted to balance gravity, giving the students something to bat around. On the highest seat of the blue bleachers, I spotted Mrs. Hall in her trademark white-collar blouse. She seemed to be scanning the dance for trouble. I began climbing up the seat steps.

"Monique," she said as I reached the top. "What happened? Are you hurt?"

I realized Ethan's blood still spattered my chest, and for a brief moment, I wanted Alexis to pay for what she did. That idea passed quickly when I realized that tonight she just might.

"It was just a nosebleed," I said, which Mrs. Hall clearly didn't believe. I adjusted my strapless dress to cover more of the blood "Have you seen Victoria?"

"What is this about?"

"We had a fight. I need to talk to her."

"I am so sorry. I knew that you were having difficulty this year, but I never imagined how deep it went. I just wanted to help."

Kill me now. How this kitten meme do-gooder had ever given birth to Alexis was beyond me. Who was the father? Caligula?

"We don't have time for this," I said. "Have you seen her?"

"Isn't that her down there?" She pointed.

Below, Victoria strolled onto the dance floor alone. Her dress shimmered in the flashing lights. With odd rhythmic steps, she stalked through the crowd, which parted anxiously around her. She smiled up at me and headed toward the stage.

"Victoria, stop," I shouted over the music, but she either couldn't or wouldn't hear me.

Instead, she touched the cheek of a freshman girl, who stepped back in fear. Then she grabbed Jeff Dyson's hand and rubbed her forefinger and thumb together with a pout, as if he were a dirty, unsuitable thing. She must have mastered feeding because no one seemed to feel the jolt of her touch. With each swipe though—from Jenna Swanson to Chad Grimes—her hips swayed to the music more, until she finally ended with a twirl, which flared out her dress.

"The students are in danger," I told Mrs. Hall. "We have to get them out of the gym quietly without causing a panic."

"Are you sure?" she asked.

"See those two?" I pointed at the kids Ethan had singled out for me. "They're with the Awakeners Church."

"Here?" she said. "At our school?"

"I think they're going to try something. Just start moving the students outside now. Try to get them to go home, and let the other teachers know."

"Okay." She was already heading away.

I moved down the bleachers as quickly as my heels and skirt would allow. This dress, yeah, worst fashion choice in the history of man.

Victoria walked on the main stage into the brilliant lighting. The crowd moved up to the front. She grabbed the wireless microphone from the DJ, who pulled down his headset and faded out the music. For a long moment, she stared out at the students, who had fallen silent.

"Now that I'm here," she finally said over the PA. "We can begin the real party."

The hushed students didn't speak. Above, a few balloons that had broken free of their anchors skittered across the gym's high ceiling.

"I came back from the dead for this shit," Victoria shouted into the microphone. "And this is the best you can do?"

Thunderous applause ripped through the gym, complete with hog whistles.

"That's better." Victoria motioned behind herself. "In honor of the sugary festivities, I think we should name the Queen of Candyland. We all know it's going to be Alexis Hall, so let's just bring her out."

She clapped with the microphone in her hands, which produced punching thuds through the speakers. Alexis appeared behind her on stage. In jerked, stiff movements, she stepped forward with her knees and arms barely bent. Giant Raggedy Ann dots had been painted on her cheeks. Her fingers and thumbs on both hands were pointed forward like a doll's too. Her yellow dress and white lace elbow gloves seemed ablaze under the spotlights. She took center stage with her legs spread, arms pointed outward like Da Vinci's Vitruvian man.

"Here she is, folks," Victoria said to more cheering. "We used to call her Lexi back in grade school. Sadly, there's really nothing left of value under that pretty plastic skin. Isn't that right, Lexi?"

"Oh, yes," Alexis grunted the words. "I'm empty and soulless."

"Very true." Victoria nodded in agreement. "She makes a pretty doll to play with though, wouldn't you agree, North Hill High?"

Most of the boys catcalled and stomped their feet. Even

some girls cheered. Several teachers raced from the hallway in back, clearly on a mission to shut this down.

"I see you have fans." Victoria picked a piece of lint off of Alexis's shoulder. "Who wants to come up here and play with Lexi Hall the Sexy Flexi-Doll? I know I do."

Victoria gently pushed her head to the side. When she removed her hand, Alexis's neck remained tilted over one shoulder, arms still outstretched. Only her wild blinking eyes gave away the fact that she was alive.

"What are you girls doing?" Mrs. Hall sounded horrified from beside the stage. "Both of you come down from there now."

"Adults." Victoria shook her head with disappointment. "Always trying to kill my buzz. Tell you what, anybody over the age of eighteen who hears my voice, go home and forget this night ever happened."

Unbelievably, every teacher turned and headed for the front doors, Mrs. Hall included. A few students and their dates did as well. Some of the remaining kids glanced around nervously, as if they weren't sure if they were being punked.

"Now that they're gone, we can have some real fun," Victoria said. "Who wants to play with Lexi?"

Everybody screamed.

I reached the foot of the stage and shouted, "Victoria, stop this."

"Speaking of buzz kills." Her amplified voice made mine seem insignificant. "It appears my best friend here wants us to quit this nonsense. Do you all think that's a good idea?"

"No," everyone shouted at once. Several people booed and hit those Mylar balloons toward me.

"Anyway." She turned her attention back to the crowd. "It sounds as though we need some incentive. Lexi, why don't you help them out?"

In awkward Barbie movements, Alexis took off her underwear. They fell to the stage and she stepped one leg out of them. Screw reasoning with Victoria. A shot of my pepper spray keychain in her face would kick some sense into her. I crept around the back of the stage riser.

"If you losers aren't going to join in," Victoria said. "I'm going to have to prime the pump."

Out front, the same four meatheads in letterman jackets who had jumped Ethan climbed up onto the stage. They formed a line. All of them had blank stares. Victoria stumbled just a bit, not enough for anyone to notice, but I did. Controlling this many people was clearly taking a toll on her power. Maybe I could wear her out somehow.

"Now, I know you boys have an awful struggle with those opposable thumbs." Victoria touched each of the guys, clearly feeding from more of their energy. "Here's a little help unwrapping our new toy."

She unzipped the side of Alexis's dress.

I snuck behind the DJ. A few people noticed me and began to point. It was now or never. I flipped off the lid and raised my pepper spray.

"Drop it," Victoria said without turning to face me, and my hand went limp. The spray fell to the stage. She lowered her microphone and turned to face me. "Monique, I already told you I can see you in the dark, with my eyes closed, or even behind my back."

"Victoria, stop this now," I said. "They're going to rape her."

"What are you talking about? Lexi Hall the Flexi Doll always wants more. Isn't that right?"

"I love it." Alexis choked on her own tears. Her neck was still tilted.

"I think we should make her a star tonight." Victoria

turned to her audience and said into the mic, "Well, get your cameras out, bitches. This film isn't going to shoot itself."

More than a dozen people whipped out their cellphones. I couldn't believe it. No wonder Alexis was such a colossal bitch. Even her so-called best friends were giggling.

"Victoria, if you do this, I'll never speak to you again," I told her. "I won't even recognize you."

"Who cares?" she said away from the mic. "I can always create more friends."

"I'll tell everyone what you are. Do you hear me? I'll tell them you did this."

"Go ahead. You know what they'll say. Poor Monique is just looking for attention because her crazy mother abandoned her. Time to up her meds too."

"What the hell is wrong with you?" I demanded. It was one thing to hear that crap from Alexis, but Victoria's slur pierced my soul. "When did you start acting like these jerks?"

That's when it hit me. When *did* she start acting like the other students here? Twenty minutes ago, she'd been Carl Malakoff's creepy protégé, right after she fed off of him. Now she was treating me like everyone else at school did because— she'd just fed off of them.

All this time, I'd assumed that she'd been borrowing people's energy to live, even their emotional state, but the truth was worse. One by one, the pieces fell into place. The animal deaths and Principal Rademacher. My expulsion hearing. The bees.

Victoria's personality had shifted every single time she'd taken in somebody else's life force because she absorbed parts of their personality too. Now, after her stroll across the dance floor, she was brimming with alcohol-fueled teen sex lust, and this was the result.

I had to get her out of here. But how could I stop her?

During the bee attack, I slapped her, and that had done the job. She'd never let me get that close to her, though. A loud noise might distract her long enough to get Alexis out of here, but it couldn't be just any noise. What was the loudest thing here? Ethan had been right all along. I just hoped that he made it inside by now.

"Let the games begin," Victoria said.

"Wait," I shouted. "I get first crack at her."

"Don't play with me." She spun around and eyed me suspiciously. "My heart can't take it."

"If anyone deserves to make Alexis Hall pay, it's me. Give me the microphone."

Victoria's eyes widened. She hugged me like a TV evangelist who had just found a bushel of converts. Then she handed the mic over.

"Ethan, if you're out there," I said over the PA. "You were right before. Pull it."

Then I tossed the microphone out into the crowd in front of the speakers. Its thunk on the hardwood floor resonated the woofers under the stage. Immediately, it began feeding back. The subsonic hum roared louder, until a high-pitched squeal sounded as though it would blow up the speakers. Louder and higher it went. Victoria flinched and then covered her ears with two fingers.

Instantly, Alexis collapsed to her hands and knees. She looked disoriented. I raced over, grabbed her hand, and led her offstage. The fire alarm went off. Ethan must have heard me and bought us more time.

I got Alexis outside and said, "Go home. Lock your doors."

"What happened?" she asked through tears. "What was that?"

"Now," I shouted.

Seconds later, the rest of the students began filtering out. I raced back inside to look for Victoria, but she was nowhere to be seen.

"Monique, there you are." Ethan limped up to me. His tattered suit was drenched with his blood. His face was mangled. "The Awakeners just took Victoria."

"They kidnapped her?"

"No," he said. "I think she went willingly. They're having that ceremony in her honor tonight."

"We have to go there now," I told him. "Before she feeds from your father or any of the Awakeners."

"What's going on?"

"There's no time," I told him. "I'll explain on the way."

41

AS ETHAN DROVE DOWN Pickens Highway, I tried to calm my nerves, but I had no clue of what to do when we got to the compound. After I helped Alexis Hall escape the dance, it didn't take a genius to predict that Victoria would be furious with me. Roman would use the divide between us to get in her head, and all bets were off if she fed from him. I had to get her away from the Awakeners by any means necessary before Roman's venom could infect her soul.

"Can't we go faster?" I tried not to look at the cuts on Ethan's face. Every part of him looked raw. "We're running out of time."

"Almost there." He turned off the highway onto a cracked asphalt street that immediately gave way to mud puddles and slush.

We drove farther on the broken frontage road, which sloped down until the street above us disappeared from view.

"Where are you going?" I asked. "The compound is at least a mile from here."

"My father has guards posted at the front gate now." He parked the car and switched off his headlights. All around, darkness swallowed us. Only the glow of his dashboard provided any light. "We have to sneak in the back way if we want to get to Victoria unnoticed."

"Okay," I said. "Where's the back way?"

"Straight ahead, on foot." He pointed at the thin path that led into the towering trees in front of us. In the darkness, the craggy bark on the densely packed tree trunks looked slick and black, like it had been sprayed with motor oil. Above, needled branches blotted out most of the full moon and starlight.

"Are you crazy?" I asked. "You want to go in there at night?"

"I know these woods."

As far as I was concerned, Jason Voorhees, American Mary, Jigsaw, Michael Meyers, Samara *The Ring* girl, and Norman Bates were all sharpening their knives in that forest, waiting patiently for my black ass to go tiptoeing through it.

"I've seen this movie," I said. "It doesn't end well for me."

"Don't worry. I can protect you."

"No offense, but you can barely stand," I told him. "Besides, we don't have time for a hike. If Victoria takes the energy of just one person from the church, we can kiss all of this goodbye."

"She's been feeding for the last two weeks. A few more times won't make her that much stronger."

"You don't understand. She's not just taking energy from people."

"What do you mean?" He clutched his ribs, reached underneath the bench seat, and found a black hoodie.

"The first time she fed off of me, I wanted to get to my expulsion hearing to avoid getting kicked out of school. She showed up that night on a mission to save me from getting expelled. The next time I saw her, after she fed off dozens of animals, I found her wandering barefoot, hunting behind her house."

"You're not making sense. What does that have to do with my father?"

"Everything. Don't you see? The mob outside the school amped her personality because those people were amped. After Principal Rademacher, she turned petty like he is. The beehive colony made her violent, and you saw what happened tonight after she fed off of the sex-crazed idiots at my school."

"Actually, that makes sense." He sounded surprised.

"It does?"

"She was technically dead in the hospital. Big sections of her brain tissue are gone. With her new psychic ability, she must be using other people to fill in the gaps."

I'd never thought about it that way. I remembered the antique wheelchair that Lita had used the day Victoria had come home after the accident. When she'd spoken her first coherent words after feeding off of me, I'd assumed that her brain had healed somehow, rewired, but had she really come back? What if she'd just filled in the gaps of her personality and life from my memories? Was she even Victoria anymore or just a ghost in my machine?

"What do you want to do?" he asked.

"She isn't psychotic. Her condition can be controlled if she doesn't take in the wrong source of energy."

"Okay, so what are the wrong sources?" His eyes widened. "You mean someone like my father."

"Imagine what would happen if you combined his desire to *cull the herd* with her power to actually make that happen."

"We have to call the police," he said.

"And tell them what? She went with the Awakeners willingly."

"Sheriff Acosta might listen to me," he said. "I live up here."

"I already tried to reason with him. Next time, he'll probably lock us up. For better or worse, we're the only ones who can handle Victoria now."

"How can we possibly stop her alone, though? You saw what she did back in the gym. I wouldn't believe it if I hadn't been there."

"Since the accident, the only time she acted like herself was after she fed off of me," I told him. "We have to get her to take in my energy."

"How are we going to do that?"

"I don't know. Piss her off until she attacks, I guess."

"That's your big plan?" he said.

"What choice do we have?"

"I don't know. Smack her over the head with a rock, throw her in my car, and drive away."

"Aren't you supposed to be a genius or something?" I asked, even though my idea back at the gym to pepper-spray her hadn't been much smarter. "She can see in the dark. If we stay outside the rally area's clearing, she'll sense me even when the other members of the church can't see us. If she notices me first, I'll at least get a few words with her before your father can kick us out. That's when I can try to make her angry enough to come after me. Just tackle her or something if she starts to take too much life from me."

"That plan sucks."

"Do you have a better one?" I asked. He didn't speak because there were no good options here. "I wish there was another way."

"Well, no matter what, we can't go through the front gate," he said. "We'll never even make it past the guards to see Victoria. Our only hope is this back trail."

I glanced at it again and shivered.

"You'd better know what you're doing," I told him.

"Trust me." He handed over the black hoodie. "I brought clothes just in case. There's an extra pair of sneakers and sweatpants under the seat below you. You need to change out of your dress."

"In front of you?"

"You saw me naked," he said.

"Yeah, covered in blood and bruises. I thought you were dead."

"If we're going to get there in time, I can't have your skirt and heels slowing us down." He unbuttoned his dress shirt and took it off. When I didn't move, he said, "We may end up running for our lives tonight."

Good point.

"Turn your head," I told him, but he'd already started putting on a black sweatshirt of his own.

Against my better instincts, I began changing my clothes to get ready for this insanity. Entering a dark forest at night in an attempt to save my best friend from psychotic hill people. How had it come to this?

For the stupidity of this move alone, the Hollywood horror gods would have seen to my death, but Victoria needed me. I knew how to save her, and I wouldn't let Roman Santo have her, not as long as there was any breath left in my body.

I finished dressing and said, "Let's go before I have time to think about this."

Ethan nodded. We got out of the car and hurried down the cold path, into the gaping mouth of the woods.

42

*D*ESPITE HIS INJURIES AND THE darkness, Ethan silently navigated the rocky trail that led into the Awakeners camp. I was a different story. Branches clawed at my black sweatshirt around every turn. Pine needles constantly crackled underfoot, until I was certain that every jackbooted church crazy within earshot was already tracking us. *If karma is listening tonight, please let us get away from this place safely with Victoria.* That's all I asked. Let a couple of insignificant specs of dust in the mighty universe blow on through this forest, and we could call it even for the rest of time.

"We're here," Ethan whispered.

He reached back to help me climb up a cliff composed of gnarled roots and boulders. Mr. Grab Hands *accidentally* touched more than he should have, but I let it ride. If we lived through the night, there'd be plenty of time to let him know that one kiss didn't give him a free pass to round the bases. I wanted a serious date, and it better not be some weird hill person ritual either.

Above on the ledge, the night breeze shocked me with its warmth. A hundred yards ahead, a roaring fire seemed to silhouette the entire forest. Flames completely engulfed the camp's main clearing.

"Don't worry." Ethan leaned down next to me. "They just lit the statue to start the ceremony."

"They're going to burn down the forest."

"I promise they won't."

"Uh huh. Sure."

"I know the church's beliefs seem stupid to you," he said. "But they aren't insane."

"Scientologists believe that Xenu, the overlord of the Galactic Federation, brought aliens to earth and packed them inside volcanoes."

"What does that have to do with anything?" he asked.

"Those people are stupid," I told him. "Your father is dangerous."

"Just remember, the other members aren't like him. They might look and act strange, but they won't hurt you if you don't threaten them."

Me threaten them? Please. Despite that egghead brain of his, too much alone time in the hills cuddled up with his bong had done a number on his common sense.

"I only want to get Victoria out of here before your father infects her," I said. "So try to keep him on a leash."

"I will." He grabbed my hand. "Let's go."

We crept forward, low to the ground. At least in the new firelight, I could see enough to move quieter now. We reached the edge of the clearing behind the remains of a fallen pine, which crumbled into soft termite splinters when I accidentally brushed it. I peeked over the log and froze, unsure of how to respond to what I saw.

Maybe eighty church members formed a circle around the fifty-foot Burning Man-Zilla sculpture. Some danced around the inferno and drank. Most stared up at the white-hot human torso, lost in the spectacle, looking like teary-eyed arsonists who'd just filled their first gasoline container.

Even from the safety of the tree line, the heat against my cheeks forced me to turn away temporarily. With black smoke pouring from the sculpture's eyeholes and mouth, the giant twisted man appeared to scream out in fiery pain. Its hands of molded rebar clutched its metal head. The machines attached as its skin sizzled and popped in the toxic fumes.

"It'll all burn soon," a shirtless hippie man shouted and splashed a jig with his bare feet in the steaming river of melted snowpack that poured from the blaze. "Clean it all away."

The hippie grabbed the shoulder of a buzz-cut, desert-veteran-looking guy, who nodded and locked arms. Sitting behind them on the wooden riser, a woman dropped her shirt completely and began breastfeeding her infant in plain view of everyone. Barely hidden beyond the opposite tree line, an old couple was having sex. Disgusting ick factor bonus, doggie-style.

A toddler ran around unsupervised, wearing only a cloth diaper. She picked up a computer mouse from a pile of old tech and threw it toward the fire. Several adults laughed at the small distance. One grizzly, slit-eyed man leaned over and tossed the item into the blaze for kindling. The little girl, who couldn't have been older than two, began clapping to more laughs.

"What the hell?" Ethan whispered with wide eyes.

"I thought you told me to keep an open mind," I said quietly.

"Not for this. My stepfather's finally lost it."

"Truth be told, I was expecting worse." A stone altar and robes. Maybe some wicker masks. "Isn't this what you guys normally do up here?"

"Of course not." His whisper sounded defensive. He hid back behind the stump, so I followed his lead. "The children shouldn't be out here. Not to mention Lisa and Rick across the way."

"Yeah, I saw them." Even the fire couldn't burn that image from my mind. "Do you think Victoria is causing this?"

"No," he said. "The church is coming unhinged. We have got to get her out of here now."

"I know, but where is she?"

He glanced over the log and pointed quickly. A spray of sparks erupted from the fire, blurring my view with waves of heat, but there was no mistaking her standing next to Roman, glaring directly at me.

Twenty feet from her, a few military types faced the main highway beyond the barbed-wire fence. Probably searching for us. At least she didn't try to warn them.

"We have to do this now," I said. "While the others are distracted. It might be our only chance to get close enough to speak to her."

Ethan nodded. With my heart racing, I stood and walked into the clearing. He followed behind. Initially, none of the church members noticed us. As we reached the middle of the group, an avalanche of melted plastic crashed down from the sculpture's elbow, drawing everyone's attention our way.

"What is this?" a woman beside me shouted. I glanced over to find Lady Milk Pump finally opting for modesty by covering herself with a towel. "You can't be here."

The crowd instantly roiled and swarmed around us.

"I was invited." I shoved my way past a barrage of outstretched hands.

"She's with me," Ethan shouted, which caused a few people to step back.

That gave me enough space to push through to Victoria, who still stared at me without blinking. Her eye shadow—which appeared as if she'd been crying soot—made it impossible to tell whether she'd already fed off of Roman's energy. I suspected if she had, everyone would already be dead. Darwin stayed by her side, clearly protecting her. The wolf's eyes never strayed from me.

Roman's eyes, on the other hand, were two chips of jagged glass. His mission had never been more transparent. To hurt me in ways that even I couldn't imagine.

"Miss Robinson." He stepped forward with his hand on the knife holster on his belt. The flickering firelight cast shadows across his chin and nose. "After what happened tonight, you're not welcome here anymore."

"I only want to talk to Victoria." I held my palms up. "Then I'll leave and never come back."

"Didn't I warn you about the consequences?"

"Yes, and I'm sorry I had to come here like this," I said loudly so that every one of his followers could hear me too. "I didn't mean to interrupt your party. Will you allow Victoria to speak with me?"

His cheek twitched. Good, suck on that catch-22. Would he let her talk to me and appear weak to his followers, or would he try to ban her from speaking to me? Best of luck trying to control Victoria. He might as well attempt to put out that fire by pissing on it.

"This is her night," he finally said. "If she wants to hear you out after you betrayed her, then so be it." He turned to her. "Do you want to speak with Miss Robinson?"

"We have nothing to talk about," she said.

"There you have it." He motioned to the guards at the front gate.

They grabbed my arms.

"Get your hands off her." Ethan rushed forward, but three more Awakeners grabbed him too.

"Victoria, listen to me." I struggled to break free. "He killed that reporter you brought to my hearing."

"No one wants to hear your lies. Get her off our sacred land." Roman shoved a finger in Ethan's face. "Him too. You aren't one of us anymore."

A deep engine rumbled on the highway above us. A set of headlights barreled over the ridge onto the main driveway that led to the compound. A vehicle cloaked behind branches raced down the road, popping rocks and throwing gravel. It sped through the front gates and slid to a halt just feet from us. That was my truck. The guards who had been holding me let go.

Dad got out of the vehicle with his shotgun aimed forward. Several Awakener women picked up the children and scurried off into the forest, while the armed men aimed their automatic rifles back at my father. Other cult members in the tree line began closing in on us like a military squad.

Don't threaten them, Ethan had said. *And they won't hurt you.*

"Dad, what are you doing?" I demanded. "You have to go now."

"How did I know I'd find you up here?" he said to me. "You and that boy really screwed up this time. Do you know what time it is?"

"You drove here because of my stupid curfew?"

"I heard about what happened at the school. You swore to me that you'd never come up in these hills again. Get in the damn car."

"Dad, put the gun down." I turned to Roman, who didn't budge from the weapon aimed in his direction. "He doesn't know what he's doing. Just let us leave."

"Mr. Robinson." Roman smiled like a salesman, peddling rain to a drought-starved town. "Normally we love having visitors, but tonight is a closed occasion."

"Stay out of it, Santo. This is family business. Girls, get in the car."

"Monique can leave, but Victoria is with us now," Roman said. The towering flames behind him shifted in a spray of sparks that seemed to accentuate his point.

"I won't say it again," Dad said through gritted teeth.

"I just explained that you have only one child here, Mr. Robinson. I won't repeat myself either."

"Apparently, you can't see too good," Dad told him. "Victoria is mine too. I've wiped more snot from that child and bandaged more skinned knees than her own worthless father. Unless you want to spring a leak, I suggest you step away from both of my daughters."

"That's too bad," Roman said. "I didn't want this to end ugly."

I glanced over, and that's when I noticed Victoria. She couldn't seem to take her eyes off of Dad. The rage on her face evaporated. In that instant, she was back. At least some piece of her, and for maybe the first time, I saw her in a new light.

Despite all my efforts, I hadn't been able to reach her, the girl who had more talent, beauty, and balls than anyone I'd ever met. The girl who'd been given everything at birth except a father who loved her. But she did have someone who loved her like that, and I watched her realize it for the first time.

I didn't care if it was dangerous to touch her. I knew she wouldn't hurt me, so I walked forward, reached out, and grabbed her hand. A few seconds passed, but I felt no jolt. Her eyes welled up, and I hugged her.

"We love you." I pulled away. She finally quit looking at Dad and focused on me. "No matter what, we can figure this out. You're not just my best friend. You're my sister, and we're going home. That's final."

She nodded and took a step toward our truck.

"Victoria," Roman said loudly. "Don't listen to their lies. We're your family now."

"Let us leave peacefully, Santo," Dad said. "And we won't press charges."

"This world will burn to the ground, and you'll die in it." Roman began walking toward us.

"Get back." Dad cocked his shotgun and raised it at Roman's chest.

A gunshot rumbled the hills. Christ. What had Dad done? If he hurt any of them, we'd all be buried in the back hills before morning. I searched around. None of the Awakeners fell down. Roman wasn't hit either.

Screw this. We needed to get out of here. I snatched Victoria's wrist, turned, and began to pull her toward our truck. Dad stared at us with a shocked look on his face. He breathed heavily. That's when I saw the dime-sized hole in his white t-shirt. He clutched his chest. Blood seeped through his fingers, and he fell to his knees.

"Hold your fire," Ethan shouted and flailed his arms.

"Daddy, no." I ran to him. He collapsed onto his back, so I tried to hold up his head. I turned around and shouted, "Call an ambulance."

Nobody moved. They just stared at Victoria, who breathed rapidly. A silent rage seemed to scream from every molecule in her twitching body, until it found a foothold in her throat. She released an inhuman screech, infinitely more terrifying than the one she'd let loose in the cafeteria. I knew what was coming.

"Victoria, don't do it," I said through my tears. "Just call an ambulance."

"It would be better if you left now," she told me, and then turned to face the other church members.

Another ball of fire exploded from the statue. With her fists clenched, she began stalking toward Roman with Darwin moving silently beside her.

43

SOMEBODY HELP US," I shouted and searched through the confusion. Awakeners scrambled in every direction. Even Ethan had disappeared, leaving me alone to fend for my dad. Coward.

Victoria continued forward, clearly oblivious to anyone but Roman. Towering above the chaos, the statue fire shifted into a white-hot fury, as if she controlled it with her will alone. Roman must have sensed the danger because he shrank from her toward the wooden stage riser. I couldn't worry about them now.

On his back, Dad stared up at me with terrified eyes. I tried to keep pressure on his wound, but his blood leaked between my fingers.

"Go," he said between gasps.

"Shhh." I fumbled for my phone with one hand. No service. "I have to sit you up. We need to get you down to the hospital."

He gathered what was left of his strength, pointed toward the road, and tried to shout, "Leave me."

His voice came out barely above a whisper. He began breathing rapidly, and then his body went limp.

"Dad." I tapped his face gently. I couldn't try CPR. Not with that hole in his chest. "Stay awake. Please god, don't do this."

The shifting winds felt like a hairdryer against my face, laced with the scent of wretched black smoke, but I only felt cold inside.

All my life, I'd made a point to live in the truth no matter how ugly or painful. It was my weapon against those who'd hurt me. My protection. No matter how vicious others could be, at least I didn't delude myself.

Now, that doubled-edged honesty turned back on me and tore my insides apart. We were too far from civilization, especially with the bullet lodged somewhere near Dad's already damaged heart. I'd never wanted to hide from anything so desperately as I did the truth then, but I wasn't able to lie to myself.

So I sat alone at what might as well have been the end of the world, helplessly watching my Dad die.

Victoria stood with her back to me. She approached Roman, but I didn't care anymore. For once in this sick world, I wanted an evil son of a bitch to get what he deserved. I thought for sure that Darwin would have leapt to his defense. I don't even think she was controlling the wolf, but it had clearly chosen Victoria, the alpha of its pack.

"My child," Roman said as she walked up to him. "I'm sorry it had to come to this."

"No, you're not." She wiped a smudge of dirt from his cheek. "You don't know how to be sorry, but I'll show you."

She snatched his forehead. His arms shot down at his sides, fingers splayed as if an electric current raced from her fingertips into his convulsing body. The bluish veins under his desiccating skin began to throb, and still I didn't care. Even when sections of his cheek disintegrated to reveal his jawbone and connected molars, I only wanted him to suffer more.

His scream transformed into a choking wet sob, until his eyeballs popped into a bloody spray that coated her chest. His back muscles contracted with the force of a bear trap, snapping his spine in the wrong direction. Then he collapsed into a bloody pile.

Victoria's new power radiated off her in waves. Somewhere, hidden in his uncaring cave, God must have taken notice, and he was afraid. New competition had been born.

A tall redheaded man with a surly beard and beer gut charged Victoria with his knife raised. Before he got within ten feet, a blur of fur and teeth tackled the man, tearing bloody chunks from his arm. He barely managed to kick the wolf away for a second, and the man stood to run away.

"Stop," she said to him quietly, and he halted. His muscles shook as he tried to fight her control of his body. "Your heart just can't take this excitement." She made a small gesture with her hand and said, "Now it just gave out."

As if she'd flicked a switch, the man dropped to the ground dead, staring wide-eyed into nothingness. I couldn't believe what I'd just witnessed. She'd killed him with a thought. Nothing more.

Without looking back, Victoria headed toward the edge of the clearing with Darwin at her side. The Awakeners could hide out there all they wanted, but the darkness was her natural hunting ground now. It was too late for them, even if they didn't know it.

Something metallic clicked behind me. I glanced back. Hunched over, Ethan hid behind the bed of our truck, tapping a pocketknife against the taillight to get my attention.

"Is she gone?" he asked.

"You left us," I told him.

"No." He raced over to me and set a first aid kit on the ground. "I went to get help."

"What good can you possibly do with that thing?"

"I didn't go for the kit." He leaned his ear over Dad's mouth to check for breath. "Karen Zimmer is our resident surgeon. She's on her way now. We're going to take him back to the compound's medical bunker. We have blood bags and equipment."

"Are you crazy?" I demanded. "They're the ones who shot him."

"Listen to me." He grabbed my shoulders. "That bullet is either in or near his heart. If we try to drive him down the hill now, he *will* die, so pull yourself together, and let me handle this."

"Okay." I wiped my tears and nodded. "What do you need me to do?"

"You're the only person who can stop Victoria."

"I don't know how. Not anymore, after she just—and your father—"

"Got what he deserved." Ethan stared directly into my eyes. "Monique, she's heading toward the nursery. The other children were there tonight."

No. That toddler girl I'd seen earlier in the diaper. Victoria wouldn't hurt a child, would she? I prayed not, but she'd never gone so far before as she did with Roman, absorbing all of his life energy. That meant his personality too. I had no doubt he wouldn't think twice about killing every person on earth for his cause. I had to stop her.

I stood and chased after Victoria. Once inside the darkened forest, I glanced back at the fire, which dimmed with each step until it only cast long shadows across the dense forest bramble. Then I came face-to-face with Darwin, who gave me a solemn look.

To my left, gunfire erupted. Cries for mercy began bleeding over the top of each other, cut short by shrieks of pain so intense that my stomach felt sick. The wolf turned and padded away from the chaos. I raced toward Victoria. I just hoped that she was controlling people more than she was feeding. That might make her vulnerable. Weak enough to want my energy, which just might flush Roman out of her system.

I ran toward the screams and found another small clearing with a dome bunker entrance. Dead center, Victoria stood in the ghostly moonlight. Roman's blood still covered her chest. At least five bodies that I could see lay scattered about the clearing.

"End it," she said to a man who stood across the clearing.

He slowly held his gun to his own temple. He was fighting her, I could tell, and he was almost winning. Did that mean she'd weakened herself enough? I turned away. A single gunshot echoed through the forest, and his body dropped.

"Victoria, please," I said. "You have to stop this."

For a moment, she just glared at me. Then she swooned and leaned against a massive tree stump in the middle of the clearing.

"Monique," she said. "Help me."

I raced toward her. This was it. I could give her my energy and end this thing.

Gunfire sprayed the ground around me. I ducked and covered my head. One of the guards in camouflage was protecting the bunker entrance. He fired another volley at us and missed. She spun to face him.

"Eat," she said.

The guy dropped to his knees. He raised his automatic weapon above his head and began sucking on the barrel. Before I could turn away, he squeezed the trigger. A flurry of bullets punched out the bottom of his jaw and neck, and he collapsed.

She too fell on the ground. I reached her and pulled up my sleeve to expose my wrist.

"Help," she said, between gasps for air. "I'm dying."

I reached out for her. Then I noticed the small legs just

beyond her, wearing a knee skirt. The legs led to a body hidden behind the tree stump. Oh my god. I recognized those purple sneakers with the charms sewn into them.

I raced around the stump. Tara's lifeless eyes stared up at the stars.

"Jesus." I rushed to her side and held her head in my lap. "Not her. Take me. Take Victoria," I shouted at God. Of course, he couldn't be bothered to hear me.

"Monique," Victoria said, just above a whisper. "I'm—sorry. She came out of nowhere. You—have to believe me."

I didn't dare move. I didn't want to think. There had to be some way out of this. Maybe Victoria could put the energy back in Tara. Bring her to life or something. Just like she had done for herself.

I glanced down at Tara's body. Judging from the remorse in Victoria's eyes, she would have already done that if it were possible. Maybe in some other universe, one that wasn't filled with such pain, Tara could come back to us, jingling and speaking Pig Latin. But that wasn't the world we inhabited.

I wiped my tears. Then I gently closed Tara's eyes. My soul ached, so much so that I didn't think I could go on living like this. In this place, I couldn't rationalize or hide or pretend. This was the end, and I knew what had to be done.

I stood and walked over to Victoria. I kneeled, just out of her reach. She didn't try to beg or fight it. I think she knew too. Maybe some part of her had always known. Those best pieces of her that had defied death to come back to me. Deep down, she had probably always known what it had taken me this long to figure out. Nothing so dangerous could live in this world for very long. I had to make sure that this nightmare ended.

"Stay with me," she said. I could hear the fear in her shaking voice. Roman was no longer part of her personality. "I don't want to be alone...when it happens."

"I'd never leave you."

"I'm scared."

"Honey, you don't need to be," I said. "I don't know many things, but I do know that. You're going to be moving on soon to a much better place than this stupid world."

"Live for me," she said. "Sleep with lots of boys. Be the hugest slut on earth"

I couldn't help but laugh through my tears.

"I will."

"Liar," she whispered quietly, and then she went still.

I don't know how long I sat there after she stopped breathing. Minutes, hours. Did it matter? I would have stayed by her side forever, but this lifetime had other plans.

When I was sure that she was gone, I kissed her forehead.

Then I let her go.

44

Y CHEST FELT TIGHT as I carried the final box of clothing from my bedroom into the barren living room. I made one last visual sweep of the house. Nothing. Nail holes in the drywall and crop circles in the carpet were the only traces that the Robinsons had ever existed here. After everything that had happened, maybe that was for the best. Still, I couldn't shake this sadness all morning, which felt as though I was abandoning Victoria's memory by leaving. I pushed it away. That kind of thinking had no place in me anymore.

Truth was, my best friend never really came back from her car accident on the highway that first night. Everything between now and then had been a dream, or so I tried to tell myself during those dark moments alone when I wanted to hide.

Perhaps one day, I'd come back to North Hills when it didn't hurt so much, but then again, maybe not. Some doors were best left shut. Besides, who would be left to reminisce with me? Alexis Hall? Toothless Carl? Not in this lifetime, honey.

With my foot, I nudged open the front screen door for the last time and walked outside to a pristine morning that was surreal in a creepy Walt Disney way. Victoria was gone. Seemed that someone upstairs should have honored her with a rainstorm or something. Still, I refused to complain. Even though I lost Victoria, the Universe had more than squared the karmic books with me. The screen door opened behind me. Speak of the insufferable devil.

"Hey." Dad walked outside with that box of his college trophies. "You almost forgot these."

"Believe me, I didn't forget." I set my box in the back of the U-Haul. "And you shouldn't be lifting heavy things, either. Do you want to end up back in the hospital?"

"Nonsense." He thunked his work boots down our wooden porch steps. "You can stomp on a Robinson. You can kick a Robinson. Some peckerwoods even tried to burn a Robinson once—"

"Whatever, Dad. You're not indestructible."

"I've got a slug here that says otherwise." He tapped his jacket pocket, where he kept that stupid deformed bullet that the ER doctors removed from his chest.

I almost told him that he was lucky, but I stopped. No reason to elevate his heart rate. Besides, deep down, I needed him to be invincible right now, even if it was only in his own mind.

At the end of the block, Ethan's El Camino rumbled as it turned the corner. He pulled up across the street and got out. Darwin leapt out too and rushed over to meet me.

"Don't take too long." Dad opened the driver's side door of the moving van. "I want to at least reach Knoxville tonight. New Orleans is a straight shot from there."

Then he grunted something at Ethan and nodded. That was probably as close to approval as any boy I brought home could hope for.

Darwin raced forward and nudged my hand for me to pet her, which I did. Of all the things that Roman Santo had done wrong, this wolf was one thing he'd gotten right.

Ethan hugged me, and my vision blurred for a second. His faint green aura shifted to forest hues. I tried to blink it away, but I couldn't. Of course. Victoria couldn't have moved on from this world without leaving me the permanent parting gift of brain damage. I don't know when it happened. Probably during her numerous psychic vampire hits from me. Yeah, and seeing auras and reading emotions? Not particularly useful. Especially for a Robinson. At least I didn't feel her hunger. Yet.

"Hey," Ethan said.

"Hey, yourself." I didn't know what to do with the awkward silence.

Between burying Victoria, keeping my head down to pass the tenth grade, and spending yet another season in St. Agnes Memorial for Dad's recovery, there just hadn't been much time for him.

"So this is it?" he asked. "You guys are really leaving."

"There's nothing left for us here anymore." I realized that insinuated him, so I added, "What I mean is—"

"No, you're right. After I clean up this legal mess, I'm moving too."

"Don't tell me the cops still blame you for what happened?"

"Sheriff Acosta has been helping with that. He worked out a story with the coroner. Something about a forest fire."

"Really?" I asked. Roman's body alone should have been donated to medical science. "They bought that BS?"

"These people will believe any rational explanation so that they can forget and move on with their lives. Still, I have to stay here with the lawyers to break up the church and sell the land."

"Once you're done, come to Louisiana with us. Dad is going to be the foreman there. He can get you a job."

"Yeah." He laughed. "I'm sure your father would love that."

"You'd be surprised. Grumps Robinson even asked me to invite you to dinner last week."

"But you didn't," he said with an air of sadness.

"He was treating me like an adult for once. I didn't want to spoil the moment."

"Yeah." He glanced at the U-Haul truck. "I don't want to spoil anything either, but I will stay in touch."

He put his hand on my cheek and kissed me. Instead of the butterfly mesh of excitement, this time there was only goodbye. He stepped back.

"Call me," I told him, and he nodded.

Who knew if he would? I liked to think so, but too much had happened. To each other, we would always be a reminder of this place. Of what happened to Tara. I guess the rest of the town wasn't alone in their need to move on.

Ethan headed back to his car with Darwin and drove away. Once he'd turned the corner off of our street, I walked to the passenger side of the moving van.

"I'm ready for a good road trip," Dad said through the open window.

My vision blurred, and again I tried to blink it away. No luck. Dad's aura splashed with a bluish tint, which I'd learned over the past few months meant that he was worried about me.

"It's okay." I got into the truck. "I'll be fine."

"Of course, you will." He kissed my cheek. "Are you ready to go?"

Boy, was that ever a loaded question? I only had two options here. Spend the rest of my life looking back or turn the page. When I thought about it like that, it didn't really seem like much of a choice. Sometimes, you have to let go in order to move forward. Besides, I wouldn't let anything get in the way of the promise I made to Victoria.

Live for me, she had said. That's what I intended to do.

I would go to film school. I didn't know how to make that

happen, and I didn't care. I wanted to make horror movies. Maybe I would marry a good man someday and have a family of my own, except I wouldn't leave my daughter for any reason. This was my clean start. A chance to live the life that was robbed from my best friend on that cold, slush highway. The life I had never thought possible.

Live for me.

"I will," I whispered to no one. Then I turned to Dad and said, "Let's go."

THE END

ABOUT THE AUTHOR

Christopher Allan Poe is an author and touring musician from Los Angeles. He writes paranormal fiction, with an emphasis in themes that shed light on social problems for women and children. Read further for an excerpt from his award-winning novel, THE PORTAL, which is now available from Black Opal Books.

To learn more about other upcoming releases and other exciting news, sign up for his mailing list at:

www.CHRISTOPHERALLANPOE.com

ACKNOWLEDGMENTS

No project worth doing exists in a vacuum, and DARK SIGHT is no exception. First, I have to thank my beautiful wife, Brandi. Without you, not only would my writing career have been impossible, but it also wouldn't have meant a damn thing. I am a better man because of you and our new baby. I love you.

In addition, my writing critique group isn't just a collection of talented and hilarious mad geniuses. They are also my family. To Bonnie Hearn Hill, Hazel Dixon-Cooper, John Brantingham, Dr. Dennis Lewis, Judge Dennis Caeton, Eve Hinson, and Kathy Puckett, thank you for all of your input and advice. I am honored to sit at a table of such brilliant minds.

I want to thank Tim and Colleen Crescenti for everything you've done for me and continue to do. Tiger Baby agrees. Thank you to my dad, who first introduced me to writing, and Jeannie Hitt, for believing in me and helping wherever you can. Thank you all for teaching me how to dream.

Mike Logan, you are—and will always be—my brother. This book has you on every page, especially the Star Trek argument. Just so you know, in a heads-up battle, Borg Voyager would knock the snot out of Kirk's Enterprise :)

Finally, special thanks to Lauri Wellington and everyone at Black Opal Books for believing in this project and for running the type of publishing house I'm proud to call home.

If not for all of you, I wouldn't be here, and I'm deeply grateful.

CHRISTOPHER ALLAN POE

THE PORTAL

Cody isn't like other little boys...

1

Vivian woke to an ocean of darkness that filled her lungs to capacity. Frantically, she groped her nightstand. Something banged on the floor. Where was her inhaler? There. She puffed and puffed again, but her short breaths could only take in so much.

Her chest loosened. Exhausted, she lay back. Underneath the splash of raindrops outside, Cody's muffled voice came from the hallway. Her bedroom door creaked open, and a sliver of light blinded her.

"Mommy?" His silhouette clung to the doorknob with one hand. The other dragged Mister Vincent on the floor behind him. "Are you okay?"

"Everything's fine." She lifted her blanket. "Come to bed."

Seconds later, he cuddled against her chest. She breathed deep the scent of baby shampoo. God she needed to be more careful. Just one slip and he would be alone in this world. Then what? Some chemical substitute to fill the void? Crime? Jesus, she would never let it come to that.

"Mommy," he whispered.

"Yes, sweetie."

"Mister Vincent is sorry."

She closed her eyes and prayed for sleep. Although Mister Vincent painted the kitchen walls in shades of peanut butter yesterday, whatever mess lay beyond her door could wait until morning. "It's fine."

"He didn't mean to let him in."

She almost sat up to check. No, everything was locked. The Trenton Security System was armed, and the dead bolts were three feet above the door handles. Well beyond Mister Vincent's reach.

"It was just a bad dream, baby," she said. "Not real."

He sat up on his knees and put his hands on her cheeks.

"Mommy," he said.

"Go to sleep."

"I have to tell you something, but I promised not to say it out loud."

"Fine," she said. "But then you'll lie down."

He nodded, leaned over her, and whispered in her ear, "Daddy's home."

She jumped up and turned on the light. It crashed to the floor. Her car keys! She needed them. They had to get out.

"Where is he? Where did you see Daddy?"

"Ouch," he cried.

She looked down and realized how hard she'd grabbed his shoulders.

"I'm sorry, baby," she said. "I didn't mean it." He lowered his head. "This is really important," she continued. "Like when Mommy needs her inhaler." He nodded. "I need you to tell the truth. Where did you see Daddy?"

"Walking in the trees."

She pulled up the mini blinds and wiped away the condensation on the window with her hand. Their van was parked next to the forest, at least thirty yards from the cabin. She put on her shoes and grabbed her keys.

"Come here," she said.

He ran in front of the toppled lamp. Shadows raced across the walls. She leaned down, and he wrapped his arms around her neck. In the hallway, her knees nearly buckled. The front door swung back and forth in the wind. Leaves blew through the living room into the hall.

Cody clutched his bear. "He didn't mean to let him in."

"I know he didn't, sweetheart. Don't worry. We'll make sure Mister Vincent stays safe." She hugged Cody's head against her shoulder. "We all need to be very quiet now."

Carefully, she stepped over the creaky second floorboard. Slowly. Don't panic. The power in the cabin went out. Shit. Following the meager light from the front door, she picked up her pace.

"I can't see." Cody's voice seemed to thunder.

"Shhh, you have to stay quiet."

The basement door directly behind her opened and clicked shut.

"Hello, Vivian." Jarod's voice froze her in place. His footsteps thumped close. Breath smothered the nape of her neck. "'Till death do us part. You do remember, don't you?"

She steadied her legs. Cody needed her to be strong.

"Honor and obey, too." Her joke, their joke failed to produce any laugh. He just kept breathing, heavy and slow in the darkness.

"I told you it was an accident," he mumbled, as if something filled his mouth.

"Cody almost died, you son of a bitch."

"You stole my fucking son," he shouted.

She bolted down the hallway. In her wake, his footsteps shook the cabin. She reached the front door, grabbed the handle, and slammed it shut behind her. A thud rocked the house. He must have smashed into it.

She almost continued, but stopped. He'd run three miles a day when they were married. Every single day. And she was carrying Cody. He could barrel them down within seconds.

She fumbled with her keys and locked the top bolt. Last month, she'd installed the dual key dead bolts to keep Cody from opening the door. Fat lot of good that did, but now they had a use far greater. There was no turn latch on the inside.

Only a keyhole. And the bars on the windows meant that Jarod was now locked inside.

The door rattled. A thunk rumbled through the mountains. She took off for the car. Above, the storm clouds broke. Flashes of lightning exposed his Humvee parked off the driveway. They were more than an hour from any town. Visions of their capsized minivan, forced from the road by the military vehicle, filled her head.

Thwack. The repetitive cracking gave away Jarod's position as she raced to the Humvee. Inside the left wheel well, she found Jarod's magnetic Hide-A-Key. Thank god some things never changed. She unlocked the gigantic door and lifted Cody into the backseat.

"Put your seat belt on," she said.

"I'm sorry," he cried.

"Now."

She opened the driver's door and climbed into the vehicle. Switches and panel readouts sat all around her. Could she even drive this stupid thing? Where was the ignition? There. She turned the key. The engine roared.

"Mommy," Cody shouted.

Something snapped the glass. An explosion of nuggets sprayed her face. Jarod reached in and grabbed her sweater. She screamed. Broken and jagged, some fused together, his teeth dripped saliva.

The corners of his lips twisted as he shouted, "He's mine."

She punched the accelerator. Mud puddles sprayed over the windshield, blurring her view. Running alongside, Jarod yanked the steering wheel. The Humvee lunged toward a tree trunk and sideswiped it.

His shriek, guttural and inhuman, echoed through the cab. She slammed on the brakes to regain control. Something brushed her leg. His severed hand twitched in her lap.

Forcing back her nausea, she slapped the thing onto the passenger floorboard and punched the gas.

At the end of the driveway, she turned left. Where could they go? Erika's house? No. If Jarod had found her here, he might have people waiting for her there.

For the last year, she'd planned for this, and none of it mattered. Along with their clothes and cash, she'd also left every inhaler behind as well.

In the backseat, Cody sobbed.

"It's okay, sweetie." She reached back to hold his hand but found only a toe. "It's over. We're safe now."

They could get out of this if she could just get down the mountain. Tammy probably still lived in Los Reyes. That was only a two-hour drive. They could *still* get out of this.

A blue dashboard light knocked back her hope as she sped around the final bend of Chesterfield Road. She closed her eyes and prayed over the sound of Cody's sobs. The gas gauge flashed empty.

cont...

Available now on Amazon
and Barnes & Noble.